ENCARNITA'S JOURNEY

ENCARNITA'S JOURNEY

JOAN LINGARD

This edition first published in Great Britain in 2006 by
Allison & Busby Limited
13 Charlotte Mews
London W1T 4EJ
http://www.allisonandbusby.com

Copyright © 2005 by Joan Lingard

A catalogue record for this book is available from
the British Library.

10 9 8 7 6 5 4 3 2

ISBN 0 7490 8229 1

Printed and bound in Great Briatin by
Bookmarque Ltd, Croydon, Surrey

JOAN LINGARD is the acclaimed author of over 40 books for both children and adults. She was born in Edinburgh and brought up in Belfast, the inspiration for many of her novels, including the compelling *Across the Barricades*. She was awarded the MBE in 1998 for Services to Children's Literature.

Also by Joan Lingard

The Kiss
Dreams of Love and Modest Glory
After Colette
The Second Flowering of Emily Mountjoy
Sisters by Rite

For Rob, Elspeth and Drew,
amigos de Nerja.

PROLOGUE

Celia Marjoribanks is beginning to think she may have made a mistake by allowing these two unknown Spanish women to come into her house. She hovers, tidying a few magazines, pretending to be occupied, while keeping an eye on the older woman, the mother, whose name is Encarnita. Encarnita pauses in her dusting of the bookcase and turns, then jabbing the spine of a book with a blunt forefinger she says, 'I know that woman.'

Celia Marjoribanks goes over to look. She frowns as she peers to read the title. *To the Lighthouse.* '*Really*? You know her? Virginia Woolf? I mean, you *knew* her? She's dead.'

Encarnita nods. 'Dead. She must be dead. She older than me.'

Celia has been wondering what age Encarnita is ever since she presented herself at her door with her daughter. At least eighty, she thinks, if not more. Her face looks weathered and it is scored by many lines but her eyes are dark and arresting.

'Yes, I knowed her,' says Encarnita.

'That is interesting,' says Celia, who is finding this difficult to believe, though perhaps Encarnita might have worked for Virginia Woolf. She tries to calculate how long ago that might have been to see if it could have been possible. Didn't Virginia Woolf die not long after the beginning of the Second World War? Wasn't she depressed by the war, amongst other things? She seems to remember that she was but then her memory is not as good as it used to be. And she's not much over fifty. But aren't the brain cells supposed to start dwindling early? Cuthbert is eight years older than her yet he appears not to have a diminished memory. Not that he would not admit to it if he had.

'I have this book,' says Encarnita, stabbing *To the Lighthouse* again.

'You have it?' But could she have actually *read* it? Celia

does not like to ask. Surely not. The woman's command of English can hardly be good enough to cope with Virginia Woolf.

'She wear nice shoes with buttons. Nice leather shoes. Soft. I feel them.'

Celia gives Encarnita an uncertain smile, then she trawls along the shelves looking for a biography of Virginia Woolf. Ah, yes, she thought that they would have one. It's by Quentin Bell. She pulls it out and blows dust off the cover.

'I dust,' says Encarnita, holding out her hand.

'No, it's fine,' says Celia, drawing the book away. This woman is proving much too invasive. She cannot understand how she did let the two of them enter the house. Cuthbert won't understand it either. She flicks through the pages until she finds *Chronology*, then, with Encarnita squinting over her shoulder, obviously not taking the hint, she finds that Virginia Woolf died on the 28th of March, 1941. More than sixty years ago. It might just have been possible for Encarnita to work for her.

'Did you work for her?' Celia asks. She is conscious of speaking slowly and clearly as if to a child, the way one tends to do to someone whose native language is not English.

'Work?' Encarnita shakes her head. 'No, not work.'

'How then......?'

'She come to my village.'

'In Spain?' Celia is beginning to see a glimmer of light. 'Did she by any chance come to visit the writer Gerald Brenan?'

'Don Geraldo, we call him. He teach me English.'

'How very fascinating. My husband will be most interested. He teaches English literature.'

'He teach this woman?'

'Yes. Not *her* herself, you understand. Her work. Her books.'

'I knowed this man too.' Encarnita points now at *Eminent Victorians*. She had seen it in Don Geraldo's house.

'Lytton Strachey?'

'Yes, Señor Stratchee.'

'My goodness, what a good memory you must have! It must be a long time ago?'

'Yes, very good memory.' Encarnita taps her forehead. 'My mother say everything what goes in my head stay in my head from very early age.'

'Your mother, she's not alive too, is she?' Celia feels she would not be surprised by anything now. Perhaps Encarnita's mother is waiting outside to come in and join them.

'No, she dead many years. Die young. She have the hard life.' Encarnita goes back to *Eminent Victorians*. 'Señor Stratchee come to my village also, with two friends. He no like to ride mule. He have piles.'

'How unfortunate.' Celia stifles a giggle.

'Yes, not fortunate.'

'So, remind me, the name of your village is —?'

'Yegen.'

'Of course! I should have remembered. In the Alpujarra, the foothills of the Sierra Nevada.'

'You correct.'

'My husband and I spent a couple of weeks in the Alpujarra a few years ago. Beautiful part of the world.' She must have photographs somewhere. She's been meaning to sort out their holiday snaps for years and put them in albums.

'You went to Alpujarra?'

'Yes, indeed. Marvellous far away from the world feeling. Wonderful air, so clear and clean.'

'Not when all the fires in village smoke.'

'Well, maybe not. We went to Yegen and saw the house Gerald Brenan lived in. We read his book.'

'Al sur de Granada.'

'Yes, indeed. Though we read it in English.'

Celia had been rather disappointed in the village and couldn't understand why Brenan had chosen it to live in when there were much prettier places around in Andalucía, especially the white hill *pueblos* further west, although, as Cuthbert had pointed out, they might not have been quite so pretty in 1920, before the onset of mass tourism. Yegen was a Berber village and the houses looked rather like boxes with flat roofs stuck together, reminiscent of ones they'd seen on a trip to Morocco. The Yegen houses had been whitewashed when they had seen them but Cuthbert had said that in Brenan's day most of them would probably have been grey, since whitewash cost money and it was a poor village. The view had been marvellous, for the village stood at twelve hundred metres above sea level; they had looked out across a great sweep of mountains, valleys and villages, edged by the distant sea. It had been siesta time on a humid summer's day and the silence had been immense.

'I not live in Yegen now,' says Encarnita. 'I move to Nerja, on coast, many years ago.'

'We went to Nerja, too. We had a wonderful week there, staying in the *parador*.'

'You were in Nerja? And I not see you!'

'Even if you had seen me you wouldn't have known who I was.'

'Oh, but I would. I sure I knowed you.' The woman sounds distressed.

'I don't see how,' says Celia gently.

Encarnita stares back at her with those large dark eyes, unnerving her a little.

At that moment, the telephone rings and Celia goes to answer it in the hall, leaving the drawing room door ajar so that she can still see Encarnita. After all, she doesn't know the women, she cannot blame herself for being watchful, even if they do seem very open, perhaps even too open. They did bring a reference with them but it was from a woman she had never heard of. Typical of you, Cuthbert would say, though not sharply. He can go back in time to recall instances when she has allowed someone to take advantage of her. He is seldom angry but he can be reproachful, showing it by just a little look over the top of his glasses. Sometimes she thinks she would prefer it if he were angry for then she could respond, and defend herself. If she tries he says, let's forget it, dear, let's not make an issue out of it, it's not that important, which leaves her with a slight feeling of resentment. He is a well balanced, well modulated man, who is never tempted to have that extra drink, whereas she is. It is difficult to argue against a policy of moderation.

'You are too trusting, you know, love,' he'd say if he were to come in now, which – fortunately – he is unlikely to do. He has tutorials until lunchtime. 'One day —' He would leave the possibilities to hang in the air.

But when she opened the door to the women she had felt as if she had seen them before, somewhere. The daughter, especially.

'Celia Marjoribanks,' she says now, watching Encarnita dust *To the Lighthouse* with a kind of reverence. 'Ah, Lilias. No, I'm not particularly busy, I can talk. I'm doing my Oxfam stint this afternoon.' She lowers her voice. 'Actually I've just got a couple of new cleaners in... Yes, I'll let you know if they're any good.'

Encarnita has replaced *To the Lighthouse* and is dusting another book. Possibly *Mrs Dalloway*. That is one of Cuthbert's favourites. Celia realises it's a long time since she has read any Virginia Woolf; she read her at a certain time in her life, with pleasure, she would have to admit, but she is not sure if she would want to go back to her now. The film *The Hours*, however, has rekindled a new spark of interest.

'They're Spanish,' she informs her friend Lilias. 'No, they do speak English, well, after a fashion. But I don't think they'd know it well enough to understand what I'm saying. They're mother and daughter. Daughter's called Concepción – yes, *Concepción*. You know how the Spanish tend to have all these odd Christian names. Ascención and Maria-Jésus, names like that. Concepción must be all of sixty. The mother's called Encarnita. Short for Encarnación. Wonderful, isn't it?'

The dusting of the books is continuing at a slow measured pace, each one being scrutinised before it's replaced in its slot on the shelf. From upstairs comes the growl of the vacuum cleaner and the occasional thud as Concepción shifts a piece of furniture out of the way.

'How did I get them? A flyer was put through my door, you know the way the odd one comes through about executive housekeeping and so forth. No, this one didn't offer that. It said: "Mother and Daughter Team. Two for the price of one. Mother will do dusting and cleaning of silver and brasses. Daughter, all other work. Phone Connie." It gave a number in our area so I thought it would be handy if they lived nearby, no bus fares for a start. I didn't actually get round to phoning. Then, this morning, they just turned up on the doorstep and asked if I would give them a chance. They had an excellent reference from a woman in St Stephen Street. They actually offered to give me a free trial run, not that I would dream of not paying them.'

The noise has stopped overhead. Concepción's fuzzy greyish-blond head appears over the top bannister. 'No find plug for electrics in study,' she yells down to Celia.

'Don't touch study!' Celia cries in alarm. Cuthbert can't stand people messing about in his study. She did tell Concepción not to go in there but she must not have understood. 'It's my husband's study. Leave, please, leave!' Now she is beginning to talk like them. Concepción's head has withdrawn. Celia goes back to her call.

'I suppose it was a bit of a risk but, to tell the truth, I felt rather sorry for the two of them, at their ages, having to trail round houses looking for work. Can you imagine if you had to do that? So I thought, what do I have to lose?' Encarnita is still engrossed in the bookcase. 'Well, of course I suppose I could lose something but I rather think they're honest.'

The vacuum has roared into life again overhead. Celia

hopes it is not in Cuthbert's study. She wonders if the women in Yegen have vacuum cleaners. Lilias is reminding her of the amethyst necklace she had once had stolen by a former 'cleaning operative', as thus she had described herself.

'These two women don't have a shifty look to them the way that one did. They both look you in the eye, very directly, though I have to admit that there is something a little unsettling about them, I can't explain it.' Celia, catching sight of herself in the hall mirror, sees that she is frowning and makes a conscious effort to relax her forehead. She says in a more decided voice, 'I am sure they are absolutely fine. They'll have finished, anyway, before Cuthbert gets back.'

In the heart of Edinburgh's Georgian New Town, in a warm, elegant drawing room, scented with yellow freesias, delicately arranged in a shallow orange-coloured bowl, Encarnita continues with her work. The sun streaming in through the three, almost floor-length windows warms her back. She moves from the bookcase to the grand piano on top of which stand a series of photographs in silver frames. Family photographs. Groups of various kinds on days of celebration. There is Celia on her wedding day with her husband. That must be her husband Cuthbert. She is wearing a white silky-looking dress with a long train that has been arranged in a swirl around her feet like a big comma. She holds a sheath of red roses against the white dress and she is smiling. The man is wearing a kilt with knee socks and a black jacket with silver buttons. He has a straight back and a small, neat moustache. He looks proud to have such a lovely bride on his arm. It is not possible from this picture to know what kind of a man he is but Encarnita will find out when she meets him for she is certain that she will. The next photograph is of three small children, a boy and two girls. She has seen none of these people before but here is a young man whom she once knew and recognises still even though he had wild tangled hair and a beard when she knew him and in this picture he is clean-shaven. He is sitting under a silver birch tree on a summer's day, with a book on his lap. The leaves above his head are shimmering in the sunshine lighting up his golden-red hair. He is smiling directly at the camera. He is smiling directly at her. She gently slides the duster over the glass and replaces the frame on top of the shiny piano.

Out in the hall, Celia Marjoribanks carries on talking to her friend in a soft, low voice, too soft and low for Encarnita to make out what she is saying. But she is content. She has completed her journey and when Celia has finished talking to her friend and comes back into the room then she, Encarnita, will tell her story.

CHILDHOOD: YEGEN

Encarnita was born only minutes into the new year of the new decade. Her birth took place in the lower *barrio* of the *pueblo* in one of its poorest dwellings. The upper floor of the house having long since fallen into disrepair, Pilar, Encarnita's mother, lived on the lower one which formerly had been a stable and still served partly as such. Births in stables were not unknown. In the corner, tied to a stake, stood their goat, Gabriella, restless witness to the birth along with a neighbour, Isabel, who had borne many children herself.

The confinement went well in the end in spite of Pilar's exhaustion at having laboured for twelve hours and more. Isabel encouraged her, holding apart her knees, crying out, 'It comes! It comes! I see the head. Push one more time!' With that Pilar grunted and willed her body to eject the child within her. She had made no noise throughout except to utter a small groan or whimper. She was a quiet, unassuming woman who never wished to attract attention. After Isabel had helped ease out the dark matted head the baby slithered quickly and easily onto the bloodied straw between her mother's legs. Isabel seized her by the ankles and holding her aloft delivered a hearty to slap to her shrivelled bottom. Encarnita responded with an angry roar and opening wide her dark, soot-black eyes she glared at her assailant. Isabel laughed and said this child would have a will of her own, like her youngest, Juliana.

Once the afterbirth had come cleanly away she wrapped the baby in a piece of new cloth purchased from the pedlar and placed her in her mother's arms. Pilar gazed with wonder into the shadowy face of her child. The candles had sunk low and soon their flames would gutter and die but they had served their purpose and in a few hours dawn would come.

'My little dove,' murmured Pilar, though the baby looked

little like one for even in that poor light it could be seen that her skin was dusky and her hair, curling in soft fronds around her face, was as black as pitch. Pilar had not revealed the identity of the father but it was rumoured that he was a gypsy from Guadix, which was more than possible. Gypsies came regularly about the village and Pilar had a weakness for their men, especially those who sang haunting love songs. The women in the village said it was a pity she had not paid more attention to the songs that spoke mostly of ill-fated love which ends in grief. Especially for the woman.

A more surprising event than the birth of a new child in the village was the coming of a tall, fair-haired young Englishman to live in their midst. His name was Gerald Brenan and he soon became known as Don Geraldo. He rented the largest house in the *barrio* and began to make changes. One of the first things that he did was to white-wash the outside walls while his housekeeper Maria dodged to and fro underneath mopping up the drips. This said a great deal in itself. Only a small handful of villagers could afford whitewash and, even less, a servant to mop up drips. He then had two thousand books brought up by wagon from the coast down in Almería nearly a hundred kilometers away. Two thousand! Could anyone ever read so many books? The neighbours stood and gaped as they were unloaded, Pilar among them, with her newborn child in her arms. Few were able to read though there was a school which some children attended when they were not needed to help in the fields. There they learnt to recognise and write a few letters, count up to a hundred, recite the names of the continents and sing hymns and prayers. Not all parents could see the value of it though Pilar knew that when the time came she would make sure her child learned to read and write. It was something she had always yearned to do herself.

Don Geraldo settled into his house like one who intended to stay for a long time. He had furniture made by local tradesmen and bought up all the best pots and pans he could lay hands on. He stocked his larder with bags of almonds and raisins, as well as fourteen kilograms of honey, forty of figs, and three huge hams. As the villagers watched the food being carried in they sensed that life in their *pueblo* would never be the same again.

In the spring, the first of Don Geraldo's many visitors from England were awaited. These were important people who were coming, stressed Maria, who seemed to draw importance from that herself. The arrival of the group, consisting of two men and one woman, was overdue, which was heightening the suspense. There had been a buzz of excitement in the upper *barrio* all day. Women appeared in their doorways at intervals to peer down the street and speculate on possible reasons for the travellers' lateness. They might have missed Don Geraldo who had set out to meet them on the road. Or they might have fallen into the hands of bandits though that seemed less probable. More likely was that Don Geraldo himself had fallen by the wayside for he had not been well when he set out and Maria had been worried.

'These travellers will have come over land and sea, Encarnita,' said Pilar, shifting her daughter higher onto her shoulder so that she could have a better view. For three months, the baby had an amazingly strong neck and could hold her head up. 'It would be fine to make such a journey, would it not?' It was thus that the idea of making a journey first entered Encarnita's head.

Encarnita always listened intently to her mother's voice. Sweet and low, with a special timbre of its own, it came over more like song than speech at times and had an almost hypnotic effect on her. Later, when she is grown, she thinks that is why she has remembered so much of what her mother told her. Its resonance remains with her throughout her life.

They moved closer to Don Geraldo's door when a pedlar came cantering up the hill on mule-back. Steam rose from the animal's flanks. The pedlar had brought news of the travellers, which was a relief to Maria. He had come across them when they'd stopped to rest and eat. They had set out the day before from Órgiva but on reaching the Rio Grande they had found it swollen to a dangerous height. They had decided, nevertheless, to attempt the crossing, but when the mules had plunged in the elder of Don Geraldo's two male friends had been thrown into a panic and they'd had to withdraw and return to Órgiva to spend another night in the *posada*.

'They might all have drowned,' said Maria and a neighbour who'd come to listen crossed herself.

'The man who panicked was in a foul mood,' said the pedlar. 'He rides ill on mule-back and so he walks much of the time, except, of course, when they have to cross water.'

'He will be walking because of his piles,' announced Maria. 'He is sorely troubled by them, poor man. He is a writer of books, so Don Geraldo says.'

'Perhaps he sits too long,' suggested Pilar.

'It is possible. Don Geraldo asked me to find a soft pillow for him.'

'He is a long thin sort of man with a high, squeaky voice,' went on the pedlar. 'And he has a beard and spectacles and a large red nose.' He mimed each attribute, enjoying being the centre of attention. Encarnita, too, was smiling, as if she were following every word and her mother would not have been surprised if she were. 'I think if his nose had not been so large his spectacles might have fallen off when his mule was bucking. He was riding side-saddle.' The pedlar had a poor opinion of that.

'Look, that is the man.' Maria pointed to the top name of three written on a slip of paper and Pilar craned her head to look even though she could not read. Encarnita turned her head, also. 'Señor Lytton Strachey,' said Maria, pronouncing the surname as 'Stratchee'. Don Geraldo had gone over the names with her so that she would know how to address the visitors. The other man was Señor Partridge but Don Geraldo had told her she could change his name to the Spanish, Señor Perdiz. He'd said that would amuse his friend though Maria had not been able to see why. They liked jokes, Don Geraldo had explained.

The third traveller was an unmarried lady called Señorita Dora Carrington. Don Geraldo had been quick to reassure Maria that by travelling with two men unrelated to her, the *señorita* would not ruin her reputation. Early on in her acquaintance with the Englishman Maria had come to realise that life in England was in many ways different to life in the Alpujarra. No well-bred unmarried woman in Spain from a good family – which this *señorita* must be – would travel with two men, for that would compromise her. Mothers liked to keep a strict eye on their unmarried daughters. A boy and a girl might glance at each other during the *paseo* but no more than a slight touching of the hands should take place. Once a girl allowed her reputation to be called into question no decent man would marry her. There were village girls who did not follow these rules, but then it could not be said that they came from good families.

Don Geraldo had told Maria that the differences were what he enjoyed though it remained a mystery to her and most of the other villagers as to why he would want to live in their poor village without electricity when he might have a fine house with bright lights and a flushing toilet in his own country. When he said he was poor and could not afford such a house in England he was not believed.

'Today, the travellers took the longer route,' said the pedlar, 'so that they could cross the river by the bridge.'

'It's a long walk from Órgiva to Yegen,' said Maria. 'It takes most of a day.'

And the last part from Cádiar would be hard going, especially if the travellers were to decide to come straight up the mountainside, which they might be forced to do if the light was beginning to fail. It would mean a climb of about six hundred metres up a steep path, with the ground plunging away sharply on either side. The terrain was wild and rugged.

'I think the big-nosed man might not have the nerve for

it,' said the pedlar with relish.

'It is beautiful there, though,' said Pilar, who had walked the route only once in her life, with a man from Cádiar, before she had met Encarnita's father. 'Especially now that it is spring.'

It had been spring when she had walked with the man and the wild flowers, yellow, white, purple, had been strewn across the hillsides, with the scarlet poppies adding their own startling splashes of colour, while further down in the valley shreds of pink and white almond blossom had still been clinging to the branches. Spring was Pilar's favourite season but it would not be Encarnita's; she would come to prefer the deep heat of summer, the sultry days without a breath of wind, with bees buzzing over the lavender and gorse, and the warm evenings when you could stroll in the streets until midnight and beyond.

The sun had gradually been lowering in the western sky, streaking it with bands of vivid pink and red. The houses, too, were touched with colour. The air was cooling rapidly. The goats were coming home from the *campo,* as were the mules and donkeys, toiling up the steep, cobbled streets, their bundles of grasses and sacks of oranges and lemons piled high on their backs. By now most of the women had gone indoors to make a meal for their husbands and children. Soon smoke was rising from the chimneys. The scents of burning rosemary, lavender and thyme stole through the narrow, twisting streets and a gauzy film spread over the rooftops. Pilar stayed where she was, for she had no husband and could feed her child where she stood. She was full of milk now. That, at least, was free. She unbuttoned her blouse and Encarnita snatched greedily at the engorged nipple.

The stars, too, were coming out.

'Where can they be?' fretted Maria, retying the black kerchief round her head, while pacing restlessly up and down. She was a spry, nervy woman who found it difficult to be still. 'I hope they have not fallen down a precipice. Let us go inside, Pilar. We shall have something to eat, too, while we wait.' She felt sorry for Pilar who had to depend on the favours of men to feed her. She was fortunate since, as Don Geraldo's servant, she was fed and also paid a *peseta* a day, more than most people in the village could hope to earn. There was little paid work of any kind to be had.

They went into the house, rented by Don Geraldo from the landowner Don Fernando, though his beautiful wife, Doña Clara, was even richer than he, with property in Granada. To own property was every villager's dream but they were not so ignorant as to think that that in itself would bring good fortune. Doña Clara was a delicate woman who kept giving birth to sickly children, none of whom survived childhood. At eighteen Maria had been taken into their house as a servant and become Don Fernando's mistress, subsequently bearing him a child, a puny girl, called Angela, who did survive and was now nine years old. Don Fernando had gone to live in Granada with his wife while retaining a room in his old house, in addition to the ground floor where he continued to stable goats, a pig and a cow.

The smell of manure was rank and flies buzzed about the animals but none of this was noticed particularly by the two women as they passed through. Pilar saw that a fly was try-ing to settle on her child's milky, half-parted lips and flapped it away. They followed Maria up the stairs to the first floor, which opened out onto a garden and a courtyard at the back. There were nine rooms of various sizes on this level, sparsely furnished, in the Englishman's eyes, if not in Pilar's. Some families in the village had little or no furniture and ate sitting on the floor. As Maria said, the foreigner was used to different ways.

'It is just as well we have so many rooms,' she said, as she trimmed a paraffin lamp and set it on the table, 'since Don Geraldo has so many friends who are willing to travel long distances to visit him.'

The kitchen was not overly large but it boasted a stone

sink, cupboards of dark walnut, a row of charcoal stoves and an open fireplace, with a bakehouse and a water closet off it. Maria had shown the latter to Pilar before and she had marvelled at its seat of fine-veined marble. She had peered down into the depths of the closet to the chicken run six or seven metres below. Flushing toilets such as Don Geraldo spoke of were not known in Yegen. He had come to accept that.

The room smelt of chicken stewing with garlic and herbs, making Pilar feel giddy with hunger. Saliva ran in her mouth. But the chicken was for the visitors, she understood that. Maria set out a heel of bread, some shrivelled green olives and a small plate of cold fried sardines glazed with yellow oil. With the food, they drank a cup of the rough local wine, which Don Geraldo had said would be too sour for his guests. For their coming, he had bought some special wine down in Cádiar.

As they were finishing eating, they heard voices below.

'They've arrived!' cried Maria, leaping up and darting off down the stairs.

Pilar cleared their dishes into the sink, holding the baby, who was now sleeping, against her shoulder. She waited, too shy to go down and meet the new people. Don Geraldo would not be annoyed to find her there; he mixed freely with the villagers and invited them into his house. He gave them anis and wine and encouraged them to tell their tales.

When Maria returned she was accompanied by Don Geraldo and the woman traveller. The others were following on behind. The *señorita* did not look so very young and Pilar wondered that she would not have a husband. She was brushing herself down with her hand and wriggling her shoulders to ease the stiffness out of them.

'What a journey!' she exclaimed, though her eyes were dancing, as if she had not minded it at all. She had very blue eyes, a fine skin and a thatch of hay-coloured hair cut short round her ears. She glanced around the room. 'So this is your hideaway, Gerald. What fun!'

Don Geraldo introduced her as Señorita Carrington and she came forward to shake Pilar's hand. Pilar felt embarrassed at the sight of her own rough brown hand with its broken fingernails nestling in the Englishwoman's smooth white one. Encarnita had wakened and was also taking an interest in the stranger. The lady came up to her and chucking her under the chin, said, 'What knowing eyes you've got, little one!' Don Geraldo translated for Pilar, who had often thought this herself. When she talked to Encarnita she felt as if the child understood every word.

Pilar left soon afterwards, going first to the fountain beside the *plaza* to take a drink. Feeding her child gave her a fearsome thirst. She would fetch water for the house in the lower *barrio* later. The water was good in Yegen, and plentiful. Sometimes, in spring, when the snows were melting, it would cascade down the street. Another woman was at the fountain drawing water, Maxima, one of the two acknowledged prostitutes in the village. Pilar, although she received men in her house at times, did not consider herself to be a part of them for she made love only with men that she liked. However, if they did offer her a few centimos or some food from their *cortijo* she was not too proud to accept it. She was too poor not to accept it. The other prostitute, known as La Prisca, an old name for a peach, was a clever woman who could read and write. She had written a letter for Pilar to the man from Cádiar but he had not replied, although he had claimed to be able to read and write. The muleteers favoured La Prisca, so tonight, once Don Geraldo's visitors had all arrived, she might have business. She had two children whereas Maxima had half a dozen and needed to fill two pitchers and come often to the fountain. She was tired, always.

Lulled by the rise and fall of the women's voices, Encarnita dropped off to sleep again. In the nearby Bar Fuente men were arguing. About politics, of course. A new government, led by the Conservative politician Eduardo Dato, had just taken over, following on from a bloody year

throughout Spain, rife with strikes and unrest and assassi-
nations on all sides of the political divide. Martial law had
been declared in Andalucía and troops had been sent to
crush the strikers on the big estates though Yegen itself had
remained calm. 'Listen to them!' said Maxima, as shouting
erupted. 'They'll be at each other's throats before long.'
Grumbling about men and children and the hardness of her
life, she stumbled off down the street, with water slopping
from her cans. Pilar had resolved to have no other child but
Encarnita and had decided that if she were to fall pregnant
again she would go to a woman in her *barrio* who would
help her. She shifted the baby onto her other shoulder and
then she, too, set off for home.

The village was quiet. Most people would have gone to
bed. The only sign of life was the odd blink of light at a window where the shutters remained open. Few houses in the
village had glass in their windows. When Pilar reached the
church in the broad stretch of land that separated the upper
and lower *barrios* she stopped, hearing hoof-beats
approaching. She waited in the shadows until the mules and
their riders came into view. She could not make out their
faces but she was able to identify the man with the piles, for,
indeed, he did look to be very long and thin and he was
hanging onto his mule as if his life depended on it. None of
the travellers saw her. They passed on by and went labour-
ing up the hill on the last lap of their journey, the muleteers
spurring them on with their cries. Both beasts and riders
must be tired. Pilar filled the pitcher she had left at the
fountain earlier and made for her home in the lower *barrio*.

The people of the two *barrios* did not mix much, not
because of any great dispute; it was just that traditionally
they had always tended to keep to their own areas. The *barrios* were small, tight communities, the total population of
Yegen being only a thousand. Pilar was one of the few who
went between the upper and lower village, mainly because
Maria had befriended her and had known her mother.

She pushed open the door of her dwelling, redolent of

goat. Gabriella was braying, her teats heavy with milk, as Pilar's had been earlier. Shortly, after Encarnita was settled, she would milk her. She had walked her during the day so she had been well fed. Although thin-flanked, the goat produced enough milk for their needs.

Pilar laid the sleeping baby gently on the blanket spread over their bed of lavender and thyme and then she lit a candle, which she placed on the earth floor, taking care to keep it well away from the straw. Shadows danced across the rough walls. One day she would whitewash them, just as one day she would buy furniture and make her house pretty. She went now to attend to Gabriella. Once the milk was in the pail, Pilar scooped out a cupful and drank, then she went outside to relieve herself in the yard. When she returned she extinguished the candle and lay down beside her daughter. There was an opening high up in the wall that let in the moonlight. She bent her head close to Encarnita's. The child's breathing was deep and regular. It was a sound that stirred her heart.

Pilar herself was on the edge of sleep when she heard a footfall. She lifted her head. A man's dark shape filled the doorway.

'Jaime,' she said. She was fond of the lad, she would not turn him away, and he always brought her eggs fresh from his father's *cortijo*.

Encarnita, too, wakened, and as she stirred her limbs, she became aware of the heaving bodies on the blanket beside her. She gave a little startled cry but they did not hear her; they were making too many noises of their own, noises that she had heard before. Someone seemed to be hurting her mother but she knew that she could do nothing about it. She quietened and closed her eyes though she did not go back to sleep until the turmoil stopped and the man got up and stumbled out into the night. Her mother relit the candle and went to look in the little bag Jaime had left by the door. 'Two large speckled eggs,' she murmured. She seemed content.

Señor Strachey was giving Maria a great deal of bother. When Pilar and Encarnita called she was ready with a string of grumbles to pour into their ears.

He made such a fuss about his food! He hated Spanish cooking, his stomach was delicate, his nerves were delicate. She struggled to please him and was offended when he peered at his food as if he suspected her of trying to poison him and then he would mess it around on his plate and leave most of it untouched. He hated beans, *tortilla* and salt dry cod. What was she to do?

Pilar had no advice to offer. She had no experience of such eating habits, either. 'No wonder he is so thin and looks so unhealthy.' She smoothed Encarnita's cheek with her finger and the child's face broke into a smile. 'Don't you think she has a good colour, Maria? And the whites of her eyes are always clear.'

Maria was more interested in Señor Strachey's colour. 'He's afraid of the fresh air. He doesn't want to go out. I can't understand why he has come at all. He says the smell of the stable makes him feel ill. He opened the bottom door a crack yesterday and squinted into the street as if he was about to be attacked by a wild beast. Then he shut it again.'

'Perhaps we would do the same if we went to his country.'

'Us? Of course we would not, Pilar!'

Pilar had to agree; she had only been trying to think kindly of the man and his fears, for he must be fearful if the idea of walking about their village terrified him. Little harm could befall him here. She knew that if she and Encarnita had the chance to journey to the *señor's* country they would spend every moment of daylight outside, making sure they missed nothing.

Señor Strachey, whether he was outside or inside, would appear to be a man who encountered misfortune at every turn. 'He says he's been bitten by bedbugs,' said Maria, scratching her waist at the thought of it, though it was possible she did have some bites herself. Few in Yegen escaped them. 'Here! In my house! He must have got them in Granada before he ever came to Yegen.' Everything had happened to him in Granada! He had caught flu, almost trod on a snake, suffered a bad stomach upset, injured his knee and mislaid his pyjamas. A man who attracted misfortune, that was obvious. And not, therefore, a good guest to have in the house.

'The nights are still cool for him to sleep without pyjamas,' said Pilar, who had never owned nightwear of any kind. 'He needs a woman to keep him warm. And to look after him.'

'He has the *señorita*,' said Maria slyly.

'She is *his* woman? I can't imagine it. He is an old man.'

'Forty, Don Geraldo says. But he looks fifty.'

'Or more. The other man is much younger and much more handsome. I would prefer him.'

'Señor Perdiz. You would be lucky to have a man like that! I can't make them out, the three of them. Half the time they're squabbling; the rest, cooing like doves at each other. Sometimes I think that *she* is the woman of one and then the other.' Maria lowered her voice. 'She fusses over Señor Stratchee like a clucking hen. Is he too hot or too cold? He needs a rug. She runs to get one. He needs a window opened because he is almost fainting from the heat. She runs to open it.'

'She has a kind heart, perhaps.'

Maria shrugged. 'Yesterday morning, I saw her kissing Señor Perdiz. And, in the evening, would you believe, Don Geraldo! I think he is in love with her.'

'I'm surprised he would want a woman of her age.' It was already known in the village that Don Geraldo liked young girls. And prostitutes. They'd heard he'd been in the brothels of Almería and Granada. 'She's not all *that* young, is she?'

'She is not! I asked Don Geraldo for he doesn't mind if I ask questions about his life. He says that most of the villagers are not interested in what he is doing but I don't think that's true. But I would be, wouldn't I, when I work for him? He asks me about my life too. "We can study each other, Maria," he says and he writes down some of the things that I tell him.'

'So what age is she?'

'Twenty-six, the same as himself. Nearly as old as me!' Maria had passed her thirtieth birthday but whereas her body was supple and firm, her face, which she washed only with aniseed spirit, made her look more than her years. The spirit dried it to the texture of leather. She had a phobia about letting water touch it. Pilar wondered if it had something to do with her belief in witches.

'That isn't young,' assented Pilar, who herself was twenty years old.

'It seems to me that she has an attachment to all three of the men.'

'I suppose that could be possible.'

'But tiring,' said Maria, who had found Don Fernando sufficient. 'They are a strange lot.'

Pilar nodded. 'Quite strange.'

'I hope all that kissing won't have harmed Don Geraldo for she has a dreadful cold and he is just recovering from another bout of flu. They seem to be ill quite often, these people.' Maria lifted a bottle from the table and, uncorking it, invited Pilar to smell. 'This is her medicine. It smells like an old barn. And what a fuss she makes when she drinks it! You'd think she was being poisoned.'

'So where are they now?' Pilar glanced around as if they might be lurking.

'Señor Stratchee is still in bed – he spends half the day there – and the others have gone for a walk. They like walking, for no particular purpose. Like Don Geraldo himself.' Sometimes he walked for as much as twelve hours at a stretch, another of his habits they could not understand.

'Perhaps they enjoy the flowers,' suggested Pilar.

Maria sniffed.

The door opened at their backs, and the tall thin one put his head round. He was scratching his midriff and they could sense his irritability even from across the room. Maria jumped up and Encarnita lifted her head to see what was happening.

'Señor Stratchee. *Desayuno*?' Maria held out a loaf of bread and pointed to a bowl of black olives sitting in a bowl in a puddle of yellow olive oil.

He shuddered and shook his head. '*Café*,' he said and left abruptly.

'He doesn't care much for our coffee, either,' said Maria as she set water on the stove to boil. 'He says it tastes of barley.'

Pilar had no opinion on the taste of coffee; it was only occasionally that she had the chance to drink it. The smell of it was making her nostrils twitch and after Maria had taken a cup to Señor Strachey she poured a small amount into two cups for themselves.

'You would think he might be hungry,' said Pilar.

'Don Geraldo says he is a brilliant man.'

'In what way?'

'He writes books. And he thinks a lot.' Maria tapped her forehead. 'Don Geraldo seems much in awe of that. And the *señorita* is a brilliant artist. She draws and paints.'

They reflected on such brilliance, uncertain as to whether Don Geraldo could be considered to have it himself since he spent much of his time reading books or walking on the hills.

'Perhaps he can be called a brilliant walker,' suggested Pilar, getting up and hoisting Encarnita onto her hip. They must fetch Gabriella and walk her on the hill.

The goat came willingly. Pilar looped her rope around her neck and led her up through the two *barrios*. The fish vendor was lugging his baskets from door to door, followed by a squad of mewling village cats. His fish, mostly sardines, clams and calamares, would have been brought up from the coast by mule the night before. Pilar loved fish and would buy whenever she had a few centimos to spare. She shook her head at him today. *Mañana*. Perhaps tomorrow.

The hill up to the top of the village was winding and steep but Pilar's legs were sturdy and the slope did not trouble her, even with Encarnita to carry. The baby jogged along on her hip enjoying the ride. Pilar sang softly to her, a *copla* about a young girl and her true love, who, in the end, is killed by a rival.

Gabriella was happy when they reached open country. Pickings were good for her at this time of year. The fresh grass shoots were green and sweet and in amongst them lurked tender spring flowers and even some thin stalks of wild asparagus. Once she was tethered to the trunk of an old olive tree Pilar sat down with Encarnita. A soft breeze grazed their cheeks. Pilar plucked a sprig of lavender and rubbed it between her fingers to release the bouquet before holding it to her child's nose. 'Smell that, Encarnita. It's lavender, my favourite smell in the world.' The baby's nostrils twitched and for a moment her eyes looked serious as if she were trying to decide. And then she smiled and her mother laughed and hugged her close.

'*Buenos dias*, Pilar!'

She looked round to see Don Geraldo standing further up the hill with Señor Partridge and his woman friend. She felt flustered. They were coming down to join her, running, galloping almost, throwing their arms up in the air. They were in high spirits.

'No, don't get up, Pilar! Stay where you are. My friend would like to draw you and your baby. And your goat.'

'My goat? But she's just an ordinary goat.'

'That doesn't matter. In fact, it does matter, for that is what the *señorita* likes about it. So, would that be all right?'

Pilar did not know what to say. Why should the *señorita*, who was a brilliant artist, want to draw them?

'You just have to relax, that's all. Don't pay any attention to her. Don't even look at her. You talk to us.'

Don Geraldo dropped onto the ground where he lounged, leaning back on his elbows. Señor Partridge joined him. Pilar thought he should have had the name of a more splendid bird than a partridge, an eagle or a falcon perhaps. Partridges were rather dowdy and meant for the pot, if you could be lucky enough to trap one. The men's long legs were sprawled across the grass. If she moved her foot she might touch one of theirs. She was conscious that her feet did not look very clean in their rope sandals. Tomorrow, she would go and bathe in one of the irrigation ponds up on the mountainside. Or else she might go down the path that led to Yátor, to a small pond reputed to have been used for bathing by women back in the times of the Moors and which was usually referred to as the women's bath. The water, there, was shallower and, therefore, warmer. She visited the baths more often than most of the villagers, sometimes going every other week. Some of them bathed themselves properly only two or three times a year. Maria had said that her guests were forever sluicing themselves with water and asking for it to be *hot*.

Pilar's cheeks were warm and her armpits felt damp. She wiped her forehead with the back of her hand. Did they really expect her to *talk* to them? What could she say that they would want to hear? She knew so little of the world. She knew about the plants that grew on the mountain and the birds that flew high above it, but that was all. Meanwhile, the *señorita* was sitting on a rock a short distance away and drawing feverishly on a large white sheet of paper, whilst lifting her head every other second to stare directly at them with her astonishingly blue eyes. Pilar felt as if she could see right through her, into her soul.

'My friend asks if your goat has a name, Pilar?' said Don Geraldo.

'Gabriella,' she mumbled, keeping her eyes lowered.

The friend said something else and Don Geraldo translated. 'He says that is an angelic name. Is your goat an angel? A gift from God?'

What was she to say to that? Gabriella an *angel*? Given to her by God? Was he making fun of her? The man then wanted to know the baby's name. She said she had been christened Encarnación, which seemed to amuse Don Geraldo's friends. Pilar wondered what they might be saying. She felt uneasy, not knowing. She wished she could learn their language so that she could teach it to Encarnita for then her child would be able to go out into the world and travel.

'I shorten it to Encarnita,' she added.

'It is a fine name!' declared Don Geraldo. 'As fine a name as any child could wish for. Look at the funny name my friend has! Who would want to be a *perdiz*?'

The three English people laughed again. They laughed a great deal while they bandied words to and fro.

Gabriella was getting restless and making it clear that she wanted to move on to new pastures, but the men told Pilar that she was not to move; they would go and gather fodder for the goat themselves. They sprang up before she could protest and came back with armfuls of grasses and even some corn shoots taken from someone's plot. Gabriella was happy, though Pilar was beginning to feel restless herself.

Finally, the *señorita* was finished. She got up and came across to show her drawing.

'Excellent!' said Don Geraldo. 'You've caught all three of them. What do you think, Pilar?'

Pilar was surprised to see how real the drawings of Encarnita and Gabriella looked. About herself, she could not be so sure. She had no mirror so seldom saw herself, except as a wavery reflection in the river when she bent over to wash her clothes. The woman in the picture had heavy black eyebrows and thin cheeks. 'Do I look like that?'

'It is a good likeness. My friend asks if you would like to have it?'

'To keep?'

'Yes. Would you?'

Pilar nodded. Of course she would! No one had ever offered her a picture before. The *señorita* signed her name at the bottom of the drawing, then she came across to Pilar and offered it to her.

'*Gracias*,' said Pilar shyly, taking it into her hands. Encarnita turned her head so that she, too could look. '*Muchas gracias*,' added Pilar and the painter responded with '*De nada*,' for she knew that much Spanish. It's nothing. Don't mention it.

Pilar looked at the signature. *Carrington*. 'Just one name?'

'That is what she likes to be called,' said Don Geraldo. 'Simply Carrington. One day, Pilar, when she is famous, this drawing might be worth quite a lot of money.'

He spoke to the *señorita* in their own language and she said something in return and once more they all laughed. Pilar envied them their laughter, which spilled out so freely.

The three friends left but Pilar sat on in a slight daze. Gabriella, too, was content to laze for her belly was full and the sun was at its height.

'We have had our pictures drawn by a real artist, Encarnita,' said Pilar, continuing to gaze at it with wonder. 'What do you think of that?'

Encarnita was scrutinising the picture, too; with approval, her mother thought.

Virginia and Leonard Woolf came to stay in Yegen when Encarnita was three years old. Since giving birth to another child the year before Maria had allowed herself to slump into periodic states of disarray, and the house with her. Dishes waited to be washed, food stains spattered on the table, the floor needed to be swept.

Pilar had come in to give her a hand.

'You'd think I had enough to do without more visitors coming,' grumbled Maria. 'All these people expecting to be fed and waited on. These ones are called Señor and Señora Lobo. *Perdices* and *lobos*, what funny names Don Geraldo's friends have.'

Partridges might be one thing but wolves quite another. Encarnita's eyes widened. Were wolves coming to stay in the village? It was said that they roamed the high mountains and shepherds claimed that they took their beasts at times. Maria was full of stories. She had seen many strange things in her life. She had seen witches flying through moonlit skies above the village rooftops. Every time there was a moon Encarnita looked hopefully up at the sky and once was sure that she did see one.

'And they're coming for two whole weeks!' Maria went on. 'But perhaps they will cheer Don Geraldo up.' He had been gloomy of late, missing his friends, the painter-woman in particular. 'You remember her, don't you?'

'Of course. She's the lady who did our picture, Encarnita.'

Encarnita nodded. They had the picture pinned up on the wall where they could see it from their bed in the morning light.

'Sometimes, when he's feeling a little lonely, he likes to talk, especially at night,' said Maria, dropping her voice. Encarnita settled in to listen. She loved to listen to the stories that passed between Maria and her mother.

'Night is a good time for talking,' said Pilar.

'He told me he was attached to a lady who, although she returned his affection, was attached to another. I'm sure that's the *perdiz* man. Don Geraldo writes long letters to her, pages and pages at a time. And then he has to walk all the way to Úgijar to post them and he brings back big long letters that she writes in return.'

'Love is strange.' Pilar looked pensive.

'But why does he bother about her when there are prettier women to be had here in the village? And I don't mean Maxima, though I'm sure he's been with her. She charges two eggs.'

'I heard that La Prisca charges a *peseta*.'

'She has her head fixed firmly to her shoulders, that one.'

'She can read.' La Prisca had been teaching Pilar, who by now could recognise all the letters of the alphabet and some simple words. Words like *casa, calle, pueblo*. Encarnita was following the lessons, too.

'What good do you think that will do for you?' asked Maria. 'Don Geraldo reads till his eyes are ready to plop out. Dull looking books, with not even a picture in them. It's no wonder he's forever getting headaches and flu. He sniffles and coughs up gobbets of phlegm into cloth handkerchiefs. And then I have to wash them. Why doesn't he spit out in the yard?'

It was true that Don Geraldo suffered much from colds and flu, which puzzled them, since he lived in a dry house and ate the best of food. At regular intervals Maria would announce, with a certain amount of satisfaction, the onslaught of yet another bout. Pilar said she did not think it could have anything to do with reading books, unless some of them were dusty and the dust was entering his lungs. Maria was peeved by the suggestion that dust might be allowed to collect in her house.

'I have a feeling Don Geraldo is a bit nervous about having these *lobos* here. They're not close friends like the others. I don't suppose they'll run about the hills telling jokes and laughing so much. They are *very* brilliant, it seems. Much cleverer than he is. So he says. The lady writes wonderful stories. Don Geraldo speaks as if he is much in awe of her.'

The two women set to to clean the kitchen and Encarnita was given a rag so that she could dust surfaces within her reach. She wiped each ledge carefully since the lady who wrote stories sounded as if she would be very particular.

From the stair came the sound of scurrying footsteps and Juliana, the daughter of Isabel, who had been present at Encarnita's birth, burst into the room to cry out the news that the visitors were approaching. They'd been spotted on the lower path. Pilar and Encarnita left at once and hastened after Juliana out into the street. A few of the neighbours had already gathered.

'I hope Señor Lobo doesn't have piles, the way Señor Perdiz did,' said Pilar. 'Perhaps all the men from their country suffer from them.'

'Don Geraldo rides a mule without trouble,' someone pointed out. 'He sits easily on a mule or a horse.'

Juliana wondered if the lady would be wearing a silk or a satin dress, but Pilar thought neither. Not when riding a mule.

Juliana, a plump nine year-old, had frizzled hair and slanting, rather sleepy eyes, but she was cheerful and good fun and Encarnita liked her. Juliana often took her along when she was going out into the *campo* to gather asparagus or fennel. Her family lived in Casa Narisco, the last house in the village, a poor affair in a state similar to Encarnita's own. Juliana's father had died in a mining accident in Linares leaving her mother to raise eight children.

They did not have long to wait. First came Don Geraldo, followed by the lady and then her husband. They were all on mule-back and none were showing signs of being in agony, so they concluded that the gentleman could not have piles after all. He wore a tweed suit and between his clenched teeth held an unlit pipe. Encarnita's eyes were drawn, however, to the lady's buttoned shoes, which were level with her eyes. She wiped the back of one bare foot against the calf of the other, hoping to scuff away some of the dirt, whilst wishing that she could have shoes made of such fine leather. In the village most people wore *alpargatas*, rope-soled shoes.

The muleteers helped the riders to descend and Encarnita's eyes followed the lady's feet until they touched the ground. Then, slowly, she began to inch towards them. She paused for a moment. High above her head the visitors were talking with Don Geraldo in their strange tongue, paying no attention to her. Stretching out a hand Encarnita touched the nearest shoe, with just one finger. The leather felt as smooth and as soft as the inside of her own arm. She let her finger slide right round the tip of the shoe, leaving a snail's trail in the dust that had gathered during the ride. When she encountered the bump made by the lady's big toe she stopped and looked up. The lady was looking down at her.

'Encarnita!' cried Pilar, scandalised, rushing forward to haul her back. She had not noticed what the child had been doing, she had been too busy looking at the lady's face, such a different kind of face to the women's faces in their village, which tended to be broader and squarer. This face was rather long, and the eyes were neither brown nor black, but an unusual shade of grey, and huge. And they were, at this moment, solemnly contemplating her daughter.

'It's all right,' said Don Geraldo, putting out a hand to bar Pilar's way. 'The *señora* says she does not mind.'

But it was obvious that Pilar did. Encarnita could see that she did when she glanced up. Her mother was frowning and scratching the flea bites on her waist. Encarnita's eyes were drawn back, though, to the shoes. All the onlookers were now watching her as she squatted on the ground stroking the foreign *señora's* foot and some of the children were sniggering. The two Englishmen were looking on, amused.

Don Geraldo then announced that they would have to be

going inside; his guests were tired after their long ride and needed to rest. He cleared a passage so that he could escort them into the house.

Encarnita released the *señora's* foot and the *señora* smiled at her, again rather gravely, but not unkindly. Her husband tipped his head to acknowledge the crowd and stood back to let her enter the house before him. Another gentleman, obviously. Encarnita watched the *señora's* shoes until they were gone from sight and the door of the house had closed. She wished she could go with them, through the barn and up the stairs into the house and see what the lady was wearing under her long coat and what food she liked to eat. Maria would tell them everything in due course but that would not be the same as seeing for herself. Perhaps, when she was grown up, she could get a job working in a house like Don Geraldo's.

'They have such good manners, the Englishmen,' observed Maxima. 'They are different from our men. Ours would have gone barging ahead.'

'The lady, too, was nice,' said Pilar. 'She wasn't cross at all. But you shouldn't have done that, Encarnita! I don't know why Maria thinks Don Geraldo is nervous about them coming.'

When Maria had a chance to report she was able to tell them that these particular visitors were pleased with everything! They ate the food and didn't complain, they were amused by the toilet arrangements and admired the view from the rooftop of the house. And they liked walking on the hills.

Juliana and Encarnita had discovered that for themselves for whenever they saw the three English people setting out from the village they followed them, keeping a safe distance behind so that they would not be seen. On a couple of occasions the foreigners did spot them and waved and the children, a little uncertainly, waved back.

'Don't tell your mama we've been following them,' warned Juliana. 'That is to be our secret.'

Juliana loved secrets. She relayed to Encarnita bits of gossip she had overheard passing between her mother and other women and Encarnita listened carefully. Paquita, the daughter of Frascillo, the mason, was mad. The priest, Don Horacio, visited the baker's wife when the baker was not there. Don Horacio came to see them, said Encarnita.

'But he is in *love* with her,' said Juliana triumphantly. She liked to talk about love. 'Paquita is in love with all the men in the village, especially when she has her mad fits. Then she is like the animals. Her father cannot stop her so he has to take her into his own bed.'

Since many of the children slept alongside their parents Encarnita did not see that there was anything strange about that.

The next time they saw the English visitors they were down by the stream where the women did their washing. Encarnita and Juliana were helping Pilar. Don Geraldo and his two friends stood and watched as if they had never seen women doing their laundry before. The women knelt on the bank and pummelled their clothes, their shoulders and forearms working vigorously, amid much rinsing and splashing and chatter. Today, with the visitors watching, their tongues dried and they concentrated on their work.

'The *señora* would like to know what you're using to make the paste,' said Don Geraldo, bending over Pilar. 'She is interested in your lives.'

'Wood ash,' said Pilar, embarrassed once again in the presence of the strangers. In Don Geraldo's house they had soap. Maria liked to brag about it. Pilar could also see that Encarnita's eyes had strayed to the *señora's* shoes and her eyes were round and wide open. She looked mesmerised, as if she might be about to make a move towards them. Pilar frowned at her and shook her head.

'And does it clean the clothes?' asked Don Geraldo.

'Quite well. The sun does the rest.'

He nodded and soon the English people wandered off.

'When I grow up I will live in a house where they have

soap,' declared Juliana.

'You will be lucky!' said Pilar.

Juliana smiled.

I, too, will have soap, thought Encarnita. And shoes, like the lady.

With the coming of summer Pilar was able to earn a little money working in the fields and when she helped bring in the harvest Encarnita went with her. On occasions, Don Geraldo helped too. He enjoyed the work. He joked and laughed. Encarnita liked the sound of his laughter. She roamed around the field where her mother was working, watching the men and women scything the corn. Often they sang *coplas*, and that she liked, except that they were usually sad in the end, and she wondered why that should be. Sometimes a man and a woman would disappear behind a hedge and she would hear noises similar to the ones that went on when her mother had a night visitor. There would be a lot of giggling and scuffling and then the two would emerge with blotchy faces and their clothes all over the place. They had been rutting like cats on heat, said Juliana.

'Don't wander away too far,' cautioned Pilar, but Encarnita liked to wander.

In September, after the harvest had been gathered in, there was a bit of excitement in the village when General Miguel Primo de Rivera proclaimed himself Dictator. He had the support of the army behind him so who was going to challenge that? The king, Alfonso XIII, was not pleased since it reduced him to playing second fiddle. The villagers did not know whether it was an occasion for celebration or not. The previous regime had been corrupt, as most regimes appeared to be, a fact they took for granted. Would this one be any less so? Justice and equality were words that held little meaning. Pilar and Encarnita hovered in the plaza listening to what the men had to say. Some argued that the general, being an Andalus himself, from Jerez, would understand the problems of the south better. At least he was saying that he wanted to improve the condition of the poor.

And Andalucía was one of the poorest provinces in the country. Few believed, though, that the landowners would give the general their support. They were too greedy. Life in the *pueblo* would no doubt go on in the same old way, regardless of who was in power in Madrid. The people of the *pueblo* were not much interested in national politics. The mayor was more important to them. It was he who sorted out disputes and recorded births, marriages and deaths.

Don Geraldo was showing little interest in what was happening in Madrid, either. His feet were itching. He packed a bag and took himself off.

'He's gone travelling again,' said Maria.

'He is lucky,' sighed Pilar.

'He thinks he might go across the sea to Morocco. He said he would go where the fancy takes him.'

Encarnita liked the sound of that. One day, perhaps, she would be able to go where the fancy took her.

It was quieter in the village with Don Geraldo away but when the days had shortened and the nights had become long he came back, his hair bleached and his skin tanned from the North African sun. Lamps glowed once more in the corner house and visitors returned. Señor Partridge and Carrington, the painter-woman, who were now man and wife, came for Christmas.

The weather was unseasonably warm and so the *señora* chose to sleep on the roof, under the stars, something else that Maria could not understand since there was a proper bed for her in a proper room. Also, Señor Partridge did not sleep up there beside her. What was one to make of that?

'Foreigners are odd,' said Maria. 'She might be married but she still encourages Don Geraldo. She'll upset him before they leave, you'll see! I don't trust her.'

During the day the men went out walking together while the *señora* drew and painted out in the open air, attracting the village children, among them Encarnita and Juliana, who would creep up behind her and stand gawping over her shoulder at the easel. When she looked round and caught sight of Encarnita a light dawned in her eyes.

'Encarnita, *si*?' she asked.

'*Si*,' said Encarnita.

'You were just a baby when I saw you last but I recognised you by your eyes! You have such a grown-up look for a small child.'

One day, Encarnita and Juliana saw Don Geraldo carrying Señora Partridge's painting materials out onto the hill for her. They followed at a distance. It would be nice to have a man to do things like that for you, said Juliana, an Englishman like Don Geraldo. Spanish men did not do such things. After Don Geraldo had set up the easel he turned to look at the *señora* and in the next minute he had her in his arms and they were kissing. The girls squatted behind a bush but after a few kisses the *señora* pulled away and Don Geraldo made his way back down to the village, his shoulders drooping.

'He looks sad,' sighed Juliana. 'He must be in love with her.'

Maria said that at times the atmosphere in the house crackled as if an electric storm was brewing, but the thunder and lightning never arrived to clear the air.

Don Geraldo decided to give a dance. He loved holding dances to which he invited the villagers. They came willingly, especially the girls, who sat beside their mothers casting demure glances at the young males from beneath their long dark eyelashes. Pilar took Encarnita, who liked clapping in time to the music. Don Geraldo plied the gypsy guitarists with anis, which helped to keep their fingers strumming.

'Don Geraldo gives good dances,' said Pilar. 'The best in the village. See, Encarnita, how the English visitors are enjoying themselves.'

Señor and Señora Partridge appeared to be, at least in the beginning. They smiled as they glanced around the room. But as the evening went on it became obvious that there was a certain amount of tension between the two Englishmen. The Partridges danced together. Don Geraldo watched. He never danced himself.

'I don't know why they don't go out into the yard and sort it out, like men do,' said Maria.

A knot of men had just come in; they would have been drinking in the bar. Jaime was amongst them. He ignored Pilar at first, then he came shuffling over and stood in front of her without saying a word. She stood up.

'You stay with Juliana,' she told Encarnita.

The children watched from the sidelines as the couple edged onto the floor. They danced sedately and without saying a word, as did most of the other dancers. Maria was different; she liked to fling herself about, wave her arms in the air and make her body writhe like a snake. Some said she went a bit crazed in the head when she danced.

Juliana sighed. 'One day we will dance.'

'Why can't we dance now?'

'*Chicas* don't dance together! Encarnita, do you think your mother is in love with Jaime?'

Encarnita did not answer since she did not know. Sometimes her mother would say, 'Jaime is kind. Look, he has brought us some eggs!' Was that what Juliana meant?

Pilar and Jaime disappeared for a while later on. Encarnita was anxious.

'They'll come back,' said Juliana. 'I expect they've just gone out to the yard.'

They came back separately into the room. No one except the two children had noticed their absence for now the whole house was teeming with people. Don Geraldo always left the door standing open.

'I hope he doesn't go away again soon,' said Juliana. 'More things happen when he is here.'

'I hope he stays in Yegen for ever and ever,' said Encarnita.

But he was restless after his guests had departed and in March he decided to make a visit to England.

'Imagine,' said Maria, 'he is taking presents for Señora Perdiz and she a married woman now! He is actually taking four chairs. *Four*! And a heap of plates – why would he take *plates*? They're just things to eat off. And some chintz. *And* he has bought her a beautiful bodice made of brocade. He is going to take all of that across the sea.'

'He must love her very much,' said Pilar wistfully and Encarnita looked anxiously at her mother.

Maria sniffed.

'Can't they buy those things in England?' asked Juliana.

'What is England?' asked Encarnita. She was always hearing the name, yet could not picture it. Her mother said she would ask the schoolteacher to show her on the globe in her classroom and when she did Encarnita was baffled to see that it was just a little patch on the round sphere of the world whereas Spain, where the teacher said they lived, was much bigger.

Pilar went with Encarnita and Juliana to see Don Geraldo setting off. They loved to watch arrivals and departures, though the former, of course, were what they preferred. There was always a feeling of emptiness after they'd called out their good-byes. *Hasta pronto*! But would they see him soon?

It was chilly on that March morning as they stood in the street watching the cart being loaded up outside Don Geraldo's house. Maria fussed over the packing, clicking her tongue at the carter when he wasn't careful enough and warning him not to drop the parcel of plates.

'He doesn't want to arrive in England with them in a thousand bits!'

Don Geraldo emerged in his best clothes, his cravat neatly tied and the gold pin in place. He was ready to depart.

'I'll be back soon,' he promised the little group that had come to wave him off. 'Take good care of the house for me, Maria.'

But he was not to return for five years, by which time many things in the village would have changed.

Don Geraldo would come back in May to find that five cherry trees had been planted in the *plaza* by order of General Miguel Primo de Rivera. His dictatorship, which had been relatively popular for the first three years, had, in the last three, been running into trouble. His plans for the poor, as expected, had come to nothing. His health was now failing and rumour had it that he was drinking nightly in the bars and cafés of Madrid. When he was heard issuing decrees on the bar's spluttering radio he often came over not only as garrulous but drunk. The cherry trees were seen, by those who thought about it, to be an effort on the general's part to get back into favour with the people. But, as the labourer doing the planting had said to Encarnita while she sat on the wall to watch, a few trees would not change anything.

'He'll not last long, Rivera. None of them ever do. Nor the monarchs either. Alfonso will go the way of the rest of them.'

'What way is that?'

'They abdicate. The last four kings have. Good riddance, too.'

Encarnita had heard someone call the man an anarchist though she did not know what that meant. But she thought the *plaza* looked the better for the cherry trees.

What was to matter to Don Geraldo more than the unstable political situation was the fact that Don Fernando had died in his absence and Maria was under the impression that she had inherited the house and was now his landlord.

The day before he was due Pilar advised Maria to clean up the house. It was in a dreadful state. The place stank and there were fleas everywhere. Since being in sole control Maria had moved in a whole colony of animals, goats, sheep, rabbits, hens, and even a cow and a donkey. She herself was no cleaner than the house. Her black skirt and bodice had a greenish sheen from dirt and wear. She looked demented. A lawsuit concerning her sister's will – or lack of it – was obsessing her. Her sister had died intestate without a direct heir, her only son having predeceased her. According to Maria, her sister had gifted her property, worth not much more than thirty *pesetas*, to her on her deathbed, just as Don Fernando had. People conceded that the first claim might be true, but not the second. Doña Clara, Don Fernando's widow, was, without question, her husband's inheritor.

'Always try to keep yourself neat and clean, Encarnita,' Pilar said to her daughter after she'd drawn her attention to the state of Maria's clothing. 'If you want to travel to far-away places you must look and smell nice or people will not want to know you.'

Encarnita, now nine years old, dreamed of distant lands. She spun the globe in the schoolroom and repeated the names of the countries to herself. In her mind she travelled to them, scaling their mountains, sailing down their rivers. She was a fluent reader, the best in the school, said the teacher, who gave her whatever books and periodicals she had. Encarnita read the weekly Granada paper to her mother, whose own reading had not progressed as far. She listened carefully, too, to the stories of the shopkeeper, José Venegas, who had spent five years travelling around South America, trading with Indians. His stories, full of danger and adventure, were more amazing than anything to be found in the Granada paper. What also surprised Encarnita was that José himself did not seem a very interesting or daring man. She had thought that anyone who had travelled as he had would be both. He recounted his stories in a dead-pan voice as if he were describing walking down the street in Yegen on a dull day.

She told her schoolfriend about José's travels in countries like Brazil and Peru but Luisa was not interested. She said the people there were savages.

'They live in the jungle and go about with nothing on.

That's why the missionaries collect money to buy them clothes.'

'They don't all live in the jungle. Mama's friend Federico has been to Argentina and he says it's a wonderful place, with hot water and fine houses. He says we're like savages beside them.'

Unlike Encarnita, Luisa had no wish to travel. She hated the idea of crossing the sea, not that she had ever seen it, except in the distance. But to cross *water*!

'You don't want to stay in Yegen all your life, do you?' asked Encarnita.

'I might go to Motril.'

'I shall go further than that,' declared Encarnita.

Her head, then, was filled with thoughts of foreign lands when Don Geraldo did finally arrive back in Yegen. He was not amused by the menagerie on the ground floor of his house and the buzzing of the flies, nor by Maria's demands for rent.

'You want *me* to give *you* money for the house?'

'I am your landlord now.'

'Nonsense!' he retorted and after making some remarks about being expected to live in a stinking pit, he stormed out and went for a walk up the hill, where he came across Encarnita grazing her goat. She had tied Gabriella to a stake and was reading *Don Quixote*, a shortened version, for children.

'It is Encarnita, isn't it? You've grown! Well, of course you would, wouldn't you? And this is the angelic Gabriella?' He dropped down onto the ground beside her. 'So what is it you're reading? *Quixote*! You must be a good reader. Not many in Yegen are. When I'm next in Granada I'll look for some books for you.'

She thanked him shyly, amazed that he would do this for her, then with a little rush of confidence she added, 'I wish I could read your books. I wish I could speak your language.' She blushed, worried that she had said too much.

'Why do you?'

'I want to go to England one day. I want to go on a journey.'

'Ah, yes, a journey.' He smiled.

'You go on many.'

'I love travelling. I always feel excited when I set out on a journey.'

Encarnita knew that she would, too. 'Where do you go?'

'France, Greece, Morocco...'

'Tell me about them, please!'

While the midday sun beat down on them and Gabriella grazed Don Geraldo talked to Encarnita about his travels to exotic places.

'And England?'

'It's green, much greener than Andalucía, and the mountains are not so high nor the weather so fierce in winter or so hot and scorching in summer. It's a much more moderate place, tamer. Less wild, less extreme.'

'Which do you like best? England or Yegen?'

'I'm not sure yet. But, Encarnita, look at what's around you! Why would anyone want to go anywhere else? Look at the space! And the *sierras*! Aren't they magnificent? Feel how still the air is. You'll never see anywhere in the world more beautiful than this. But you don't believe me, do you? Of course you don't! You want to see for yourself. That is why we travel.'

She had known that he would understand.

'Why don't I teach you some English?' he said.

They began that afternoon and when she ran down the hill afterwards, tugging Gabriella behind her, she went straightaway to find her mother, who was sitting in Don Geraldo's kitchen with Maria and her daughter Angela. Angela had turned seventeen and was a pretty looking girl.

'Don Geraldo is teaching me English,' Encarnita announced, breathless. She was able to say "tree, flower, goat, clouds", as well as, rather hesitantly, "My name is Encarnita and I am nine years old".'

Her mother was impressed, Maria less so. She was too

consumed by her own affairs to be interested in anyone else's. She had two on her mind: her sister's will, and the making of a marriage for her daughter. She made it no secret that she wanted Don Geraldo to marry Angela. He was in search of a wife, she said that was obvious, the way he was casting his eyes around the girls, though Pilar pointed out that might not mean he wished to marry any of them. But Maria felt sure that he would. He was thirty-six years old after all, no longer a young man. She had enlisted the support of Doña Clara, who had become fond of her stepdaughter Angela, the only surviving offspring of her late husband.

'Doña Clara has offered to make over all Don Fernando's property in Yegen, the house *and* his cattle ranch, to Don Geraldo, if he marries Angela,' announced Maria and sat back to to enjoy the others' astonishment.

For some time Angela had been saying her prayers in front of an image of San Geraldo, which a papal missionary had procured for her from nuns in Granada. She was a religious girl and never missed Mass on Sundays.

'Not only that,' Maria went on, 'when Doña Clara dies, she will leave him *all* her property in Granada. You will be a rich woman, Angela, and live the life of a real lady. You'll be Doña Angela! And when you are you must not forget your poor mother who has slaved all these years to bring you up.'

'But will he agree?' asked Pilar.

'Why would anyone refuse such an offer? He's always saying he's short of money. She is a rich woman, Doña Clara, richer than Don Fernando ever was.'

'He won't marry Angela,' predicted Pilar on their way home.

'Why not?' asked Encarnita.

'Who would want Maria for a mother-in-law? She's becoming more *loca* by the day.'

Encarnita could see that for herself. Nevertheless, she was intrigued by the idea of Don Geraldo marrying Angela. She did not think Angela worthy of him but, on the other hand, if he did marry her that would keep him in the village.

Encarnita returned to the same place on the hill next day with Gabriella and read *Don Quixote* until he came.

'Do you remember what I taught you yesterday?'

They had another English lesson and he told her she was a good pupil, which made her blush with pride.

Glancing down, she saw Juliana on the path below. The older girl did not keep company with her as much as she used to; she had other companions. The boys in the village liked her and ran after her, hoping for her favours. She spied Encarnita with Don Geraldo and waved. '*Hola*!' she called up and came to join them.

Juliana had become a young woman since Don Geraldo had last seen her. At fifteen, she was not tall but well developed, with rounded breasts and a softer, clearer skin than was usually seen in these parts. But it was her eyes that attracted attention most of all; large and expressive, they were at varying times and in different situations wide-open, at others half-closed, which was when she looked at her most sensual. Her eyes invited men, said Pilar; she knew how to draw them in, like when a cat stares down a bird, paralysing it.

Don Geraldo stood up when Juliana reached them.

'*Hola*!' she said again, smiling directly at him. Her eyes looked slanted now. 'Do you remember me, Don Geraldo? Juliana.'

'Juliana,' he repeated. He was staring at her as if he would like to eat her, Encarnita told her mother later, and Pilar said that she did not doubt it.

Shortly afterwards, Don Geraldo engaged Juliana to work as a maid in his house, having first paid a small sum to her mother to keep her happy. Juliana moved in and shared a bed with Angela. Maria, as was to be expected, was in a fury.

'She's a lazy bitch! She trails a cloth across the table as if she's in a dream and she calls that cleaning! And she eats! You should see how she eats. You can't leave anything lying but she'll have it in her mouth in a flash. She'll be fat before she's forty.'

Don Geraldo decided it was time to give a dance again and told Maria to invite all the young girls. Antonia, Paca, Carmen, Dolores and Lolita came and he flirted with them in turn but his gaze came to rest more often on Juliana than any other girl. She flirted, too, with the young men, and danced. Encarnita could not take her eyes off them. They were playing a game, said Pilar.

For the next move, Don Geraldo began to teach Juliana to read and write. Encarnita felt a pang of jealousy when she heard. He had less time for her now; their English lessons had lapsed though he did give her a book of fairy tales written in English which she puzzled over, understanding words here and there. Juliana told her that they sat side by side in the *granero*, she and Don Geraldo. He had made it into a cosy sitting room. Don Geraldo said that she was making good progress. He had brought her some nice stories to read, love stories.

'He wants me to be his *novia*.'

'Has he asked you?'

'He wouldn't *ask*, Encarnita, not like that. It is something that I just know, by the way he looks at me. When you're older you'll understand.'

'So, are you going to be his *novia*?'

A little smile curved around Juliana's lips. 'We shall see, won't we? I haven't let him kiss me yet.'

Maria, who had been growing steadily more annoyed, sacked her. Don Geraldo immediately reinstated her. The rows went on and Maria's voice could be heard out in the street. When her screeching built to too high a pitch Juliana dropped her bucket and cloth and went for a walk.

She found Encarnita on the hill. 'Shall I tell you a secret, Encarnita? Last night I let him kiss me!'

'And was it nice? Did you like it?'

'Yes, I liked it,' said Juliana and she laughed. 'And so did he! He didn't want to let me go, but I told him that he must.' So was Juliana now his *novia*? Not quite, she said. But soon, perhaps. 'He is panting after me like a dog. That is good. If he waits a little longer he will want me even more. It is good to be fifteen, Encarnita. Wait until you are! Do you know that copla?' She began to sing:

> *From fifteen to twenty a girl is like a rosebud;*
> *at twenty-five, a rose;*
> *at thirty, a scarlet poppy;*
> *at forty, a withering flower;*
> *at fifty, an artichoke gone to seed.*

'Don Geraldo likes rosebuds!' Juliana went off down the hill laughing. 'Most men do.'

It was not long before Maria sacked her again, declaring that she refused to have such a lazy useless bitch in her kitchen. 'That's what you are – a bitch on heat!'

So Juliana, still smiling, walked out again.

The situation would have to be resolved, said Pilar.

Don Geraldo paid Maria what was rumoured to be a considerable sum of money to move Angela out of Juliana's bed. He then told her to vacate the house at night-time and when she dilly-dallied he threatened to shoot her. Finally, in mid-September, Juliana joined Don Geraldo in bed. It was not a secret in the village. How could it be? Englishmen were reputed to be wonderful lovers and Juliana was known to be highly sexed so the verdict was that the union must be a great success. For the next eight months Juliana would not be seen out and about in the village as much as before nor did Don Geraldo go for his usual long walks in the hills. Maria said they didn't get up until all hours of the morning and then they had breakfast together, taking their time and cooing at each other like a couple of idiots, and after that he would sit on the roof reading while she would sing and flit about.

'I think he is in love with her,' said Encarnita.

Maria humphed. 'We shall see.'

At the end of September, Don Geraldo's friend Señor Partridge returned, bringing a different woman with him.

Señorita Marshall was younger and prettier than his painter-wife whose drawing Encarnita looked at every morning. Don Geraldo took Juliana on an expedition down to the sea with the visitors. This surprised the villagers, who wondered if they would ever understand the ways of foreigners. They did not find it odd that a man of his standing would have a girl like Juliana in his bed but it was a different matter to take her out with his friends from England. Juliana told Encarnita that she had shared a bathing hut with the *señorita*, whose first name was Frances.

'I saw her naked. Her body is very white. I saw her look at mine.' Juliana smiled.

'Were they nice to you, Señor Perdiz and his woman?'

'Of course! Why wouldn't they be? I am Don Geraldo's *novia*. I have lovely times with him, Encarnita. In the evening he plays his gramophone and I make him dance with me. And we drink the most delicious sweet green liqueur you could ever imagine.' The tip of Juliana's plump pink tongue ran round her top lip as if she were still savouring it.

'Will he marry you?'

Juliana smiled. 'Who knows? But I think I would like to have his baby.'

Encarnita went home to relate the conversation to Pilar, who said that if Juliana were to have a child with Don Geraldo he would have to support her even if he didn't marry her. 'People say she is easy-going but her head works. Well, who am I to say that is bad? We all have to do as best we can in this life. No one will give us anything for nothing. '

Another day, meeting Juliana coming out of the shop, Encarnita asked her if she had drunk that sweet green liquid again.

'Come in and I'll show it to you. I might even let you taste it. Geraldo has gone to Úgijar to collect his mail. He wouldn't mind, anyway. He likes you. He says you are a clever girl and he likes clever people.' Juliana giggled. 'I wonder why he is so fond of me!'

She led Encarnita through the kitchen where Maria was banging pots about. She scowled at the girls and said to Encarnita, 'Your mother shouldn't let you be a friend of this bitch!' Juliana stuck her tongue out at her and with a waggle of her hips proceeded up the stairs. Encarnita followed close on her heels. They went into the *granero*. There were books everywhere, on chairs, in shelves, on the floor, whilst, in the corner, sat a gramophone with a big brass horn. Encarnita went at once to the bookshelves and ran her fingers over the spines.

'You'd better not dirty any of them,' said Juliana.

Encarnita wiped her hands on the back of her skirt.

Juliana took two little glasses from a shelf, poured some green liquid into each of them and handed one to Encarnita.

'Hold it up to the light,' said Juliana. 'That is what Don Geraldo tells me to do.'

Encarnita held it up and thought the glowing green colour was beautiful, too beautiful almost to drink.

'Drink!' commanded Juliana.

Cautiously Encarnita put the glass to her lips and sipped. A tiny drop slid down her throat like a small pearl, and then another. It felt thick and sweet and unlike anything she had tasted before.

'Do you like it?' asked Juliana.

Encarnita nodded. If Juliana and Don Geraldo liked it, then so would she. She finished the glass and Juliana poured them each another. After three glasses they were both giggling.

'Will he be cross?' asked Encarnita.

'I don't care if he is,' said Juliana. 'Sometimes we quarrel but then we make up afterwards. Making up is wonderful.' She smiled one of her slow, lazy smiles and yawned. 'I think I'll go to bed before he comes back.'

Encarnita scurried round the back of Maria on her way out. Maria yelled after her, 'She's bad for you, that one! You don't want to end up a whore like her!'

Outside in the street, Encarnita felt as if her head was spinning like a top. She staggered down the village into the *campo* and collapsed. Everything in front of her eyes was shimmering, rocks, trees, the distant *sierras*, the thin blue line of the sea. She felt as if she could take off like a great winged bird and float on a current of air down to the Mediterranean Sea. She stayed until the mist in her head began to clear and the world settled itself on its axis. When she went home she did not tell her mother about the green liquid.

Maria continued to be a nuisance to Don Geraldo and to vent her jealous rage on Juliana, annoying him so much that one day he ended up hurling a *tortilla*, along with its plate, out of the window. Finally, he sacked her and everyone wondered why he had waited so long. She took her dismissal calmly at first but by the time she was ready to go she had worked herself into a new state of fury. Once back in her own house she stuck her head out of the window and yelled obscenities about her former employer and his whore.

In her place, Don Geraldo engaged another Maria, a daughter of the innkeeper in the lower *barrio*. This Maria presented a sharp contrast to the ousted one, being small and round-faced with a smooth skin, something that her employer appreciated in a woman. Fewer dramas were played out in the kitchen now and the villagers missed the excitement. The new Maria kept a clean, peaceful house. Don Geraldo dubbed her White Maria, and the other, Black Maria.

Encarnita dreamt one night about the sweet green liquid that gleamed in the light. She was holding a glass in her hand and dancing to the sound of thin, scratchy music, which she could barely hear, when a quite different noise cut across her dream, a terrible low, groaning noise, a noise filled with pain. She sat up startled, as did Pilar. It was Gabriella who was in pain.

They struggled to save the goat but there was little they

could do. She had not been herself this last while; she had been reluctant to walk up hill, had dragged her rope and at times stopped dead, refusing to go further. By the time the dawn came, she was dead. She lay on her side in the straw, eyes open, staring sightlessly. Encarnita wept.

Their life was even more difficult now than it had been before. Gabriella had given them milk, which Pilar considered necessary for a child in order to build strong, straight bones. They could not afford another goat.

Encarnita sat in a hollow, sheltered from the wind, studying the English book of fairy tales Don Geraldo had given her. Each story was illustrated, which was a help. She knew the tale of the ugly duckling that turns into a swan and there was Cinders, the poor girl who marries a prince in the end. Was that how Juliana's story would turn out? Would she marry Don Geraldo and never be poor again? Encarnita lingered over the picture of Cinders stepping into a glass coach, waved off by her fairy godmother.

It was March, and still cold. Snow lay thick on the tops of the *sierras*. Encarnita sat with her knees up and her skirt covering them like a tent to keep her legs and ankles warm. She rested the book against the slope of her knees.

'You were far away in your head.' She looked up, startled, to see Don Geraldo standing in front of her. 'It's a good feeling, isn't it, being transported into a different world?' He glanced around. 'Gabriella not with you today?'

'She's dead. She was sick and we had no medicine to give her.'

'I'm sorry, Encarnita! You'll miss her. Are you going to get another one?'

She shrugged. 'We have no money.'

'Would you like me to read you a story in English?'

'Please!'

'Which shall I read? Cinderella?' He sat down and they bent their heads together over the book. 'Once upon a time,' he began. He read slowly and clearly and her lips moved as she silently mouthed the words with him. Finally, he read, '"And they lived happily ever after." So it has a happy ending! That's what we like about stories. Happy endings are not so easy to come by in real life. At times one thinks one is about to achieve one. And then it slips away.'

'But if you have money?'

'That doesn't solve everything, Encarnita. One of the

problems can be not knowing what you want.' He was staring into space and for a moment she thought he had forgotten she was there. He turned back to her. 'I'm going off on
a journey again. To Morocco. Will you take care of Juliana
for me while I'm away? My friend Paco is going to look
after her, too.'

She wondered why he could never stay long in one place.
He left the following day.

When Encarnita went looking for Juliana, White Maria said
she had gone home to her mother's house. Encarnita carried on down the hill to the Casa Narciso. The door was
open. No one locked their door in the village though they'd
heard that some people up in Granada did for fear of
thieves. No one here had much to steal. She went inside.
There was no sign of Juliana's mother or of anyone else.
Then she heard a noise. Of Juliana giggling. She was in the
loft overhead. With Paco. Encarnita recognised his voice.
Other noises followed, which she also recognised. She left,
feeling slightly guilty that she had not done a very good job
of looking after Juliana, though she knew, when she talked
it over with herself, that she could not have stopped her
going up to the loft with Paco. No one could stop Juliana
from doing anything she wanted to do. It was soon common knowledge that she was sleeping with Paco. Pilar had
a word with him. She had known him since they were children together.

'You shouldn't have betrayed Don Geraldo, Paco. He's a
decent man. He trusted you as a friend.'

'I have to protect her from the village boys. If she was
not with me they would all have her. Don Geraldo would
like that less.'

Pilar had no answer to that.

Don Geraldo heard the news as soon as he arrived back
in Yegen and angry scenes ensued. Juliana wept and took
refuge with Pilar and Encarnita.

'Why does he make such a fuss? Do you think he's been
faithful to me in Morocco? He'll have visited the brothels,

I know he will.'

'It's his pride that is wounded,' said Pilar. 'Everyone knows you've been with Paco. He sees all the young men after you and it makes him feel old. Especially since he's beginning to lose his hair.'

'And his teeth,' said Juliana with a giggle. 'One or two. He doesn't like that. But I'm going to go back to him now that he's here. We have good times together.'

'You'll have to let him see that you're sorry, then. Otherwise he might not want you."

'He'll want me. He says I'm better at making love than any girl he's ever had before. He told me that sometimes he's had trouble to make love, even with prostitutes. But not with me. He says I unblocked him.' Juliana had perked up. She smiled and stretched and made her way slowly back up the hill to Don Geraldo's house.

'She will try to make sure she has a baby soon,' predicted Pilar. 'While she has the chance.'

Don Geraldo took Juliana back but the relationship was not as it had been before. He was restless and went walking alone again more often and when he met Encarnita he took time to stop and teach her a little English and read to her.

One day, after he had closed the book he said, 'I've decided to go to London, Encarnita.'

'For ever?' Her heart was thudding. He had said it in a very final way.

'No, I'll come back sometime.'

But not for a while, she thought sadly. Not when he says *sometime*. It was a word that suggested away in the distant future, or perhaps not at all.

Before Don Geraldo left he gave Juliana his gramophone and seven hundred *pesetas*, which became the talk of the village. Imagine such a sum! She had known what she was doing, that girl! Don Geraldo then sent Juliana off with her mother and Paco to stay with her sister in Motril, down on the coast. They departed in good spirits, despite Paco being due to go off soon to do his Military Service.

Don Geraldo also had two presents for Encarnita. One was a book of poems called *A Child's Garden of Verses,* written by a man called Robert Louis Stevenson. The other gift was a motherless four-week old kid with soulful eyes and wobbly legs.

'Do you mean she's for me to keep?' Encarnita could hardly find the words to thank him but wanted to do so in his own language. *Thank you, thank you!* She stumbled over the words and they came out in a tangle.

'*De nada,*' he said. 'What will you call her?'

Encarnita did not hesitate. 'Cinderella. I will call her Cinderella.'

And so Don Geraldo departed, yet again.

His absence left a hole, as always, in the life of the village, but especially for Encarnita, who felt sad whenever she passed his house. There were no dances now and no visitors arriving for people to watch and gossip about. She would have felt even more lonely with both Don Geraldo and Juliana away if she had not had Cinderella to look after. She went once or twice to see Luisa, who lived out in the *campo* in a a poor, broken-down shack of a house, but her friend had little time to herself. Her mother had seven children, of which Luisa, at the age of ten, was the eldest. She had to help look after them, to wash clothes in the stream, cook porridge, gather fuel, light the fire, and often milk the goat. Her father was a drunkard as well as lazy, except when it came to breeding children. Her mother was immensely fat and lay on a stinking couch with the newest baby clamped to her breast and the second youngest yowling beside her trying to get attention and his share of the milk. Encarnita never saw her on her feet and wondered if she was able to walk. More often than not Luisa could not come to school though she desperately wanted to. When her father saw her with a book he would strike her, throw the book across the room and call her a lazy bitch. Encarnita eyed him warily on her visits. Luisa often sported a blackened eye or a bruised cheek.

After school, every day, Encarnita led Cinderella slowly down the path from the lower *barrio* into the *campo* where the spring flowers were blooming and the grass was lush. The kid grew gradually steadier on her legs and her body began to fill out. Pilar was looking forward to the day when she would start giving them milk. Men did not come to their house at night now that Encarnita was older, but there were times when Pilar would get up from their bed of rosemary and thyme and go out for a while. Encarnita did not let herself think about that; she lay in the half-light thinking about the little boy in the book of poems who played with toy soldiers in his bed or else she went through the Cinderella story until they all lived happily ever after and then she would go to sleep. Sometimes she stirred when her mother came back and Pilar would say, 'It's all right, Encarnita, it is only me. Go back to sleep.'

When Juliana returned to Yegen, she was pregnant. Don Geraldo was the father, she was adamant about that. It had to be because of the dates. Believe that if you will, said Black Maria. When Juliana heard what she was saying she went to challenge her and they had a slanging match in the street.

'Wait till you see the baby and then you'll know!' yelled Juliana, tossing her head. She looked extremely well. Her skin glowed and the whites of her eyes were clear. She said that word had been sent to Don Geraldo in England and he had agreed to pay her a hundred and fifty *pesetas* a month. He was in the money! Juliana rubbed her forefinger against her thumb. His aunt had died and he had inherited. 'He wants his child to have the best.'

'There's no justice in this world,' said Black Maria, who had been paid thirty *pesetas* a month to keep his house. She was becoming more and more resentful by the day and went about the village in an unkempt state, muttering to herself.

'She will go mad,' predicted Pilar.

On the 7th of January 1931, Juliana gave birth to a girl in the house of her maternal grandmother. She named the child Elena, after Don Geraldo's mother.

The baby was bonny and fair of face. There were some in the village who were convinced that Paco was the father whereas others declared that they saw a likeness of Don Geraldo in her. Everyone wondered if he would come to see her.

There was a mild stir in the *pueblo* in April, when, following an election in the country, King Alfonso XIII abdicated. Encarnita heard the mayor read out the abdication statement.

'Sunday's elections have shown me that I no longer enjoy the love of my people. I could very easily find means to support my royal powers against all comers, but I am determined to have nothing to do with setting one of my countrymen against another in a fratricidal civil war.'

There was no great upsurge of feeling about it in Yegen. Most of the men were in favour of a republic even if political changes never did much to improve their lives. Few of the women had an opinion; they had too many other things on their mind. One or two of them were sorry for the king, in a mild way, amongst them Encarnita, whose only idea of a king came from the illustrations in her story book. She had always pictured King Alfonso wearing a crown and a red robe with an ermine collar.

'Let's hope something good comes out of it,' said José Venegas.

In May, they heard that there was rioting in Madrid, involving clashes between monarchists and republicans. Churches and convents were fired, not only in the capital but all over the country, as far south as Málaga, creating anxiety and alarm. No one was sure what exactly was going on. A man visiting from Granada said it was the work of anarchists who wanted to stir up trouble for the republic. Rumours about all the different factions that were operating continued to fly around. Encarnita overheard a group of the men talking in the *plaza* but could make little sense of what they said. The talk became heated. Two brothers, one a Falangist and the other a Socialist, almost came to blows and would have done had the other men not held them back. Pilar said it would all die down in time. There was little that ordinary men could do to change things. Life in Yegen ticked over much as before.

Sometimes, when Encarnita called at Don Geraldo's house, White Maria would allow her to go upstairs and sit in the *granero* and look at his books, as long as she first washed her hands and took care when turning the pages. Sitting in his big chair, wrapped in the stillness of the room, the world far removed, Encarnita could almost feel his presence and hear his voice talking to her.

In the shelves, she found some books by Señora Woolf. She remembered touching her lovely soft shoes and the lady giving her a serious but not annoyed look. She laughed about that now. One day, perhaps, she would wear such soft shoes herself.

'Encarnita!' Eventually White Maria's voice would disturb her and break the trance. 'Your mother's looking for you. It's getting dark, child. You must hardly be able to see.'

Encarnita liked the long, light evenings of summer when she could be out and about until late. Pilar, who found the heat tiresome, was glad when it was replaced by the milder days of autumn. By then, Don Geraldo had been gone for more than a year. Juliana was untroubled by his absence; she had money to spend and as many men as she wanted and the child was growing and developing as all children should, eating and crawling and trying to stand. Also, she confided to Encarnita, she was worried that Don Geraldo, if he did come back, might want to take Elena from her. In spite of her wild ways, she was fond of her child and cared well for her, keeping her as clean as it was possible to keep a child clean in a poor house without running water.

'But he can't do that!' said Encarnita. 'Take Elena. She's yours.'

'It was a pact, we agreed. He said if he gave me a baby I could keep her until she was weaned.'

'And then?'

'He would take her to England where she would have a better life.'

Encarnita was silent. It must be true that the child would have a better life in England. How could anyone deny that? She would grow up in a nice house, eat good food and wear fine shoes on her feet and clothes on her back, and go to school every day. But Juliana was her mother.

'He couldn't make you, could he?'

Juliana sighed. 'I don't know.'

'You should ask the mayor.'

But Juliana did not, fearing that the mayor would be on the side of Don Geraldo.

In the winter, Pilar developed a cough. It came on mostly at night and she would sit up banging her chest with the back of her hand until she had coughed up a gobbet. Encarnita saw that there were streaks of red in the phlegm and fear clutched at her heart. 'It's this damp house,' said Pilar. She went to see a woman in the *campo* who boiled up some herbs for her. These quietened the cough a bit but it persisted right through to spring.

The year turned and rumour had it that Don Geraldo would return in the summer, but that came to nothing. White Maria kept the house spick and span and whitewashed the outside walls so that it continued to shine amongst its drabber neighbours. Juliana was pregnant again; by her current boyfriend, Amador, or so she said.

Pilar had a talk with her daughter who, at twelve and a half, was starting on the passage from childhood to maturity.

'You must not let yourself grow up to be like Juliana, Encarnita. Going from one man to the other. She has no pride when it comes to men. It's not good for a woman to live like that. She will come to a bad end if she's not careful.' Pilar paused. 'I know at times I have had to do things I would rather not do but I have tried to keep my dignity.'

Encarnita had never heard her mother make such a long

speech.

Pilar cleared her throat and said, 'Encarnita, there is something else I want to to say to you. About your father.'

Encarnita caught her breath. She had often wondered who he was and had imagined him to be a prince who would come galloping into the village on a white horse to rescue them, or a sailor who sailed the seas and went to far-off lands, or an Englishman like Don Geraldo who owned two thousand books. That was her best daydream of all.

'He was a gypsy from Guadix,' said her mother. 'You look like him. You have the same black hair and eyes. He was handsome. He was a singer who sang from the heart and a dancer who danced like an angel. His name was Gabriel.' Two red spots burned brightly high up on Pilar's cheeks.

Encarnita waited, hardly daring to breathe.

'I fell in love with him.'

'And he?'

'Fell in love with me.'

'Why then —?'

'Did he leave me? He was married to another.'

Encarnita found her full voice now. 'I shall go to Guadix and find him!

Pilar shook her head. 'He was killed in a brawl.'

Encarnita put her face in her hands and howled. Her mother comforted her and they cried together and after a while they dried their tears and sat quietly.

'You must keep yourself for a good man, Encarnita,' said her mother. 'One who is free and will take care of you and give you a good life.'

Encarnita looked at the scruffy boys who hung around in the *plaza* and who had started to call after her and she could not see any who would be capable of giving a girl a good life. Most of them had never been to school. She would never take a man who could not read and write.

And then, in October, after being away for two and a half years, Don Geraldo returned. With a wife.

Gamel Woolsey was American, and a poet. The fact that she came from the United States of America, a country where the buildings reached the sky and the streets were paved with gold, caused a stir in itself. Anyone they'd ever heard of who had emigrated to North America had made a fortune. Half the village would have packed up and gone, given the chance, though few could actually imagine doing it. It was a far and distant land, appearing much more distant than Argentina where, at least, the people spoke Spanish.

Doña Gamel was not young, perhaps no younger than Don Geraldo himself, which caused surprise, considering his tastes. It was decided that she must have money. When that rumour reached Don Geraldo's ears, which it inevitably did, he laughed and shook his head. He told White Maria that there were poor people in America just as in most countries.

'But you don't mean Doña Gamel was as poor as a woman like Pilar,' said White Maria, somewhat shocked.

'No, of course not. It's all relative, I suppose. I mean, it depends on what one is used to.'

He introduced his wife to Encarnita when they met on the path below the village. Doña Gamel nodded in recognition when he said Encarnita's name. 'I've told her about you.'

'You speak English, I believe?' The American woman had a soft, low, dreamy voice. Her hair was very black, as black as Encarnita's own, but her skin was much paler. Don Geraldo repeated the question in English.

'*Un poco*,' Encarnita answered, staring down at her grubby feet. Then she lifted her head and added in English, 'A little.'

'You like to read, don't you?'

'Yes, like to read.'

'So do I.'

'How is Cinderella?' asked Don Geraldo.

'She well.'

'She *is* well,' Don Geraldo corrected her gently. 'You see, you can have a conversation in English. You haven't forgotten during all the time I was away.'

'I never forget,' said Encarnita.

Don Geraldo put a hand under his wife's elbow and guided her on down the path. She trod on a stone and her ankle went over just a little and he was immediately concerned, asking if she was all right, and she was reassuring him. They smiled at each other. Encarnita watched them go. It would be nice to have a man who would look after you like that. Most of the men she knew would go ahead of their wives and never thinking of putting out a hand to support them. She turned and went back up into the village.

Juliana was standing in the doorway of Casa Narciso. Since Don Geraldo's arrival Elena had not been visible in the village. Pilar suspected that Juliana might be keeping her out of the way so that she could bargain with Don Geraldo should he want to see the child. But would he, when he had a new wife with him? In Pilar's opinion, it would be better for him, and his new wife, if he were to let sleeping dogs lie and let the child think Paco was her father. He had made no attempt so far to see her even though he was continuing to support her. There were some in the village who still maintained that he was not the father. Most were agreed, however, that he was a fool to go on giving Juliana all that money.

'What were they saying to you?' demanded Juliana as soon as Encarnita reached her.

'We were talking about reading.'

'You will burn out your brains! What use are books?'

'He taught you to read.'

'I only liked to read when he was sitting beside me. But it's useful, I suppose.' Juliana shrugged. 'But her, what did you think of her?'

'She seems nice.'

Juliana sniffed. 'But she's quite old, isn't she? Soon she'll be a withering flower. He always said he liked young, fresh girls.'

'Perhaps, for his wife, he wanted someone different.'

'You don't think she's prettier than me?'

'Are you jealous, Juliana? But you've got Amador.'

'Amador! I am going to get him back, you'll see.'

'Don Geraldo?'

'I've bought some love philtres.' Juliana held up a phial. 'You go into his house sometimes, don't you? Will you put this in his wine for me?'

Encarnita took a step back.

'You're my friend, aren't you? Oh, go on, Encarnita, do this for me,' wheedled Juliana, her bottom lip sagging into a slack pout. 'He'll want me again, I know he will. She won't be as good for him in his bed as I will, I can tell.'

'He's my friend too,' said Encarnita and ran off.

'Bitch!' yelled Juliana after her.

It was no secret that she was trying to tempt Don Geraldo with love potions. The woman who made them up for her had a tongue that wagged. White Maria had warned Don Geraldo to touch nothing that came from Juliana.

Encarnita met him another day when she was with Cinderella. This time Doña Gamel was not with him. He stopped to admire the goat. 'You're obviously taking good care of her.' His voice changed a little, dropping a register. 'Do you still have Gabriella's picture? My friend – my friend Carrington who drew it – she is dead.' His voice cracked as he said it.

'Dead?' echoed Encarnita. 'How can that be? She was not very old.'

'No, she was not old. But she was very unhappy. Because Señor Strachey – you remember him? – died. She didn't want to go on living without him.'

Encarnita was confused. 'She loved *him*, then?' The long thin man with the piles and the big nose who complained about everything? But Señorita Carrington had married

Señor Perdiz, who was younger and much more handsome. And had she not also been in love with Don Geraldo?

'Yes, I know it's difficult to understand, Encarnita.' Don Geraldo sighed. 'Relationships between people often are.'

To her, the story was a muddle, but she supposed that Juliana's love life was, too.

'I'm very sorry,' she said.

'Thank you.' He looked away from her, up towards the mountains.

After a moment, she ventured, 'Doña Gamel is nice.'

He nodded. 'She is, very nice.'

'How long will you stay this time?'

'Perhaps for ever.'

Encarnita's face broke into a smile. They had heard a rumour that he had been talking to Doña Clara about buying the house and that she was more than willing to sell it, since she would never want to live in it again herself.

The Brenans began to have work done. They had a big fireplace installed in the living room and screens fitted on the windows to keep out the insects in summer. Doña Gamel had been used to such things in America. She and Don Geraldo roamed the countryside buying furniture. They loved going on shopping expeditions and on their return Encarnita would run up the hill to see what they had brought back.

Once Doña Gamel had got used to the village she went out walking in the *campo* on her own. The terrain was rough and boulder-strewn under her delicately arched feet but Don Geraldo had obviously decided that he need not watch over his wife quite so closely as he had been doing. Her health was not good; she had had tuberculosis when young and part of one of her lungs had been removed.

Encarnita would often see her when she was grazing Cinderella. She sensed that the American lady liked to be alone. At times she would not even notice Encarnita, who wondered if she might be writing poems in her head. And then, another day, Doña Gamel might be in a different mood, and would stop to talk. They would exchange a few words in both English and Spanish. Doña Gamel said they could help each other for she had much to learn too. She told Encarnita that she was coming to love Spain, and although the country did seem to be somewhat unstable politically, and a bit worrying because of that, she did not want to go back and live in England.

'It's cold and damp there in winter.'

Doña Gamel was soon to find that it could be cold and damp in Yegen, too, in December, when the rains came. There were days when it poured relentlessly and water ran down the streets in torrents, flooding the lower floors of houses that were badly placed. You couldn't put a foot across the threshold without getting drenched within seconds. White Maria said the Brenans were feeling depressed; they hated the morning-to-night greyness and they were missing their friends. The news depressed Encarnita. She had so much hoped that Doña Gamel would like Yegen and would want to stay. Pilar warned her not to rely too much on her friendship with the Brenans.

'You know what Don Geraldo is like. He's restless. It seems he always has to keep moving.'

He took Doña Gamel to Granada for Christmas and when they came back they were in better spirits and immediately started to arrange for friends to come and stay. Encarnita was pleased. She loved the arrival of visitors from England. She would wait for the sound of the mules approaching, eager to see what the people would look like, what they would be wearing, and what their voices would sound like.

In February, came the elderly Señor Roger Fry and his wife with his very much younger wife. White Maria told Encarnita he was a painter and that he wrote things as well, but what she did not know.

'You are such a nosey child,' said Maria's sister, Rosario, good-naturedly. She had been taken on by the Brenans as cook, so now the sisters worked together. 'You were from the day you were born, isn't that right, Maria? Your eyes were everywhere.'

One day, when Encarnita was down at the stream washing clothes, Don Geraldo came past with his friend. They were so absorbed in their conversation that they did not see her. Señor Fry was talking intently and gesticulating. He sounded distressed. Encarnita caught some English words that she could understand, words that she had come across in the fairy tales. *Poor. Miserable. Hovels. Poverty. Rags. Barefoot.*

She looked down at her skirt. There was a rent in her skirt and the hem was ragged. Her feet, too, were bare.

'It *is* the year 1932!' said Señor Fry vehemently. 'It's unbelievable! And in Europe!'

What did he mean by that, wondered Encarnita.

The men went on by.

After the visitors had left, Don Geraldo sought her out. He was hesitant at first as if he had something to say and did not know how to say it. He began, 'You remember my friend Señor Fry who was here? He has given me some money to distribute amongst a few people in the village.'

'Why should he do that?'

'He wanted to make a gift to the village since he had enjoyed his stay here. So, Encarnita, I want you to take this.' Don Geraldo put fifty *pesetas* into her hand. 'Don't thank *me*! Just take it.'

She remembered the words Señor Fry had spoken. *Poverty. Rags. Barefoot.* She looked down at her own bare feet and felt her face heating up. For the first time she was seeing herself as another saw her and now she knew why Señor Fry was giving them money.

'Buy yourself a new dress, Encarnita,' said Don Geraldo hurriedly and left her.

When she showed the money to her mother Pilar said, 'But what is it for?'

'For nothing. It is free.'

They both had new skirts when the pedlar called, and for

Encarnita there were two bodices, as her breasts were beginning to strain against the cloth of the old ones. They had some money left which Pilar hid in a corner of the stable.

Don Geraldo finally went to see Elena, and when he did, according to Juliana, he recognised at once that the child was his daughter.

'I know myself that she is! When I look at her eyes I see him. Can't you see it too? She is not from Paco.'

'Did he speak of taking her to England?'

'He wants to.'

'What did you say?'

'I told him I didn't want to give her up.'

'And then?'

'He said I could have more children.'

'Will his wife not have a child?'

'Maybe not, since she's not strong.'

'He will offer Juliana money,' said Pilar, when Encarnita reported the conversation to her.

'But she can't sell her baby!' Encarnita was horrified.

'Poor people do things that the rich would not do.'

'But she gets money from Don Geraldo now.'

'He might stop that if she doesn't let him have Elena.'

Encarnita felt upset that he could do this to Juliana. It was not as if he knew and loved the little girl and she knew and loved him. They were strangers to each other. Also, Encarnita did not want him to leave Yegen, but if he were planning to take his daughter to England he must intend to live there himself. How dull the village would be without him and his hundreds of books and the dances that he gave and his strange visitors who were so clever and who strode around the *campo* laughing and talking! Always talking. She loved hearing their voices echoing around the valley and sometimes she would catch and understand the occasional word in English and when she did she would feel that she was preparing for her journey. One day she would make it; she was sure of that. 'You and your journey!' Luisa would say when she talked of it.

Encarnita, thinking still about Juliana and her child, took the path out of the village that led to Úgijar. People said she was getting to be like Don Geraldo, going for long walks into the *campo*. It was not a thing the villagers did without a reason. Pilar was not easy about her walking alone and warned her that there could be bandits about. But they tended to roam the higher hills. The almond trees were shimmering with pink and white blooms and looking so pretty that Encarnita's eyes were dazzled even though she had seen them every spring of her life. But, then, blossoms last for only a short time before they wither and drop.

Further along the path, she met Don Geraldo. She had thought that she might for she had seen him heading off in that direction earlier in the morning. He would have been going to fetch his mail.

'*Buenos dias*, Encarnita. It's a fine day, isn't it?' He had an open letter in one hand and he was smiling. 'This is from my publisher. My publisher! He is to publish my first novel in October.'

'You've written a book??'

'It's called *Jack Robinson* and it's about a fifteen-year-old boy who runs away from home to go travelling.'

'I wish I could read it!'

'I'll bring you a copy when I come back.'

'You're leaving? Soon?'

'Quite soon. We have things to arrange in England. But we'll be back.'

He was always coming and going. She feared the time when he would go but not come back.

That winter, Pilar's cough began to trouble her more. At times she was racked by it so badly that after it had calmed she had to sit upright for a long time, with Encarnita supporting her, gasping as she struggled to find her breath. Increasingly there were streaks of blood in her phlegm but she said it had come from her throat because she had been coughing so fiercely. Encarnita walked up to the village of

Válor where she sought out a woman who was reputed to be good at brewing herbal potions for bad chests. Encarnita thought that if Pilar could make it through to the spring she would be all right for then the sun would help her to regain her strength. Encarnita also took a few centimos from their savings and went into the *campo* to buy eggs and cheese for her. Jaime came by from time to time and left them a couple of eggs. For no payment. After Encarnita had milked Cinderella in the evening she would hold a cup of warm milk to her mother's lips and encourage her to drink.

'It will soothe your throat, Mama, and quieten your cough.'

Pilar did make it to the spring but she looked hollow-faced and black round the eyes.

By then, Don Geraldo and his wife were on their way back to Yegen, though their arrival was delayed because he had been taken seriously ill himself when travelling in Portugal. A message came to say he had flu, which had then developed into pneumonia.

'You see, Mama,' said Encarnita, 'even rich people who live in dry houses and can buy medicine get ill.' But they knew that the rich would always have a better chance to recover.

At length, the Brenans arrived and Don Geraldo went to see Juliana to discuss the future of Elena. Juliana claimed that while he was there they'd made love with the child looking on. Encarnita was not sure whether to believe her or not though, knowing Juliana as she did, it was possible. But it looked as if Don Geraldo had not changed his mind about taking Elena to England. Pilar wondered how Doña Gamel would feel about that. 'After all, Elena speaks not a word of English.' And she urinated wherever she stood.

When Encarnita met Don Geraldo in the *campo* she saw that he looked at her in a different way, the way a man might look at a woman, and she blushed. He commented that she had grown up in his absence to be a young lady, a pretty young lady. She glanced away, too embarrassed to meet his gaze, yet flattered that that a man like him should think her pretty.

He had heard about Pilar's illness and expressed his concern and insisted on giving Encarnita money to buy food and and medicine. He also gave her a copy of his book *Jack Robinson*. She was delighted.

'But it doesn't have your name on it!'

'George Beaton is a pseudonym. A made-up name. Same initials, that's all. G.B.'

'But why?'

'I might want to write different things under my own name. Non-fiction. I might write about Yegen.'

'But Yegen is not an important place.'

He smiled. 'It is very important to me,' he said, though, even then, he was planning to leave it, for good.

Encarnita put the book carefully away in the box where she kept her special things, Señorita Carrington's drawing, the English fairy tales, the poems by Robert Louis Stevenson and *Don Quixote*.

To her dismay, the Brenans came to the decision that living all year round in Yegen would not be good for Gamel's health. They began house-hunting. After travelling the length and breadth of Andalucía, looking along the coast and in the hinterland, they bought, in the end, a house in a small *pueblo* called Churriana, close to the city of Málaga. The winters, there, would be milder than in the Alpujarra. It was a long way from Yegen.

Before moving to Churriana they had to go to England, to settle their affairs, but they would come back to Yegen one more time, in order to collect their furniture, as well as Maria and Rosario, and Rosario's husband Antonio, who were to go with them to look after their new house. They took with them the little Elena, whom they renamed Miranda Woolsey Brenan. Before they left Don Geraldo gave Juliana a thousand *pesetas* – worth about fifty pounds sterling in the year 1934 – with the promise that he would send her two hundred and fifty *pesetas* a year.

The villagers did not judge Juliana harshly for taking the money. Few knew what they would do themselves in the same situation, especially the women who struggled to feed and clothe three, four, five children or more in miserable hovels. They were sorry for her when she wept afterwards.

The Brenans came back in November to pack up their belongings, having dropped off the little Miranda at a friend's house in Torremolinos, not far from Churriana.

They toured the village to say their goodbyes and Don Geraldo invited Encarnita to come up to the house to choose a book. She hesitated before saying that she would like one by the lady who had worn the soft leather shoes. For a moment he could not think whom she meant, then he laughed and said, 'Do you mean Señora Lobo?'

'Could you spare one? Only if you can.'

'Let me see. You know, I think I might have two copies of this one.' He pulled *To the Lighthouse* from the shelf and put it into her hand.

She thanked him, saying that she would keep it for ever, and the other books he had given her.

'You have a difficult time ahead, I think, Encarnita. I hear your mother is very ill. That's hard. Losing people is difficult. I know that myself.'

Don Geraldo gave her fifty *pesetas* before kissing her on both cheeks. 'Don't argue with me now! That's to help you out. You'll need it.'

'Perhaps I'll keep it for my journey.'

The Brenans loaded up two lorries with their possessions and then climbed on board themselves with Maria, Rosario and Antonio. There was a road passable for wheeled transport into the village now.

Encarnita did not go to wave the travellers off. This was one departure that she did not wish to see.

Encarnita was fifteen years old on the first of January. By now Pilar was very weak. She had to be helped out into the yard to relieve herself. And she could not walk as far as the church, which grieved her even more. Her condition had worsened over the winter and she had been given the Last Rites twice, rallying afterwards each time.

'Don't let yourself be too sad, Encarnita. Think about going on a journey. This might be the year to begin it. You might try to go and find Rinaldo.'

Rinaldo was a half-brother of Pilar's of whom she had been fond. He had gone off down to the coast some years back to seek work and a while afterwards had sent them a letter, which he had got someone to write for him. The letter was in Encarnita's special box.

'I'm not going to leave you, Mama!'

'But I might be going to leave you. We both know that.'

Encarnita held tightly onto her mother's hand, willing her to live, fervently praying that she would, but with little hope. Just before first light she felt the last traces of strength ebb from the fragile body. Pilar had slipped away as quietly as she had lived; she had never been one to raise her voice or make a fuss. She was thirty-five years old. Her daughter sat beside her, frozen like a statue until Isabel, Juliana's mother, came in and found her.

The neighbours were good to Encarnita; they were willing to share what little food they had and they mourned with her and helped to bury her mother. Pilar had been well liked in the village. She had never spoken ill of anyone and she had had a kindly manner. She was buried in a shallow grave in the part of the cemetery known as *la olla* – the stew pot – where the poor resided after death, their relatives being unable to afford one of the masonry niches in the walls. She was conveyed there in the communal parish coffin whose hinged bottom opened to allow the corpse to drop through.

Encarnita shed tears with Juliana, who was mourning her own loss. Juliana said her arms felt empty. She would never forget her daughter but her daughter would not remember her! She was too young. Why had she let her go? But it was too late now. What was done was done. Encarnita, trying to comfort her, said, 'Think of the good life she will have in England,' but even as she said it she knew it was cold comfort. Both of the girls felt cold, chilled, through to the bone.

Encarnita spent time, too, with Luisa, whenever her friend could snatch a little time away. They embraced, holding on tightly to each other, reluctant to let go. They did not speak much of their troubles; there was no need to. But during those short visits the girls grew close.

When alone, Encarnita went walking in the *campo* for hours at a time and the neighbours worried that she might become demented like Paquita or Black Maria, but she was sane enough and talked calmly. She was often to be seen sitting in the doorway of her house reading her book of English Fairy Tales. She no longer believed that a fairy godmother with a silver wand or a prince in shining armour would come but the stories comforted her nevertheless and made her feel that there was always the hope of things changing.

In a short space of time she had lost the two people that had fed her life. Her mother was the biggest loss of all for they had lived together for fifteen years, sharing the same bed, never spending a night apart; but Encarnita missed Don Geraldo, too. She missed the possibility of meeting him in the *campo* and stopping to talk. She missed the life he had brought into the village, the very unpredictability of it. Every time she had crossed his doorstep she had felt a little spurt of excitement, not knowing what or whom she might find there. The house was closed up now and when she passed she turned her head.

Life in the village had little variety on these dark wintry days. People complained of the rain and lack of money and envied Maria and Rosario who had had the luck to be taken out of it to live in a better place. There was little prospect of anyone doing anything in Yegen to make life better. The fish vendor went on crying his few wares, as did the pedlar, but Encarnita was unwilling to spend much of her savings on either. She ate sparingly, lived mostly on maize porridge and Cinderella's milk and the occasional scrap of cheese or sausage which the shopkeeper pushed across the counter to her free of charge. She was saving for her journey.

Juliana had money to spend but she was not in a buoyant mood. She still shed tears daily for her lost daughter. She was living with her mother and her son in a small house that had been bought for her by Don Geraldo. Her boyfriend had gone off to do his Military Service but she planned to marry him on his return. In his absence her mother was keeping a close watch on her and any young men who might come near.

'Do you think you will ever make your journey, Encarnita?' asked Juliana. 'You keep talking about it. You've talked about it ever since you could speak.'

'I will, come summer.' That would be the time to go, when the days were warm and the nights mild, for then one could sleep out in the *campo*.

Encarnita had decided that she would try to find Rinaldo down on the coast. It would be a start. She took his letter, discoloured from age and damp, and smoothed out the creases. It said little, other than that he was well and living in the fishing village of Almuñecar and hoping to find work. It was not much to go on but Encarnita thought that it should be easy enough to find him as long as the village was not large. Provided, too, that he was still alive. She did not take for granted that he would be. She folded up the piece of paper and put it carefully away, then she went up to the school and asked the teacher if she could look at the atlas. Yegen was not marked on the map of Spain, nor Almuñecar, but Úgijar was, and Granada and Motril. And there, to the west, lay Málaga, with a bigger dot to its name. The teacher said that Almuñecar was somewhere on the coast between Motril and Málaga.

'It doesn't look too far,' said Encarnita.

'Not on the map. It would be a long walk, though.'

But Encarnita liked to walk.

During the harsh weeks of winter when it was cold and the light failed early she held on to the thought of her journey. She put her travelling money safely away and resolved not to touch it, knowing that if she did she would never be able to replace it. There was no work to be had at this time of year. No one in the village could afford to pay a servant now that Don Fernando was dead and Don Geraldo gone. Neither the shop nor the *posada* did enough business to need an assistant. The traders lived on the poverty line themselves. At times Encarnita had to rely on charity, scraps that others could afford to give her. Juliana helped her and occasionally Jaime would come by and leave her an egg without expecting anything in return. She knew it was for her mother's sake. He had married and his wife was expecting a child.

One night, she wakened to see the dark outline of a man framed in the doorway. She tried to let out a scream but it became strangled at the back of her throat and emerged like the squeak of a mouse. She tried again but could make no other sound. It was as if her voice had frozen. In the corner, Cinderella became agitated and trampled her straw.

'That's right, just you keep quiet,' said the man. 'I have a *peseta* for you if you'll give me what I want.' She knew him. He was the father of Luisa. She had seen him earlier, eyeing her in the street. He had called out to her and she had looked away. 'A *peseta*'s a lot of money for a *chica* like you. You've not had a man yet, have you? It's time.'

'I don't want to.' She cowered back against the wall. He was coming closer, his bulk blotting out the small amount of light that there was in the room. She could smell his foul breath and hear his laboured breathing. She found her voice now but nobody would come. 'Go away!' she cried. 'Leave me alone!'

He was on top of her then, a solid weight crushing her body into the bed of rosemary and thyme as he forced himself into her. The pain made her head swirl and she blanked out and when she came round the man was lying on her, spent. After a moment he pulled himself up and saying not a word stumbled out. He did not leave the *peseta*.

Encarnita cried herself to sleep and in the morning went to talk to Juliana, who said it was better not to fight it.

'Men don't like to be refused.'

'I hate him! I'll kill him if he comes back,' vowed Encarnita. She would do it for Luisa as well as herself. 'I mean it!'

She was worried that he might have made her pregnant but Juliana said she thought it unlikely, the first time. 'Come to me at once if you think you are.' Encarnita did not reveal who the man was, nor would she ever tell Luisa.

When Juliana had gone she set off down the path to Yátor, to the small pond known as the women's bath, where she had bathed often with her mother. In February the water was cold but after she had stripped off her bodice and skirt she plunged straight in and submerged herself up to her neck and stayed there until she felt her teeth begin to chatter and her feet to grow numb.

After her bath she kept to the house for several days, afraid to go out in case she would meet him in the street. He came into the village to drink in the bar. She could not bear the idea of his eyes on her face, on her body. At night, she barricaded the door, using an old piece of rusted machinery that she'd found in the *campo* and dragged up the street. Beside the door she kept a solid piece of stone which she would use against him if she had to. He did come back another night. He put his weight to the door and she thought he might splinter it but after a couple of tries he gave up and went off cursing her.

Not long afterwards, he got into a drunken brawl and fell, or was pushed, onto a spike, which pierced his thigh.

His troubles were not over for the wound went septic and for many weeks he was laid up in agony flat on his back. It was said that his groans could be heard far and wide in the *campo*. Encarnita did not hear them herself for she did not go anywhere near his house, but she rejoiced. She had an uneasy feeling that it might be wicked of her to feel such joy in her heart, but that did not stem her sense of satisfaction. Surely he had been punished for what he had done to her, and to Luisa? She did not think she should go so far as to thank God for punishing him. He might not like it, especially since He was supposed to forgive sins, but only if the person repented. She could not imagine him repenting of anything.

She went into the church and lighting a candle for her mother she knelt down and began to talk to her. The little flame helped to calm her. She told her mother the story of the man from beginning to end and when she had finished she knew what Pilar would want her to do. She had been a religious woman and believed in the power of the confessional. She had always said it was bad to keep ugly thoughts locked inside you. So Encarnita went to confess her sins to the priest, who asked if she was sure she had not enticed the man. The question shocked her.

'No, I did not.' She had to clasp her hands together to stop them trembling. She was sure that she never had. When she had seen him looking at her in the street hadn't she glanced away?

'A young woman can entice a man in different ways. Just by the way she looks at a man. Or by the way she flaunts herself.'

'But I didn't! Flaunt myself.'

'You must learn humility, child. You must learn to take responsibility for what happens to you in your life. In such matters as this it is seldom that it is one person who is at fault.' She tried to speak but he hushed her. 'If you look into yourself you may find that your conscience will tell you that you are not guiltless. Few of us mortals are without guilt. We harbour sinful thoughts. Sometimes lustful thoughts. That is the way of the flesh.'

She could not deny that at times she had sinful thoughts, but she was not going to confess to having wanted to break the sixth commandment. Thou Shalt Not Kill.

'It is the duty of a young Christian woman to dress soberly and behave with modesty at all times. Have you forgiven this man?'

'How can I? He is a horrible man. He hurt me.'

'He is a child of God, as you yourself are.'

'He is a monster.'

'To harbour hatred is a sin also.'

She was silent. She thought that what he said might be right but she did not want to acknowledge it, not to him, anyway. She felt spent.

'I ask you again – have you forgiven him?'

'It's difficult,' she muttered.

'To follow the way of the Lord is difficult. For the third time, I ask you – do you forgive this man?'

If she did not say, 'Yes', that one small word, her sin would not be absolved.

'Do you?'

'Yes.' She forced it out in no more than a whisper but it was heard. Her sins were absolved, according to the priest, and she was given five Hail Marys. She left the church knowing she had committed another sin. She had lied. In her heart, which was what mattered, she had not forgiven the man. If he were to die from his wounds tomorrow she would not be sorry. If that meant she was wicked then she could not help it. But she did the Hail Marys, anyway, just in case the priest knew what he was talking about. She had begun to doubt that he did.

Now she could roam freely around the village again, without the fear of meeting the man, and as time went on she realised that if their paths were to cross she would be able to stare him down without flinching. Something inside her had resolved itself and she was determined that no man would ever treat her in that way again. When she said so to Juliana her friend advised her to get a boyfriend of her own.

'That's the best way to keep other men off you.'

But Encarnita was not interested in having any of the young men in the village as a boyfriend, not in the sense that Juliana meant. Her mother had told her to keep herself for someone special. She did not expect to meet him in Yegen but perhaps she would, on her journey.

WOMANHOOD: ALMUÑECAR

Encarnita waited until midsummer to set out. The days, now, were hot, but that suited her well. She thrived on heat, due perhaps to her gypsy blood, so her mother had thought. She washed her spare set of clothes and tidied the house where she had spent fifteen and a half years of her life. As she worked she was watched anxiously by Cinderella, who sensed that something was afoot. Once her chores were done, Encarnita went down to the women's bath and soaked herself in the warm, limpid water, letting her hair float free. She lay on her back, gazing through half-closed eyes up into the sky, watching the white clouds scud across the wide expanse of blue, and she thought of the journey she was about to make. She would be leaving this place that she knew so well, and the people she knew, but the sky would still be the same sky above her, and that was a comfort to her.

'Are you sure of what you're doing, Encarnita?' asked her neighbours, many of whom had never been as far as Motril, let alone further west. Military service had taken the men to places further afield. 'You're young to travel alone,' the women said. 'Think of what could happen to you!' She might meet with bandits. Fall over a cliff. Starve by the way-side. Find that her uncle was long dead. Find that he was alive but had a wife who did not want her.

'Nevertheless,' said Encarnita, 'I am going. I have to go. We are going.' For she intended to take Cinderella with her. There was no question of leaving her behind, any more than she would her water bottle, her blanket, or the bag that contained her books, Rinaldo's letter, and Señorita Carrington's drawing. The goat, as well as being her companion, someone to share the journey with, to talk to, and sleep beside at night, would have a practical use. She would supply her with milk. And goats were good at walking. Goatherds regularly walked their flocks from dawn to dusk.

The day before she was set to go, Encarnita left Cinderella behind and walked out to Luisa's *cortijo*. She stopped before she reached it and let out a long whistle, a signal to let Luisa know that she was there.

Luisa emerged, carrying a child. He was naked and had a cluster of sores on his stomach. He was fretting and trying to scratch them and his sister was doing her best to keep his hands away.

'I have been trying to heal them,' she said worriedly, when she saw Encarnita looking at them. 'I got some herbs and made a paste but it hasn't helped.'

'There's a woman in Válor who is good.'

'I have nothing to pay her with.'

Encarnita gave her two *pesetas*.

'You can't do that! You'll need all your money for your journey.'

'Take it! Please, Luisa. It's part of the money Don Geraldo gave me.'

They broke off as they heard the roar of Luisa's father's voice from within the house. 'What are you doing out there, you lazy bitch? I want food!'

One of the boys came out and yelled, 'Papa wants you, Luisa!'

'I'm coming!' Luisa turned back to Encarnita. 'I wish you weren't going.'

'I must! I've always promised it to myself.'

'I'll miss you.'

'I'll miss you too, Luisa! I wish you could come with me.'

The girls looked at each other and for one crazy moment it seemed as if it might be possible. Then Luisa's shoulders slumped.

'I can't.'

They promised to write to each other and vowed that they would always be friends and never forget each other. They embraced and then they parted. Encarnita sensed Luisa's eyes watching her as she walked away, but she did not look back. Her own eyes smarted with tears.

Before leaving the *campo* she picked a bouquet of wild flowers; blue delphiniums and pink dianthus, along with a few sprigs of lavender, Pilar's favourite herb. She had always said it was a calming, soothing herb. On her way down the hill Encarnita called in at the shop and bought half a loaf of bread and a lump of cheese, and a collar and bell for Cinderella. She had never belled her before but she had to be sure that the goat would not slip her stake and wander off while she herself slept. It was not likely that Cinderella would want to stray but the smell of some delicate plant reaching her on the night air might tempt her. And who knew what desires a goat might have once she was embarked on a journey. She might scent freedom.

'So you're off tomorrow?' said José.

'First thing.'

'Looking forward to it, are you?'

Encarnita nodded.

'You can always come back,' he said gloomily.

Two women were standing outside the shop gossiping. They turned their heads to greet Encarnita. '*Vaya con Dios!*' they said. Go with God.

Encarnita smiled and thanked them, a lump in her throat. She could not believe that this would be the last time she would walk down through the village.

When she reached the church she slipped inside and lit a candle for her mother. She talked to her. 'Mama, I am not leaving you. You will go with me and Cinderella. And as soon as I get to Almuñecar I will go into the church and light a candle for you there, too.' On her way out she passed the priest and nodded to him but did not stop to speak.

She went round the back of the church to the graveyard. It was a pitiful looking place, so sadly neglected and going to rack and ruin. Encarnita felt ashamed that her mother should lie here. She laid the wild flowers on the mound that was her grave. They were wilting already, from the heat of her hand, and soon they would die; she knew and accepted that. One of her regrets was that she was leaving the grave behind but was comforted by the thought that it was only the husk of her mother that lay there.

The only person left to say goodbye to was Juliana. The girls embraced, with little more to be said now, except to wish each other luck.

Encarnita left early the next morning, when the day was still fresh and the air cool.

'We are going on a journey, Cinderella,' she told the goat as she led her out of their home. *Don Quixote* came into her mind and she smiled. It would have been good to have had a Sancho Panza with her, a comforting sort of uncle, but the book itself would keep her company and, in the evening, if she were not too tired, she would read a little before sleeping. She had packed all her books, as well as Señorita Carrington's drawing, in her bag.

They took a path leading out of the lower *barrio*. The going was steep but both travellers were sure-footed and used to the terrain. They descended down through cliffs of soft red sandstone, bordered by plunging ravines, stopping for a few minutes to look at the view when they reached the Piedra Fuerte, a large rock where a Moorish castle had stood, many centuries before. They had to stop from time to time to give Cinderella a chance to graze undisturbed. Below them grew orange and lemon trees, apricots, peaches, olives, figs and prickly pears, the fruit glowing warmly in the sunshine. A traveller need not starve with fallen fruit to lift from the ground and fresh milk from a goat's udder.

Cinderella was especially pleased when they reached the more fertile ground of the valley. Her pickings were sweeter here though much of the undergrowth was dry. They by-passed the *pueblos* of Yátor and Cádiar, moving steadily southward and westward, the goat's bell tingling gently as they walked. Encarnita looked back once at Yegen, perched now high above them, but only for a second.

They met a few people on their journey: men working in

the fields mostly; one or two children who ran alongside them for a while with outstretched hands, hoping for an offering which Encarnita could not afford to give; a woman trying to wash clothes in an almost dried-up stream. Cinderella was glad of the trickle of water. They rested in the shade while the midday sun burned overhead and Encarnita allowed herself a few small sips from her water bottle. Later, they met a man driving an ox cart, piled high with sugar cane. He had come up from the coast, having been walking for two days. His paired oxen lumbered slowly between their shafts, their flanks alive with insects. The man knew Almuñecar; he said it was a poor living for the fishermen there. Don't expect much, he told Encarnita. He thought they were better off in the *campo*, where they could grow their own food. A little disheartened, she moved on. People had often talked about going down to the coast as if life would be easier there. But soon her spirits picked up again for the day was beautiful and everything was new to her. The land was softer than higher up in the *sierra*.

She stopped for the night somewhere between Cádiar and Órgiva, in a grove of old olive trees, whose gnarled, twisted branches looked like witches' arms and made her think of Black Maria. Had she been on her own she might have made it as far as Órgiva in the day, but not with Cinderella, who had her own speed and way of walking. Encarnita's backpack, too, was heavy, and her shoulders ached. Once she had milked the goat and tied her to a stake she was able to eat her own meal in peace. She was ravenous. She tore off a hunk of bread and ate it with the cheese which had gone soggy and slightly rancid in the heat but still tasted good. A drink of milk, a handful of wrinkled black olives and an orange completed her meal. The sun was gradually dropping behind the *sierras*, but soon it was gone and the light in the valley dimmed and it was too dark to read more than the first few lines of *Don Quixote*.

She began to prepare for the night, first making sure that

Cinderella was firmly secured. Then she took the knife from her pack and placed it by her side where she could reach it quickly, after which she wrapped herself in her blanket and settled down in a patch of lavender. As she drifted into sleep she heard a nightingale begin its plaintive song.

Awaking to a grey dawn, a panic overtook her. She leapt up and glanced around, startling Cinderella, who had been quietly grazing. For the first time in her life Encarnita had woken in strange surroundings. She felt confused and could not think where she was. It took a few minutes for her alarm to subside. The thought of returning home, to Yegen, intruded, and appealed, but only briefly, before she dismissed it. She ate and drank and by the time she was ready to move on the sky had cleared again to an azure blue.

She reached the coast that day, at sundown, and went down to meet the sea. The vastness of it astounded her. She stood barefooted in the gritty sand, transfixed, the frilly white edge of the Mediterranean washing over her ankles. The coolness of the water was soothing after the harsh heat of the day. 'Look, Cinderella,' she said, 'look how far and wide the sea stretches! It goes on forever and ever.' They watched together as the great expanse changed colour with the lowering of the sun, turning from a shimmering orange to a milky pink to a very pale lilac until, suddenly, it had no colour at all. It was very quiet then.

Encarnita shivered, the feeling of alienation returning. She was uncertain as to where to spend the night. Putting her back to the sea she surveyed the beach, but it looked too open, and she was used to enclosures. She decided to retreat into the *campo*.

On the way there she stumbled across two members of the *Guardia Civil*. She had seen their tricorn hats looming up out of the twilight, too late to draw back.

'Where are you going at this hour?' The voice was curt.

'To visit my uncle in Almuñecar.'

'Almuñecar is that way.' He pointed along the coast road. 'Yes, I know,' she faltered, 'but it's getting dark.' She feared these men and knew that if they were to push her down she would not dare try to use the knife.

'So what is your plan? To sleep rough?'

'I thought I'd wait for a few hours and go on when it is light.'

'Have you papers?'

She fumbled in her pack and produced them.

'Born in Yegen, I see, Encarnación. You know my cousin Jésus-Maria Rodriguez?'

'Yes, yes, I know him!' She seized on the connection, in spite of it being a foul one. 'He is the father of my best friend, Luisa Rodriguez.'

'Luisa? I have not seen her for many years. She is your friend?'

'My best friend. We always sat in school together.'

'So she went to school? She is a clever girl, then?'

'Very clever.'

He handed back her papers. 'Take care where you pass the night. And make sure you find your uncle in the morning. A girl like you should not be out alone. I am sure my cousin would not let his daughter wander about in this way.'

'With a goat!' said his companion and he laughed. 'Maybe we should look after her for a while, Diego? A girl like her might do better with a bit of company.'

'No, let her be. She is a friend of my cousin's family, after all.'

Encarnita did not stop trembling until their hats had faded into the darkness and their voices dwindled.

1935

She came into Almuñecar at its eastern end, by the long straight beach. A few battered-looking fishing boats were drawn up on the grey sand and, close by, fishermen were mending nets. Other men, older, with dark, lined faces, sat watching and smoking thin cigarettes that smelled of burning leaves. They lifted their heads to look at the girl and her goat but she kept her eyes averted from them. She did not want to have to account for herself until she had had the chance to take a look at the village. Cinderella was unhappy; she did not like the smell of the sea or the feel of the sand underfoot.

Further along the beach, they came upon a small white hotel sitting straight onto the sand. The Hotel Mediterráneo. Encarnita hesitated for a moment before plunging Cinderella's stake into the sand and going inside. The lobby was empty. She cleared her throat a couple of times and a short, chubby young man with a practically bald head and a little black moustache appeared. He looked her up and down and then asked what she wanted, in an abrupt though not unkind voice, but realising obviously that she would not be a customer.

'I'm sorry, we don't need any housemaids at present,' he added. He spoke Spanish with an unusual accent.

That was a pity. She would have welcomed such a job. She told him she was looking for her uncle, Rinaldo Benet.

'Ah, Rinaldo? Yes, I know him quite well.'

'You do?' She felt like hugging him, it was such a relief to know that Rinaldo was alive and here, in Almuñecar.

'He lives up the hill in Calle Carmen. Come, I'll show you.'

She followed him outside. Turning to face inland, he pointed to a narrow opening. 'Take that street and follow it right on up. There's a ruined fortress at the top. They call it an *alcazaba*. Rinaldo lives up there, not sure which house, anyone will tell you. Part of the *alcazaba* is a cemetery now. Creepy place it is, too. They put their dead in drawers and slot them into cement niches. Maybe you're used to that? Where I come from we put them in the ground. More civilised, if you ask me.'

'Where do you come from?'

'Germany. Heard of it?'

'Of course. I've seen it on the globe.'

'You've been to school, then? Can you read and write? Half of them here can't. Your uncle can't, can he?'

'I don't know.'

'You don't know?'

'It's a long time since I've seen him.'

'I see. Is he expecting you?'

'No.'

'You'll be a surprise then. Come to stay with him, have you?'

'I hope to. For a little while. My uncle – is he married?'

'Never heard of him having a wife. So, what do they call you?'

'Encarnita.'

'Funny name. But you're a a pretty girl, Encarnita. My name is Jacob but everyone here calls me Jacobo. The maids call me Don Jacobo.' He giggled.

'The hotel belongs to you?'

'No, I wish it did. Herr Christien is the proprietor but he relies on me a lot. He's Swiss.' He looked back at the beach. 'See that fat man walking along by the sea. That's him, taking the sea air, for his nerves. He's the nervous type. washes his hands until they're nearly rubbed raw. And he keeps changing the locks, thinking we're going to be robbed.' Jacobo had been eyeing Encarnita while he was talking and moving a little closer to her so that she began to feel uncomfortable. She wanted to get away but did not like to be rude when he had been so helpful. He was fingering his little bristly moustache. 'Perhaps we might take a walk along the beach together sometime, Encarnita, you and me?'

'Perhaps,' she answered and bent to untie Cinderella.

'Is that your goat? I hope she hasn't fouled the sand. I cleaned it just a little while ago for the sake of our guests who don't like goat shit on their shoes. It stinks.'

'I'll clean it,' Encarnita said quickly, noticing a few round black balls on the sand.

'It's all right, I'll do it. You can be nice to me in return when we go for our walk. You will, won't you? You look a kind girl.' He gave a little giggle again.

She thanked him, without engaging his eyes, and led Cinderella to the street called Calle Carmen. It was cobbled and steep, but there were wide side-steps for donkeys and goats, already well fouled by animal excrement. A warren of streets sprawled upward, winding their way round the hill. The houses looked in poor condition; some were half-broken down and appeared abandoned. The streets themselves were deserted but it was the siesta hour, the time to stay indoors out of the heat of the sun.

She pressed on, encouraging Cinderella, who was lagging behind and becoming stubborn. She needed food and water, as did Encarnita herself. A scraggy hen skittered across their path and Encarnita had to hold Cinderella back. In a doorway an old man sat on a low chair, with one of his trouser legs pinned up at the knee. Encarnita stopped.

'I'm looking for Rinaldo Benet's house,' she said.

The man stared back at her with glazed, rheumy eyes and she wondered if he might be deaf. She muttered that she was sorry to have disturbed him, even though she had not. He did not move his head to watch her go. The silence in the street was beginning to unnerve her but when she turned the next corner she could see the ruin of the *alcazaba* ahead. She passed the few remaining houses, hearing the sound of men's voices, loud, raised voices, coming through the unglazed window of the last one. She wondered if one of them might belong to her uncle but hesitated to knock without knowing.

She climbed on up into the ruin of the *alcazaba* which lay sprawled over a wide area, with some of its outer and inner walls still intact. Its size surprised her. She staked Cinderella so that she could wander among the stones on her own. She began to visualise the layout of the fortress. Some shapes must have been rooms, and other long narrow ones might have been baths. Their teacher had told them about the Moors who had built grand palaces and castles with baths and fountains. They had loved water. There was none here now. Weeds grew amongst the tumbled stones. At the top she had a marvellous view of the sea on one side and, on the other, the *campo* leading to the *sierras*. The place might no longer be as splendid as when the Moors were here but Encarnita thought it a magical place where a child might play and hide in the nooks and crannies.

The cemetery occupied a space at the far wall. A squat, middle-aged woman in a black dress and headscarf was dusting the outside of one of the niches while, in her left hand, she held a crucifix. She looked startled when she saw Encarnita.

'I used all my savings to give him a proper funeral,' she said.

'You did?'

'I wasn't going to let him lie in the ground and have the dogs gnaw his bones, was I?'

Encarnita swallowed and put a hand to her throat. 'No.'

'Are you all right?' The woman came a step closer to her. 'You've turned a funny colour.'

'It's just the heat. I need some water.'

'Come and sit down on the wall.' The woman guided her. 'I don't know you, do I? You're a stranger here?'

'Yes. I'm looking for Rinaldo Benet. He is my uncle.'

'Your uncle? Didn't know he had any family. He's never spoken of anyone. You don't look like him.'

'I've been told I take after my father's side.'

'So where is he now, your father?'

'Dead.'

'Thought he might be. They're either dead or they've gone off somewhere. A gypsy, was he?'

'How do you know?'

'You have the look and the hair. Black as a raven's, isn't it? I hope you've not got any of the gypsy ways? Thieving, and that.'

'I don't steal! I'm sure my father didn't, either.'

'Except your mother's heart! All right, don't fly off! I was only asking. You're obviously not a full-blooded gypsy. They can sing, though, I'll give them that. I bet he sang love songs in your mother's ear.'

'Can you tell me where I can find my uncle, please?'

'He lives in the end house.' The woman pointed the crucifix downward, then she gave it a last quick dust before placing it on the ground below the niche which Encarnita presumed held the body of her relative. 'Everything's dusty here. It's the sand, especially when the wind gets up.'

'I heard voices in my uncle's house when I went by.'

'They're always arguing, those men! About politics.'

'Politics?'

'They want to change the world. Not much chance of that!'

'It would be difficult.'

'Difficult! We are born poor, and poor we shall die. It is the rich who run the world and nothing will ever change that. They call the tune. What can we do? Now here am I talking politics myself! It is my son Pedro I have to blame for that. He is a friend of your uncle. Rinaldo has put ideas in his head, along with Manolo. Manolo's the leader of the group.'

'I'm sorry,' said Encarnita.

'It's not your fault, is it?'

'What kind of ideas do they have?'

'That the workers should rise up! Overturn the state. And get themselves killed while they're doing it. The army and the *Guardia Civil* are not going to stand by watching, are they?' The woman took a last look at the niche before turning away. 'He died twenty years ago, Alfonso, my husband. Chose his time to go. The day after Pedro was born. He'd had a lung disease. It was terrible listening to him at night.'

'I'm sorry,' said Encarnita again.

'So what is it you want with your uncle?'

'I'm not sure.' Encarnita shrugged. 'Before my mother died she suggested I might come and find him. She was his sister. They were fond of each other.'

'So you think he might take care of you, is that it? He has no money, I can tell you that straightaway. He earns a bit on the cane-cutting now and then but that wouldn't feed the two of you. Doesn't feed him.'

'I don't expect him to pay for me. I'll try to earn some money.'

'Doing what?'

Encarnita felt her head drooping, from the heat and lack of food and water.

'He's a kind man,' the woman went on in a softer voice. 'I'm sure he'll do what he can for you. My name's Sofia. And you?'

'Encarnita.'

'Come, Encarnita, I'll take you to him.'

Encarnita collected Cinderella and Sofia led them down to the house of Rinaldo. They reached it as two men were emerging. Sofia introduced them. The younger man was Pedro, her son; the other, the older, was Manolo. They greeted the women politely and went on their way.

It was quiet inside the house now. Sofia pushed open the broken door.

'Rinaldo,' she called out. 'I have a visitor for you. A surprise.'

A tall man with a gaunt face and dark, greying hair came to meet them.

'Your niece has come to visit you,' said Sofia and left them.

Rinaldo, after the initial shock, greeted Encarnita with a

warm embrace. He kept saying that he couldn't believe it, he still thought of her as the tiny baby he had last seen. When he heard the news of Pilar's death he was overwhelmed, for he had always hoped to see his sister again and now felt guilty that he had not.

'I should have done! The years go by in a blink.'

He took Encarnita into the kitchen at the back of the house, a dark room, where the only furniture was a scored wooden table and three chairs. On the table sat a bundle of grey leaflets printed with large letters in red and black. Inclining her head Encarnita read, 'WORKERS UNITE.' He saw her looking at them but made no comment.

He apologised that he had only a little food in the house and not much water. 'Water is scarce up here. We have to carry it up from down below. I'll go down to the fountain shortly and draw some.'

'Give what you have to Cinderella, please. She needs to drink.'

He insisted that Encarnita drink, too. He was eyeing the goat dubiously. 'There's a bit of grazing at the back but it drops sharply down the hill.'

''She's used to steep slopes and I can take her into the *campo*, too.'

'Very well. In that case,' said Rinaldo, 'you are welcome to stay with me.'

One day, while roaming about the *campo* with Cinderella, Encarnita came upon a ruined house. She knew straightaway that she wanted to make it theirs. It would be their secret home, a place to retreat to away from people. She would tell no one about it, not even Rinaldo. It was isolated, far from any main paths, with not another building in sight. She threw out the carcasses of a dead rabbit and several birds and swept the floor with a broom made of sticks. In one corner she made herself a bed of rosemary, thyme and lavender. A small part of the roof remained so that they would have shade to rest in during the hottest hours of the day. She scavenged around the countryside and came back with a number of useful items: a chair with a broken leg that was mendable with a stout stick, some pieces of ceramic pottery she could use as dishes, a scratched enamel basin and a dented tin pail. Nearby, she discovered a source of water, a small spring issuing from between two rocks. She was overjoyed.

'Look, Cinderella, water! We'll be all right now. We have everything we need.' Tucked away in the house, she felt as if she were living inside a fairy tale.

They began to spend their days there and when they returned to Rinaldo's house in the evening Encarnita cooked a meal, when there was food to cook. Sometimes bread and olives were all they had, with perhaps a sliver of cheese or sausage, if they were lucky. She brought in fallen oranges, figs and avocados from the *campo*, concealing them in her apron pocket, in case she might be accused of theft. She thought guiltily of Sofia's suggestion that she might steal because she had gypsy blood. But this was different, she reasoned, for what lay on the ground could surely be picked up by anyone since, otherwise, it would rot. On occasions she made *patatas a lo pobre* – poor man's potatoes – by frying onions and potatoes together in oil. This was a dish that Pilar had liked.

Often, after they'd eaten, Encarnita would go down the hill and across the square to the Iglesia Encarnación where she would talk to her mother. That the church bore her own name made her feel more at ease, otherwise she might have found it too big and unfriendly compared to the one in Yegen. She told her mother about Rinaldo and Almuñecar and her secret hideaway in the *campo*. 'So you don't have to worry about me now. Cinderella and I are well.'

Coming out of the church one evening, she bumped into Jacobo.

'Ah, if it's not the lovely Encarnita! I was hoping I might see you. You were going to come for a walk with me.'

'I didn't say so.'

'You're tossing your head at me! Don't you like me? Why

don't you come for a walk with me now and you'll see what a decent fellow I am?' He stuck his elbow out for her to take but she did not do so. 'It's *paseo* time. Look, everyone is out!'

'A girl only walks with a boy in the *paseo* when he is her *novio*.'

'I could be your *novio*.' He giggled.

'But it would not be true. I don't know you.'

'You could come to know me. Hey, don't run away! I was going to offer you a job at the hotel. As a maid. One of our girls is leaving.'

She stopped.

'It would be mornings only. Six till twelve. And sometimes in the evenings, if we're having a party.'

'But you can't offer me the job, can you?'

'Herr Christien listens to me. He takes my advice. So what do you say?'

'I will have to talk to my uncle.'

When she did, Rinaldo said, 'You'll only be paid a pittance.'

'I know, but it's better than nothing, isn't it?'

He sighed. 'Of course. That is why we all do as we do. And why we will never be able to better ourselves. But I think Herr Christien would not treat you unkindly and you would have the company of the other *chicas*.'

She hesitated before confessing that it was Jacobo who worried her more. 'He keeps asking me to go for a walk with him but I don't want to go.'

'Then you must not, Encarnita. I'll have a word with my friend Manolo. He works in the hotel as a waiter and he'll warn Jacobo off. He's harmless, Jacobo. He talks, mostly. But he is well enough liked in the village.'

Encarnita started at the hotel the following day. She learned to make beds with sheets and pillows, scrub baths and toilet bowls, and set tables with knives, forks and spoons. There was not a constant stream of guests but enough to keep the place going. Most were German, but some came from England, and to those she tried to speak a little in their own language, even if it was only to say, 'Good morning' or 'It is a nice day'.

One kind lady, who worked in a library in London, undertook to teach her a little English while she was cleaning her room in the mornings. Miss Osborne had been attending night classes in London and could speak some Spanish. She had come to Spain to research into its state of illiteracy and had been appalled to find so much in a European country, in the year 1935. 'It's not as if it's South America!'

'Everyone can read in London?' asked Encarnita.

Miss Osborne admitted that some illiteracy did exist in the British Isles, which was to be deplored, though not anything like to the same extent as here. She did voluntary work at home, teaching reading, writing and arithmetic to young women at a night school in London run by an organisation for the Advancement of Christian Knowledge. She praised Encarnita's desire to learn. She told her that knowledge would lift her out of poverty.

'I take it that you are a Christian, dear?' Miss Osborne cleared a catch in her throat. 'Though a Roman Catholic, I suppose?'

Encarnita was not sure what she meant. 'I go to Spanish church.'

Miss Osborne nodded. 'Of course you would, wouldn't you? You haven't had a choice. But don't be offended by me saying so for it's not your fault. Obviously not. But perhaps when you're older you might want to think about it.' Encarnita was still mystified so Miss Osborne changed over to Spanish to try to clarify what she wished to say. 'It is just that in your church there is too much emphasis on the swinging of incense and the worshipping of idols. Statues. Rather lurid statues too, from what I've seen, with all that gilt and gold and baby blue, and then there are those thorns in the flesh of Jesus!' She shuddered. 'The waxy faces are rather vulgar, too. In very poor taste. I'm sorry to speak this way, Encarnita, but I have to be honest with you, dear.'

'You don't like them? The statues?'

'No, indeed. Besides, God is the only Being we should be worshipping.'

'Why not Mary? She is the most important of all! She is the mother. My mother always talked to Mary. She said she understood the pain of women more.'

'Yes, I've observed that there does seem to be rather a cult of Mary. Not terribly healthy, to my mind. Half the women in Andalucía seem to be called Maria!'

'I am Encarnación Pilar Maria.'

'Yes, well.' Miss Osborne cleared her throat. 'We are thinking that we might need to come over and do some mission work here in Andalucía. If so, you might like to come to our classes?'

'Oh yes!' Encarnita would be happy to go to any kind of class. 'My Uncle Rinaldo doesn't go to church any more,' she added, thinking that might please Miss Osborne. 'He dislikes the priests.'

'Is that so?' Miss Osborne brightened. 'Perhaps he has seen the light and will be ready for a less gaudy form of worship. I might talk with him.'

'I don't think he'd listen. He says there's no such thing as God, that the church keeps the people down so that the landowners can get away with murder.'

'That was a rather wicked thing of him to say, Encarnita. You must not let such poison enter your soul.'

'He says that when we have a truly free society the priests and bishops will be sacked and the churches closed. "No God, no owners, no private property." That's one of their slogans.'

'Sounds like anarchy to me! I do not think he should be discussing politics with you. You are a young girl and, because of that, impressionable .'

'Politics are the only things he talks about. He says we'll have a revolution, like they had in Russia, sooner rather than later.'

'And look what a Godless country that is now!'

Encarnita enjoyed their conversations, conducted in bits of English and Spanish, even if she could not always follow the drift completely. She enjoyed, too, the actual cleaning of Miss Osborne's room. She loved handling the lady's pretty things: her tortoiseshell-backed hair brush, comb and hand mirror, all to match; her cut-glass scent bottle which smelled of lavender water when you lifted the silver top; and the little round pot of cream, moisturising cream, for the face, to keep it from drying out, so Miss Osborne told her. Encarnita would dust slowly and carefully, spinning out the time until Jacobo would roar her name up the stairs, demanding to know what she was doing. Miss Osborne would smile and say in English, enunciating each word loudly and clearly, 'Better go, dear. I shall see you tomorrow.'

On Miss Osborne's last day in the hotel, with her packed leather trunk standing by the door waiting for Jacobo to lift, she said, 'I will give you my address in London, Encarnita. If you manage to get there on your journey you must come and see me. There are perils waiting for girls like you when they come to the city. You would have to be wary. And if you would like, we could write to each other and I could correct your letters?' She pressed twenty *pesetas* into Encarnita's hand.

'That's too much,' protested Encarnita.

'It's too little,' said Miss Osborne. 'May God bless you and keep you from all evil and protect you during the dark days ahead.'

Jacobo pushed back the door and came barging in to lift the trunk. The taxi was at the door waiting for Miss Osborne. Encarnita and Jacobo saw her off, waving until the car had gone from sight.

'I shall miss her,' sighed Encarnita.

'She gave me five *pesetas*. What did she give you?'

'That's my business.'

'So she gave you more! I thought she would. You've got

to share it with me! It's only fair. Why should you have more? I got you this job, didn't I? You wouldn't have it if it weren't for me.'

'She gave me more because I am her special friend.'

'Friend! She'll forget you as soon as she's on the boat back. They always do.'

'Oh, all right.' Encarnita pulled five *pesetas* from her pocket and passed them over. Jacobo wasn't as bad as she had first thought. She was getting to like him well enough, though not as a possible *novio*. They had called a truce on that. He said that if she didn't want him there were plenty of girls who did. Even female guests, he hinted, would leave their doors ajar for him at night. 'I'm going to write to Miss Osborne,' she told him. 'And she is going to write back!'

She also wrote to Luisa, using the hotel as her address, and a few weeks later a reply came back. Encarnita tore the envelope open eagerly. The sight of Luisa's round childlike writing made her feel homesick for Yegen. She took out the single flimsy page.

Luisa wrote that her father had died after his wound had become infected again. 'His end was bad.' Encarnita felt nothing, neither pity nor joy, but she was pleased that Luisa would not have to put up with such a man any more.

'Good news?' asked Jacobo.

'Quite good.'

'You haven't heard from your Miss Osborne, have you?'

'I expect she's been busy. She was going to Portugal when she left here to see what the illiteracy was like there.' Encarnita had written her a short letter, with considerable difficulty, in English, thanking her for her teaching.

A few days later, a letter arrived from Miss Osborne, a very long one, consisting of several pages, correcting first of all Encarnita's grammar and misuse of words, and then going on to relate all her doings, and those of the Society for the Advancement of Christian Knowledge. At the end, she urged Encarnita to keep to the ways of the Lord and not those of her uncle who, sadly, had gone astray. Redemption was always possible, however. She urged Encarnita to pray for him, but to the Lord God, and not to Mary. The letter was written in a fine sloping hand with wonderful loops and curls that made the reader marvel. She could not understand even a quarter of its contents but she kept the envelope in her pocket so that if another English guest should come to the hotel she could ask him, or her, to translate for her.

In December came a young, fair-haired Englishman, called Lorenzo, to brighten their lives. He carried a violin and he had tales to tell, which he told well. Encarnita was fascinated by his stories. He had walked the length of Spain with a violin, few other possessions and little money. A true traveller. He had earned a few *pesetas* here and there playing his violin in cafés and market squares and shared a bed in squalid inns with a weird range of people. He'd met poets and musicians, vagabonds and thieves, and had received many favours, especially from the ladies. Encarnita blushed when he spoke of that.

Herr Christien took Lorenzo on to help around the hotel. He helped out in the kitchen and fixed windows broken by the waves. He was given a bed in the attic beside Jacobo and the two became good friends. They joined together to form a band so that they could play at hotel functions. Lorenzo played the fiddle, and Jacobo the accordion. They had fun together. They practised on the roof and they laughed a lot. Encarnita enjoyed the sound of their music as she went about her work; it made her smile and set her feet tapping. They gave concerts, the programme ranging from tangos, serenades and *paso dobles* to Schubert's *Marche Militaire*. The most requested tune was *Rio Rita*. The musicians were prepared to tackle anything and prided themselves on their versatility.

Encarnita also enjoyed serving at the evening dances put on for locals, the better-off ones, not for those such as her uncle and their neighbours, or the destitute family who lived in the vaults under the ruined *alcazaba*. The girls at these entertainments were fiercely chaperoned. Their parents' eyes watched every move they made. There would be no favours granted here.

Encarnita could not imagine her uncle dancing. But perhaps he had in his younger, more carefree days. He was obsessed with meetings and pamphlets. There was to be an election in February and he was predicting that major changes would result from it. He hoped that they would; otherwise, there would be much trouble in the land. He said it would be foolish of him to be too optimistic. People did not give up power without a struggle. When Encarnita was listening to the music of Lorenzo and Jacobo she could forget Rinaldo's forebodings.

She asked Lorenzo to look at Miss Osborne's letter. He read it through to himself first of all, and laughed. 'She sounds like a very earnest lady. A bit of a frump, I'd say. I bet Jacobo made no conquests there.' Lorenzo's Spanish was not good enough to allow him to translate the whole letter. 'You don't need to know all that stuff about night classes and mission work! You're young, Encarnita. Come, dance with me! Life in Almuñecar is better.' He seized her hands and whirled her round the room until she collapsed, laughing, into a chair.

Life in Almuñecar did seem good to her, although she could not forget for long that there was another side to it. When she went home and saw the stacks of little grey pieces of paper lying on the kitchen table her stomach would turn over.

One night, when Rinaldo was out, she went into his room, thinking she heard a noise. There was nothing there. It might have been a mouse, or a rat. She saw that the bed was pulled slightly out from the wall and went to take a closer look in case an animal might be lurking. Something wrapped in sacking was wedged behind it. Gingerly, she eased back the sacking to reveal two rifles and half a dozen hand-grenades.

'What are you doing in here, Encarnita?'

She jumped and turned to face her uncle in the doorway.

'I'm sorry,' she faltered. He was angry, and she had never seen that in him before. 'I didn't mean to pry. I thought I heard a noise.' Her voice tailed off.

'Don't come in here again, do you understand! You shouldn't meddle. These are dangerous times.'

She left the room and he followed her into the kitchen. He sighed. 'I'm sorry I shouted at you.'

She shook her head. 'I shouldn't have looked.'

'You do believe in what we're doing, don't you, Encarnita?' Rinaldo took hold of her hands and the look in his eyes was fierce as he engaged hers. 'You believe we must fight for our rights, don't you? You *must*! If not, our lives will never change!'

1936

The February election brought victory for the Popular Front, a coalition of the Left. Their supporters were out celebrating in the streets, cheering and talking of freedom and fair shares for all. Those who had supported the Monarchists and Falangists and other Right-wing parties were aghast and keeping to their shuttered houses.

'Now we will have our own government,' cried Pedro, punching his fist in the air. 'This is for *us*. For the people!' The cry was taken up.

'They think they've got it all tied up,' said his mother, Sofia, meeting Encarnita on her way up to the cemetery. Sofia spent much time up there amongst the dead. 'Do they think the other lot will just sit back and take it? What fools they are! The landowners are never going to give up their estates without a fight. People are tight-fisted when it comes to land.' A few peasants had taken over some parcels of ground in the *campo* but that had not gone very far.

'She's right, of course,' agreed Rinaldo, when Encarnita repeated what Sofia had said. 'The struggle is not yet finished. I always told you it would not be simple.'

To hear this depressed Encarnita. She had been hoping that she would not have to go on worrying about him when he went out to meetings. Sometimes she lay awake until the middle of the night listening for the sound of his step in the street outside.

'Is nothing going to change?' she asked.

'We have to keep up the pressure,' said her uncle.

Some things did change. Political prisoners were released and for a while there was no censorship and books and newspapers were printed unexpurgated. The power of the church appeared to be diminishing. For a start, education was to be taken out of the hands of the clergy and given over to the state. Moral standards began to shift. Freedom was in the air. Young courting couples from decent families walked the streets without chaperones and fishermen and labourers came with their girls to dance in the hotel and were served cheap beer by a smiling Manolo. But, said Rinaldo, all of that was not enough. The poor were still poor and their children were starving. They couldn't go dancing. The political meetings went on, and the speeches. Discontent mounted. Shop windows were broken, priests spat at in the street. There were acts of sabotage, too, at the ice-making plant and the power station, both owned by a marquis no one had ever set eyes on. The tax collector, along with his wife and furniture, were thrown out of their house by a posse of elderly women, who then, amidst applause, proceeded to dump them in a cart and drive them out into the *campo*, depositing them beyond the confines of the town. Encarnita watched their eviction and was caught up in the wave of cheering but afterwards she wondered if it had been right to cheer. The taxman's wife had looked terrified. Encarnita was left with an unpleasant feeling in the pit of her stomach.

'None of this is good for business,' grumbled the puffing and sighing Herr Christien. 'When is it all going to settle down?'

'Most people from abroad don't know what's going on until they get here,' said Jacobo. 'Most people don't know anything much about Spain.'

Encarnita was with Jacobo and Lorenzo in the hotel when a boy put his head round the door and yelled that they were burning the holy images from the church on the beach. They dropped everything and went out. An excited crowd had already gathered around the fire, which crackled and spat and licked its booty. The men of the village were there, and their women and children. The children became enflamed themselves and began to chuck stones. Their mothers looked uneasy and Encarnita saw Sofia standing on the edge of the crowd crossing herself.

'The Spanish are far too excitable,' said Jacobo. 'It would be for their own good if they would all calm down a bit.

Even the girls are talking about politics!'

But the excitement carried on, taking the form of parades and strikes and, of course, speeches. The speeches stirred the blood. Fascist symbols were daubed on walls. The Republican flag was draped across the balcony of the Town Hall and, underneath, painted in red, were the words: 'We swear to defend this *bandera* with the last drop of our blood.'

The strikes, when called, were solid. No citizen of Almuñecar would dare work. Rinaldo warned Encarnita not even to lift a hand. The staff at the Hotel Mediterráneo sat idling on the beach while Herr Christien struggled in the kitchen to feed his few guests, whose rooms lay uncleaned.

Every day, a line of peasants could be seen coming in from the *campo*, on foot and on donkeys, laden with any weaponry they might have, staves, rusty pistols, flintlocks, ready for battle, should battle be necessary.

'Who are they going to fight?' asked Jacobo.

'Maybe the army,' said Encarnita uneasily.

'Whose army?'

Rinaldo was thinking, as each day passed, that conflict was inevitable. He was convinced the Right was planning a counter attack. There were regular reports of violence in the large cities, Madrid, Barcelona, Valencia. Strikes and riots were a daily occurrence. In a village along the coast, a group of Falangists, proudly sporting armbands, entered a bar and coolly shot dead five fishermen. The son of a former mayor, a Falangist, was later found in the *campo*, shot through the head. Fear crept through the streets like a poisonous gas. Lorenzo was talking of going home. He had moved from the hotel into the house of a middle-aged Englishwoman, who had taken him under her wing. Wilma Gregory was literary, according to Lorenzo, and well connected. She had come recently to Almuñecar and had bought a house next to the church with the idea of settling here but was coming to realise that she had picked the wrong time.

News of an anti-government uprising in Morocco on the 17th of July reached Almuñecar. 'The Moors have risen up, led by some general called Franco,' reported Jacobo, who had heard it on the radio. The next day there were similar uprisings in Sevilla and other cities. No one knew exactly what was going on. Rumours flew about. Villagers gathered in the *plaza*, along with the peasants and their families who had come in from the fields. With them, they had brought their beasts. Sofia moaned about the mess in the *pueblo*. 'It's beginning to look like a farmyard. And smell like one.' The police, at this point, were making themselves scarce, not knowing which side they were meant to be on, according to Rinaldo. He, along with Manolo and another man, Francisco, known as Frasco El Gato – The Cat – were organising a kind of home guard, a militia, for the protection of Almuñecar against the Fascists.

One group, led by Manolo, set up a roadblock on the coast and stopped the few vehicles that were abroad. They made a quick arrest: a car that two young men were travelling in was found to contain rifles and grenades. When a Frenchman arrived, flying a white flag, he was able to give them news of Málaga. He told them that the city was half in flames and people were fighting hand-to-hand in the street. Many were fleeing. He had been shot at as he left; the bullet holes in the bodywork of his car were proof of that. He was unable to say who had done the shooting.

Other members of the militia embarked on house-to-house searches and by the end of the first night they had stacked up a considerable pile of weapons in the *plaza*. They lit fires and sat around them, discussing tactics and keeping a watchful eye on their cache. They also made some further arrests. Young Falangist males, decked out in lacy shirts, heads held high, were rounded up and taken to the jail, as was the priest, protesting loudly.

'What harm would he do?' asked Sofia.

'Uncle Rinaldo says he's a symbol of the old regime,' said Encarnita.

'Why don't they let him be, then, if the regime is done for?'

But it was not done for, they both knew that. They went home to their beds though they did not sleep well. They were wakened at intervals by shots. Cinderella whinnied unhappily in the back yard and tugged at her stake. Encarnita went out to quieten her and stayed for a while beside her looking over the great expanse of sea below, silver in the moonlight. The world seemed so peaceful. And then a new shot rang out and made her jump. She retreated indoors.

At first light, Rinaldo came home to change his clothes. He said they were going along the coast to help defend Motril against the Fascist rebels; they'd heard they were having trouble.

'Be careful,' said Encarnita.

'Don't worry,' he said.

She pulled on her dress and ran down the hill to see him off. The men had commandeered a number of trucks and were piling aboard. They were in high spirits. Waving their caps and rifles in the air, they sang as they sped away, a song about the sons of the people being oppressed by chains. *This injustice cannot go on…* They left a deep silence behind them. Encarnita had noticed that El Gato, who was in charge, had had something strapped to his body. Dynamite, Jacobo told her, once they had gone. She shivered even though the sun was up.

She was on edge all day. After she'd finished her work at the hotel she wandered about the village, unable to settle. The men were not back by the time darkness fell. She sat on a wall down by the sea with Jacobo and Ana, one of the other housemaids, whose brother had gone on the trucks. They listened to the sound of the waves. Some people were out doing the paseo. Hearing a noise overhead Encarnita glanced up and saw a small plane circling. Aircraft were only occasionally to be seen in their skies. She shivered.

Suddenly, a bright, sweeping light, coming from the sea,

almost blinded them and made them recoil. They put up their arms to shield their eyes. The light raked the shore from one end to the other.

'It's a searchlight!' said Jacobo. 'There must be a ship out there!'

Panic seized for a moment, then the people stilled and, not knowing what else to do, waited.

The light moved up to main road.

'I can see a truck!' cried Ana. 'Look!'

She was right. The lorries were coming bumping along the coast road, sounding their horns, with the men on their feet, waving again. Their mission had not been successful, but they had survived their first encounter with the enemy. The crowd converged on them, clapping their backs, cheering, with Encarnita amongst them, relieved to see her uncle unhurt.

Then, as suddenly as it had appeared, the light from the sea went out, as if someone had pulled a switch. A sigh of relief went up. But a moment later, the shelling began. The people on the shore panicked and for a moment did not know which way to turn. Then they headed for the shelter of the hills. Children stumbled and fell and were urged up and on by their fathers; mothers carried infants bobbing against their shoulders; older people hobbled.

Within minutes, it was all over. The noise stopped abruptly, though the smell of smoke hung in the air. They halted in their tracks, frozen like statues, half way between their homes and the hill, and listened, uncertain as to what to do. After a little while, when nothing else had happened, they began to creep back down into the village. Nobody had been killed, only frightened. It could have been worse. The next morning they heard that the attack had been a mistake; they had thought the trucks belonged to the rebels. So the attacker was really on their side, a friend, they were told. Apologies were conveyed to them.

Out of the confusion came a stronger determination for the *pueblo* to show its colours. The flag of the Republic fluttered from all the main buildings, the bank and the casino amongst them. People cobbled up makeshift flags and banners and draped their doors and windows. Peasants and fishermen took over the empty houses of the better-off, with great plans for turning them into sanatoriums and nursery schools, and even a training college for girls. In this new free society girls were to be given the chance of a proper education.

The militia set off once again along the coast in lorries, but they were more muted this time. They did not sing. Amongst them went old and young men, and a band of teenage girls armed with hand grenades, showing that women could be equal to men. Rinaldo had asked Encarnita if she wanted to join them.

'I'm not sure,' she had said hesitantly. At whom would she be expected to throw grenades?

'The enemy! The enemy of the people. Surely you know that?'

'But how would you know who is the enemy?'

'It will be obvious.' Rinaldo had been a little impatient.

'I am on your side,' she had said to him as he went out of the door. 'I am for the Republican cause, you don't have to doubt that.'

'I know. You're too young, anyway, to stain your hands with blood. Better to stay at home!'

She felt a little guilty now that she had not gone to give him her physical support, but what use would she have been? Faced with a human being, could she have thrown a grenade? She knew that Pilar would not have wanted her to go. After some agonising, Ana had gone with her brother.

In the late afternoon, they saw two warships steaming eastward down the coast in the direction of Motril. Encarnita went down to the beach and joined Jacobo. As the evening sky began to change colour the ships commenced shelling the shore to the east of them. They listened to the dull thud, the steady boom, boom of the shells, and felt dull themselves, incapable of feeling. Encarnita stayed down by the sea with Jacobo after the bombardment had ceased.

'Don't you want to go home?' asked Encarnita. 'To Germany?'

'It wouldn't be so good for me there, either. I'm a Jew, you see. Our leader, Herr Hitler, doesn't like Jews.'

Encarnita had never heard of Herr Hitler.

'You're lucky. Better not to hear of him.'

There was to be no jubilant welcome for the homecoming men and women this time. When lorries returned they brought back dead and wounded along with the living. Pedro was dead, and Manolo was missing, as was Ana's brother. Ana herself had received a stomach wound, but the greater harm had been done to her spirit. She subsequently suffered a nervous breakdown and would not leave the house. As for the rebel village, it had not been quelled; the Almuñecar militia had been ill-equipped to cope with the Nationalists' defence, and the destroyers' shells, which should have helped them, had missed and landed in the *campo* behind.

Rinaldo had a wound in his shoulder, caused by a passing bullet. It was bleeding profusely and the flesh was torn right down to the bone. 'Superficial,' he said. He could not complain about something so trivial. He'd seen one of his best friends lying in an alley with his throat cut. After Encarnita had bound up his shoulder he went out and sat in a bar with El Gato and some of the other men, sunk in a mood of deep depression, trying to decide what had gone wrong, apart from the fact that those bastards of warships had let them down.

Encarnita went up to the *alcazaba* and crouching in the shelter of a wall she let the tears flow. She wished she were back in Yegen, away from this madness. But perhaps they were fighting each other there too. She knew that some in the village would defend the monarchy and the church to the last while others would not and thought their power too great. But would that be enough for them to go out and kill each other, their friends and neighbours? She could not imagine it. She wished she could talk to Don Geraldo for he might have been able to help her understand why the world had turned crazy. He knew the world. He had travelled far and wide. But perhaps he and Doña Gamel would have left Spain by now and gone back to the peace and quiet of their own country.

Hearing footsteps Encarnita looked up to see Sofia coming purposefully up the slope with a cloth in her hand, making for the cemetery.

'I have come to do my cleaning,' she announced calmly.

'Today?'

'Why not today?'

Encarnita got up and followed her into the enclave. At least the dead were not warring.

Sofia picked up the crucifix. She held it aloft for a moment, regarding it with lips pursed, then, suddenly, she dashed it to the ground, crying, 'What use are YOU? I asked YOU to look after him and YOU did not!'

Encarnita went to Pedro's mother and put her arms round her. They cried together and when all their tears were spent Sofia said, 'Now I shall have another grave to visit. If I can afford the funeral.'

'I have some money.'

'You need it.'

'No, I want to give it you. For Pedro.' Encarnita broke off, sniffing the air.

'Something's burning,' said Sofia.

She stayed up in the cemetery while Encarnita ran down the hill. The casino was on fire, blazing brightly, beyond salvation. The crowd was cheering and some had run in and pulled out pieces of furniture. Two men dragged the grand piano into the street and turned it upside down, whereupon a group of children began to stone it. The casino might not have been an important building, except that it had attracted tourists, who had brought money into the town, but it saddened Encarnita to see the flames and the venom in the children's faces. She turned away.

By the shore, she bumped into Manolo. He looked like a wet seal.

'Manolo! You're not dead, then!'

'Not quite.'

'Have you come out of the sea?'

He had escaped by swimming to the lighthouse, then he had made his way over the cliffs. 'We are finished, Encarnita,' he said limply. 'They are too strong for us.'

'But not in the whole of Spain?'

'I don't know! I just do not know.'

He went into the bar and Encarnita continued along to the hotel where Jacobo and Lorenzo were listening to Radio Sevilla.

'It doesn't sound good.' Jacobo shook his head.

They huddled round the crackling radio and at midnight heard that General Queipo de Llano was about to make a statement.

'He's for Franco,' said Jacobo.

De Llano sounded drunk, but triumphant. He had come on air to announce the fall of Sevilla. God's army had triumphed! Praise be to God! *Viva España! Viva la Virgen!* Anyone who was not with them would be shot like dogs.

'It sounds as if they've won,' whispered Encarnita.

'How can we tell?' said Lorenzo. 'He might just have captured the radio station.' That was the trouble: news came through in fractured bursts. There was never a complete picture; Spain was a big country and there were many different factions operating.

'I heard earlier that they were still fighting in the north,' said Jacobo. 'In Barcelona and Madrid. The workers won't give up so easily there.'

'Maybe they did not give up so easily in Sevilla!' said Encarnita.

Next morning, another warship was standing off-shore. Friend or foe? Shortly afterwards, a small launch was seen setting out from the bigger ship. When it reached the beach an officer, in sparkling white and with gold on his cap, stepped ashore, announcing that he was from H.M.S. *Blanche*. His Majesty's Navy – His Majesty being the King of Great Britain and Ireland – had sent them to pick up British subjects who had found themselves marooned in this difficult situation. They could come or not, it was their choice, but if it were him, he said, he would not hesitate. This might be their last chance to get out.

Lorenzo and his friend, the Englishwoman, Wilma Gregory, decided to go.

'I don't blame them,' said Jacobo.

'Nor I,' said Encarnita sadly, who wished that they could also be carried away across the sea on HMS *Blanche*.

They helped Lorenzo gather up his few belongings and escorted the two travellers down to the beach. The woman was handed into the launch first, then it was the turn of Lorenzo. He would come back, he promised, then he embraced them and said good-bye. Encarnita and Jacobo watched the little boat cutting like an arrow through the blue sea, leaving a white wake behind, growing smaller and smaller as it neared the horizon. When it was a mere smudge they turned their backs. There would be no more musical evenings in the Hotel Mediterráneo.

Encarnita went up the hill and collected Cinderella. There was no sign of Rinaldo, who was probably at yet another meeting. 'We're going to get some fresh air,' she told the goat. 'We're going to our house.'

As they neared the outskirts of the village they heard voices and the trundling sound made by cart wheels. Encarnita stopped dead, as did Cinderella. The road was swarming with people as well as animals and all manner of vehicles, moving eastward. Many were on foot carrying bundles. The old limped, some with feet bound in rags. Scattered about were pots and pans and pieces of furniture, dropped by those whose arms had grown weary. A mule lay on the side of the road its nostrils foaming horribly. Babies cried from the running sores on their limbs. An ambulance

came weaving through and arms were stretched out in sup-
plication but it was full already.

One family had pulled up on the verge while the father
was trying to mend one of the wheels of their two-wheeled
cart. He was cursing; a spoke had broken. The cart itself
was piled teeteringly high with furniture, bedding and
clothing.

Encarnita spoke to the mother, who looked as if she had
not slept for many nights. 'Where are you going?'

'Who knows? As far away as we can get from Málaga. It's
like hell on earth there, what with the shootings and burn-
ings. God knows what we've done in our lives to deserve
this!'

'You were living in Málaga?'

'A village nearby. A village called Churriana.'

'Churriana!'

'You know it.'

'No, but a friend – well, someone I used to know – went
to live there. An Englishman. His name was Señor Brenan.'

'Don Geraldo? Yes, we know him well. And his wife,
Doña Gamel, too. They are friendly people. They always
talk to us.'

'And their servants, Maria, Rosario and Antonio?'

'They're well, as well anyone can be with all this going
on! How is it you know them?'

'I used to live in the same village.'

'In Yegen, away up in the Alpujarra? Don Geraldo said
they had been happy there.'

'Have they stayed in Churriana?'

'So far. But we think they'll leave at some point. It'll be
easier for them to get away, of course. They can go to
Gibraltar and get a ship to England. Their government will
look after them. But who is to look after us?'

The father lifted his flushed face. 'It's not going to hold.'
He shrugged. 'I need some strong twine.'

'What use is a cart with a missing wheel?' His wife was
close to tears. 'What are we to do with all our things? We

can't carry them.'

Encarnita offered to go and try to find some twine in the village. She knew a man who sold it.

'But will the shop be open?'

'He lives in the room at the back.'

'Why should you do that for us?'

'Because I should like to. Since you know Don Geraldo. He is the link between us.'

The man gave her some *pesetas* and one of the children, a boy of some nine or ten years, came with her. The rest of the family said they would look after Cinderella. Encarnita found Roberto, the shopkeeper, at home; and he did have some twine left, which he was willing to sell to her. She felt that this piece of luck was a good omen and it had cheered her even to have news of Don Geraldo, as well as Maria and Rosario. She ran back to the family who waited by the road-side.

'Would you like to come with us?' asked the woman. 'Franco's men will be coming this way, you can count on that.'

'I live with my uncle,' said Encarnita. 'I couldn't leave him.'

'Of course you couldn't. We must stay with our own in times like these. *Vaya con Dios!*'

They took leave of each other like people who had known each other for a long time. Encarnita watched yet another departure and wondered how far these people would have to flee to escape the rebel armies. They might be driven into the sea in the end.

She spent a couple of hours in the *campo* with Cinderella, who was reluctant to return to the hard, barren streets afterwards. When they reached the road she strained at her rope and dug in her hoofs. Life in Almuñecar did not suit her, nor Encarnita now, either. She wished they could live in their little house remote from war and talk of war.

She found Rinaldo at home. He was tying up a bedroll, and by the wall stood a packed knapsack.

'Encarnita,' he said, looking up at her, 'I'm joining the Republican forces. They need recruits badly. I have to go and fight for our freedom. You understand that, don't you?'

Encarnita nodded.

The bells rang out and people cheered as the Risen Christ, his waxy face pale in the bright sunshine, his right hand raised, ready to bless them, was borne on high out of the church. The scuffed, workaday boots of the fishermen shouldering the heavy, flower-decked float were visible beneath the hems of their scarlet and white cloaks as they shuffled forward. *The Saviour Has Risen! Aleluja! Aleluja!* All is well with the world. It was a message that the crowd was desperate to hear. A tear or two was wiped away. The priest nodded and smiled upon his flock. Nearly everyone in the village was there; few would dare stay away. Attendance at church was mandatory now that General Franco was in power. The general was a pious man, reputed to attend mass daily and to spend hours on his knees in prayer. Where the moral standards of his citizens were concerned, he had a missionary's zeal. He was determined to lift his people out of the slack ways they had slumped into and in which they might have remained had he not defeated the Republicans. Censorship was back, the clergy had their hands on the schools again and young men and girls were no longer to be seen out on the *paseo* hand-in-hand, their bodies brushing against each other as they walked.

Then it was Mary's turn. This was the moment that the women had been anticipating. They were ready with their cheers. Encarnita, who had been standing back a little, moved forward and she, too, clapped and cheered. It was impossible not to. The men, in charge of this precious float, conscious of the watching eyes of their wives and daughters, were taking great care not to let the virgin wobble. The women tossed up flowers for their lady, who gazed serenely down at them from her lofty perch. Their faces glowed as they looked up at her. She had suffered the loss of a son, like many of them; she understood their pain. *Blessed be the Virgin of Almuñecar! Mother of the seas!* Sofia wiped her eyes

with the back of her hand. Encarnita's eyes were as dry as
the dust in the road; she had shed so many tears in the last
three years that she did not think she could ever weep again.

Once the crowd had fallen in behind the floats Encarnita
detached herself. She had told Sofia earlier that she might
go for a walk. Sofia did not like her to go walking alone in
the *campo* but she needed to get away from the crowd. And
bandits and dropouts from the war, which was what Sofia
feared, did not come down as far as the coast. Also,
refugees from the war would be Republicans and would not
harm her. 'How can you be sure?' Sofia had demanded. 'The
war has changed our people. It has brought out the bad
blood in them. Men, if they're desperate, cease to know
what is right or wrong. ' But the men tended to lie low in
the higher passes of the sierras. It was known that a number of Republican fighters were up there, awaiting their
chance to strike back, though Encarnita did not see how
they would be able to without being slaughtered. There
could not be so very many of them, and they must be ill-
equipped, and the army and the *Guardia Civil* had a firm
grip of every town and village. They were often to be seen
up by the *alcazaba*, scanning the *campo* from the walls.
Encarnita resented their presence there. She felt they had
violated a place that belonged to her and Sofia.

As she dropped back from the crowd, she felt a hand on
her arm and looked round.

'Does anything ail you, child?' asked the nun. She was
elderly and had lived in Cádiar as a girl, not far from Yegen.
Sometimes Encarnita would stop to talk to her, to reminisce
about the places of their birth. The almond blossom was
what the nun remembered most. 'Are you not coming with
the procession?'

'I was feeling a little faint, Sister. I need some air.'

'It is a very emotional experience, is it not, the resurrec-
tion of Our Saviour?'

Encarnita nodded.

'I've not seen you at mass for a while. Do you go to

confession?'

'Sometimes.' She had not been for a while. She hated the stuffiness of the confessional box, preferring to sit in the church when it was quiet. She found it more helpful to talk to her mother than to the priest but the nun would probably think that sinful. Sofia did. Sofia despaired of her state of grace, or lack of it, at times. 'I'll go soon,' Encarnita added, though she was not certain that she would.

'Good! *Vaya con Dios!*' The nun took her hand from Encarnita's arm and hurried after the procession, her skirts swirling.

On the next corner, Encarnita passed two members of the *Guardia Civil*, who swivelled round to watch her go. Automatically, she dropped her gaze. Anyone who had had family members fighting for the Republicans was regarded with disfavour and suspicion. Rinaldo had been known as a leader.

'One moment, Señorita!'

She stopped, looked round. One of the guards was coming strolling towards her, taking his time. He waddled slightly, as if his thighs were rubbing together. Her heart beat quickened.

'Your papers, Señorita?'

He knew very well who she was and where she lived. He had asked to see her papers before. She took them from her pocket and he perused them, pursing his lips, as he had done the first time.

'So you were born in Yegen? That's up in the Alpujarra.' He made it sound like the moon. He was from Madrid himself and had not been pleased at being posted to a rathole like Almuñecar. He made no secret of it. Guards never worked on their own home ground.

'What brought you to Almuñecar?'

He knew the answer to that, too.

'Somebody cut out your tongue? Let me see it! Come on, show me your tongue!'

She let only the very tip of it slide over her lower lip. He put out a stubby index finger and laid it on her tongue, holding it down. She tasted nicotine and sweat and thought she might retch.

'It's healthy enough looking, I see, nice and plump and pink. I don't like girls with skinny tongues. Seems it should be able to talk.' He lifted his finger, regarded it for a moment, then ran his own tongue over it. 'Quite sweet. Are you ready to answer me now?'

She swallowed. 'I came to visit my uncle.'

'Ah yes, your uncle.' He came a step closer until she could feel the flow of his breath on her face. She flinched as if struck by a physical blow. His breath was heavy with the stench of beer and tobacco and his face looked blotchy and red beneath the tricorned leather hat. She could see beads of sweat sitting in the open pores of his nose. 'So, have you any news of this famous uncle of yours? Or should I say, infamous?'

She shook her head.

'No?' He smiled. 'Are you sure about that? You would tell me if you had, wouldn't you? *Wouldn't* you? Come on now, answer me! Don't start playing dumb with me again. I might just get angry. You'd tell me?' He engaged her eyes with his.

'Yes,' she whispered, feeling as a bird might when confronted by a cat.

'I'm sure you wouldn't want any trouble?'

'No,' she said.

'You want to be nice to me, don't you? Of course you do. Maybe I'll come and visit you sometime. You must be lonely up there all on your own, a pretty *chica* like you, lying next to the dead. Aren't you afraid of the ghosts?'

'No.'

'You're not? I like a bold *chica*. So, tell me, would you like me to pay you a visit? I might even bring you a little present, if you were prepared to be very nice.' A blob of spittle had formed at the side of his mouth. She thought she had never seen an uglier face in all the nineteen years of her life.

'What do you say?'

'I don't know.'

'You don't know? No, don't look away from me!' He put his hand on her shoulder, letting his hot fat fingers slide down to touch the top of her breast underneath her blouse. He ignored the sniggers of his friend, who was waiting on the opposite side of the road. 'All right,' he said, 'I'll let you go.' He gave her a little push and she staggered back. 'For now,' he added.

Her legs felt like jelly as she walked away. She heard the two men laughing. The street up the hill was deserted except for four or five mangy kittens scavenging in the gutter and one old man who sat on a low wicker chair in his doorway. He was too old to join an Easter procession and even the guards left him alone. He asked her, as he always did when she passed, 'No word of Rinaldo?' She shook her head and he sighed and said what a loss all the young men were. His grandson had been killed at the battle of the Ebro and buried there. But, at least, his family knew what had happened to him. 'The *pueblo* will never be the same again.'

When Encarnita reached her house she closed and barred the door behind her. Then she sat down on her straw pallet and allowed herself to shake for a few minutes. Following on, came a bout of anger which swept through her like a raging fire. She felt the heat of it in her chest. She thumped the pallet with both fists until she felt gutted and empty. She would keep a knife by the door and if he were to come she would stick it into him as one might to a pig. If she were to confess this murderous thought to the priest would he absolve her sin? Priests the length and breadth of Spain must have had to absolve hundreds of thousands of the blackest of sins. Brothers had murdered brothers, and fathers sons. At times, surely, the priests themselves must have wept in the confessionals.

She rinsed her mouth with a small cupful of water and spat it out in the yard. Then she lifted a small canvas sack and set off again. She was going out to look for fallen fruit, whatever she could find, olives, an orange or two, perhaps even an avocado, if she would be lucky enough to find a ripe one. She would share her pickings with Sofia. Sofia had a nephew who was a fishermen; he would sometimes bring her a fish which she would then share with Encarnita. They helped each other out. The baker gave them the ends of stale loaves. Life would be a little easier, come summer, for then she might be able to find work in the fields.

She took a street that led down to the *plaza*. Before she reached it she stepped back into a doorway and waited. There seemed to be no sign of the guards. Moving quickly and quietly, she crossed the square.

Once she reached the edge of the village and could see the *campo* in front of her she began to feel a little easier. She was about to cross the road when she heard the sound of traffic. An open-backed army truck came into view, the rear packed with soldiers, each clutching a rifle close to his body, looking as if he were ready to spring out and fire the moment an order was given. The vehicle slowed and the driver spoke to her through his open window. Had she seen any strangers in the area?

'No, no one,' she said.

The army was conducting regular searches over wide sweeps of country, their quarry Republicans on the run. Sometimes, lying awake in the dark, Encarnita would hear shots. They carried out their executions at night and buried their victims in mass graves in the *campo*. It was said that the poet Lorca lay in one such grave somewhere outside Granada but no one knew where. He had been executed early in the war. It was the not knowing that the relatives of the missing found the most difficult thing to bear. Sofia had been able to put her son to rest and so could mourn him.

'If you see anyone report it at once to the *Guardia Civil*!' snapped the driver.

The engine roared into life and the truck picked up speed, foul smoke belching from its exhaust pipe. The soldiers stared back at her where she stood at the side of the road.

They could not be any older than she was, yet some of them had the glazed eyes of the old man who sat on the low wicker chair in her street.

And then, the soldiers were gone. Encarnita crossed the road and ran until she was out of breath, when she slowed her pace to a walk. Out in the *campo* she missed the company of Cinderella. The goat had died in the winter. She had no money to buy a new one and there was no chance of Don Geraldo coming to her rescue this time. In the beginning she had felt as if Cinderella's death had severed a link with him but had found that when she took out Señorita Carrington's picture of Gabriella, her first goat, and looked at it, her mind would travel back to the hillside above Yegen and she would remember the sound of the Englishman and his friends talking and laughing. They had always been so full of life. Were they laughing now? Was anyone laughing? Only the victors. In Republican houses, people were quiet, afraid even to raise their voices.

She often wondered how they were, Don Geraldo and Doña Gamel, if they were living in England, or had stayed in Spain. She thought it unlikely that they would have stayed. Luisa might have heard from Maria and Rosario's brother, but there had been no news from Yegen since early in the war. Encarnita had received one letter from Miss Osborne, to which she had written a reply, but when she had dropped the envelope into the box she had had the feeling that it might never reach its destination. The postal service had all but collapsed.

She made for an old olive grove that was no longer tended. She harvested a number of its wrinkled fruits and dropped them gratefully into her sack. Further on, she came to a ruined house that had been burned out by the Nationalists; it had housed a Republican and his family. They had all died in the fire, the parents and their three children. Encarnita hated going near the blackened ruin that smelt still of smoke, but there was a good orange tree in the garden and if she did not take the fruit it would drop and wither and Sofia and herself would go hungry. As soon as she had dropped the fruit into the bag she put her back to the place and plunged deeper into the *campo*. She was going to visit her house.

It was many months since she had been there. During the war it had been difficult to wander off the beaten path. Even now it was dangerous. She had set out to go not long ago but, before reaching the house, she had come across one of the patrols. They had waved her back with their rifles and so, without a word, she had turned and headed for the coast.

She went warily, keeping an eye open for any sign of human life. The house, standing in such an isolated position, was well away from any other kind of habitation. When the broken-down roof came into view, she felt herself smiling. It was still there! Her own special secret place. No one had burned it down. She picked her way between the brambles and thorn bushes that had grown up around it since her last visit. Vegetation had crept up the masonry, too, virtually obscuring it.

She pushed open the splintered door. The first thing that struck her was the noise after the quiet outside. It was the frenzied noise of madly buzzing insects. Many insects. Her eyes took a few minutes to adjust to the light but when they did she saw that someone – it looked like the body of a man – was lying on the floor. He was surrounded by a cloud of flies.

Could it be Rinaldo? That was her first thought, then she realised that there was no reason why it should be him any more than anyone else. He had not known the place existed. She wished now that she had told him about it for he might have been able to use it as a hideaway.

It was very hot inside the house. She swallowed to calm her rising nausea, then she forced herself to move towards the man. The flies came up in a swarm as she closed in on them and she batted them away whirling her arms round and round her head. Finally, she lifted a piece of old sacking and drove as many as she could out of the house, swearing at them as she did. She felt angry with them. They were an enemy she could attack in return.

Now she could see the man. His head and shoulders were covered with a stained, grey blanket. The stains were dark. Blood, probably. Gently, she eased the covering back from his head. It was not Rinaldo. She did not know whether to be relieved or disappointed. He was not a Spaniard at all, or like none she had ever seen in their part of the country. His tangled shoulder-length hair, and matted beard were sandy-red in colour and his skin was pale, very pale, waxy almost, like the face of the Christ in the church. He had a gash on his temple, clotted with black blood. She swished away the insects that had been feeding on it. His long blond lashes were closed. She put out a finger and cautiously touched his cheek; it felt chilled but she did not think it was quite stone cold. She jumped as he let out a small moan, more of a mew, like the noise a kitten might make. He was alive.

When she pulled back the blanket from the rest of his body she saw that he wore the uniform of the Republican army. So he was on the run. His right arm lay in an awkward position and there were blood stains on the legs of his trousers. She stayed for some time as she was, on her knees, watching him; his eyelids flickered from time to time and once or twice twitched so rapidly that she thought he was about to wake. But he did not. His lips were ridged and cracked at the sides. He was bone dry.

Her dishes were still where she had left them, beside the wall, covered with a piece of cloth. She lifted the pail and went to fill it at the spring, taking care, as she came and went, to scan the terrain for any sign of human life. A black vulture was hovering overhead, casting his shadow on the ground, awaiting his chance. It was lucky for the man that he had found her house; out in the open he would have been vulnerable to birds of prey as well as humans. When she went back to him she found that he had not moved. She dipped her fingers in the water and laid them against his lips and immediately his mouth responded with little sucking movements. She plunged her fingers into the water again and again and each time the response from his lips was stronger.

She sat very still beside him and waited, sensing that he was gradually stirring into life. The expressions on his face were changing. He frowned now as if trying to remember something. The sun was gradually moving round until its rays no longer reached into the interior of the house. Shadows were forming. She knew she should go soon or else she would be caught out in the dark. Just as she was thinking that she could not delay any longer he opened his eyes and looked directly into her face.

'Hello,' he said, in English.

She was not surprised. While she had sat there, keeping her vigil, she had begun to think that he must come from a country further north. They had heard of the International Brigades, made up of men from several European countries as well as North America, who had come to Spain to fight on the side of the Republicans.

'Hello,' she returned, using his language.

'English?'

'Me? No, I Spanish.'

'But you speak English?'

'A little. You, you are English?'

'No, Scots.'

'It is not the same?'

'No, it is not the same.'

He tried to move his arm and flinched.

'Painful?'

'Broken. Feels broken.'

'You know Rinaldo?'

'Rinaldo?' He looked blank. 'No, I don't think so. Why? Should I know him?'

'He my uncle.' She had hoped that he might have news of Rinaldo. She feared she would never see him again. It was as if he had vanished from the face of the earth, like so many others. 'He fight like you. For Republicans.'

'I see. Has he not come back? I'm sorry.' He ran his serrated tongue over his cracked lips. She put the cup to his mouth and lifted the back of his head up with her other hand to make it easier for him to drink. He drank noisily and greedily.

Dusk had gathered inside the house. Looking up at the sky through the broken roof Encarnita saw a star. Very soon it would be dark. She had to hope for a moon and a cloudless sky to see her home.

'I sorry but must go. It late.' She got to her feet. 'But tomorrow I come back .'

'Would you? Would you really? I'd be very grateful. Do you think you could bring me some food?'

'Some here.' She took two oranges and a handful of olives out of her sack and laid them beside him. 'I bring more food tomorrow. There is water in pail.'

'Thank you. You are very kind. You will not tell anyone about me?'

She shook her head and then she left him. It was only when she had put the house behind her that she realised she did not even know his name. There was only a half moon which shed indifferent light over the undulating *campo*. She was normally sure-footed but in the half dark she could not avoid stumbling into rabbit holes or scratching her legs on thorny bushes. As she drew nearer to the coast she was encouraged by the sight of the little winking lights of Almuñecar ahead.

The road was quiet so she was able to cross quickly and was soon in the shelter of the streets. She went cautiously, as she had come to do wherever she went, watching for signs of tricorned hats. There was scarcely anyone at all around. People did not venture out much after dark for fear of running foul of the patrols. When she reached Sofia's house she saw that her lamp was lit so she tapped on the door and went in.

'Encarnita! Where have you been? I've been worried about you.'

Encarnita went to kiss her. 'I was in the *campo*.'

'But it's been dark for an hour and more.'

'No harm came to me.' Encarnita tipped out the contents of her bag. 'I brought us some fruit.'

Sofia had a hunk of bread and a sliver of hard cheese. They put their food together and sat down at the table to eat. Encarnita related her encounter with the guard earlier.

Sofia knew the man. 'He's a pig, that one! He tries to get his hand up all the girls' skirts. His wife is a miserable creature. He beats her, I'm sure he does. You can see the bruises on her face. And she misses her family in Madrid. She talked to me up in the cemetery. Poor girl. She comes up there sometimes. She has no one here to talk to, with her husband being a guard. You must stay with me tonight, Encarnita. You shouldn't be sleeping up there all alone, a young girl like you.'

Encarnita stayed and woke in the morning thinking of the Scottish soldier. As soon as Sofia had gone up to the cemetery Encarnita slipped down the hill and set out for the house, collecting olives, a couple of avocados and some oranges on the way.

He was sitting with his back to the wall. His face lit up as soon as he saw her. 'I've been wondering if you would come.'

'You think I would not?'

'Why should you? You don't know me. Have you come because of your uncle?'

'I come because I want.' She set down the fruit, trying to explain in faltering English that she did not have money to buy other kinds of food.

He asked her name.

'Encarnita.' She felt shy now and looked away. He had very searching eyes of an arresting shade of turquoise-blue.

'*Me llamo* Conal.'

'*Habla español?*'

'A little. What I learned in the war. I don't think I should repeat some of the words though!'

She smiled. 'We can speak in a mixture of the two. You help me with English and I help you with Spanish.' That would be good for her, she said, since she planned to go to England one day. He countered, saying that she must come to Scotland. He was curious and wanted to know how she had come to learn English.

'You know Don Geraldo Brenan? He live in my village.'

'Geraldo Brenan? No, I don't think so.'

'You don't know him? But he famous. He has written books with the name of George Beaton. You don't know his book *Jack Robinson?*'

Conal frowned and shook his head.

'That is pity. He very nice man. You know the woman Virginia Woolf? She writes books as well. Lot of his friends do.'

Conal had heard of Virginia Woolf though had not read any of her books. 'She didn't live in your village too, did she?'

'She come for visit. She wear nice soft shoes.'

A spasm crossed his face and he closed his eyes while it passed. Encarnita went to him.

'It's my arm.' He tried to smile. 'And a few other things. I'm filthy too.'

She fetched water and let him sluice his face before she looked at his wounds. He shook his head afterwards like a dog coming out of the river. 'That's better.' He was gasping. She had brought with her an old piece of cloth and a shirt of Rinaldo's. He fainted for a moment while she was helping to ease him out of his jacket. She gave him a drink and held his head until the dizziness left him, then she went out to look for a straight stick to use as a splint. She found a branch and snapped it in half.

'You've done this before,' he said, as she bound the stick to his arm and afterwards cleaned, as best she could, the wound on his temple and two deep gashes in his right leg that had been bandaged by fraying strips of grubby cloth. She frowned at those wounds but made no comment. He was right; she had done this many times before. In the early years of the war, before they had been overrun by the Nationalists, she and Sofia had helped to tend wounds and bind up limbs of many wounded Republican soldiers.

'You are an angel,' he said.

'An angel?' That made her laugh and she realised that she had not laughed for a long time. 'No, I not think so. I am not very holy. The priest probably not say so.'

'You don't have to be holy to be an angel! I like your name. Encarnita! Tell me about yourself, Encarnita.'

'Not much to tell.'

'There must be. You've been in this hellish war too. Tell me about your uncle.'

To do that, she had to lapse into Spanish. She spoke volubly and fast, losing him at times, but holding him sufficiently so that he knew, more or less, what she was saying. 'He was good man,' she said finally, in English, and then she shed tears for Rinaldo, for the first time. Until now, she had tried to believe that a miracle would happen and he would return.

Conal put out his hand to touch hers. 'I understand. I have seen so many men die.'

'You tell me your story?'

The Scotsman told her that he had come to Spain in 1937 and enlisted in an International Brigade, having crossed over the Pyrenees from France with a number of other recruits, men who had wanted to help their Spanish brothers.

'But why? Why you come when you are not Spanish? I don't understand. It was not your war.'

'It was every man's war. I came because I hate Fascism!' He went on to talk about Hitler, the man whom Jacobo had feared, and about Mussolini, the leader of the Italians, and how they wanted to take over the world.

'The priest say the communists in Russia want to take over the world too. He say there is a man called Stalin who is very bad man and hates God.'

'I'm not a communist. You don't need to have a label. I am on the side of the poor and the underdog. You have to stand up for what you believe in in this world.'

He might have been repeating the words that she had heard Rinaldo speak in the *plaza*, his eyes on fire, the listening crowd captured by his fervour. She wondered if the Scotsman was a poor underdog himself. How could she tell? He wore a soiled army uniform and he had no money so he was poor now whatever he had been at home in his own country.

'You are brave man,' she told him.

He shook his head. 'At times I was so scared to death I was tempted to run away but I didn't know where to run.' Now that he had begun to talk he went rambling on, about battles and places, most of which she could not follow. Some names she knew, like the river Ebro, which she had seen on the map of Spain. The battle there, she gathered, had been bloody and had lasted many months. It had been his last battle. Friends had died, had given their lives. As Sofia's Pedro had, at that same place. 'For what?' Conal demanded, but she had no answer. She felt as if the soil of her country was soaked in blood. She wondered if flowers could ever bloom again in such polluted ground.

At length, he ran out of energy and slumped back. 'What good did we do?' he muttered. 'Were we idiots to think we could do something? It's all right to talk about standing up for what you believe in but in the end we achieved nothing.' He'd been left for dead on the battlefield and rescued by a family who had cared for him and hidden him until he had felt fit enough to move on. He had been hoping to make his way to Gibraltar but his strength had given out. Was Gibraltar far? he asked.

Encarnita did not know. 'Somewhere past Málaga.' She remembered Don Geraldo talking about sailing from the port.

'It belongs to the United Kingdom, so if I could just get there I should be able to find a ship that would take me home.'

It would be too far for him to walk in his present state as well as difficult with *Guardia Civil* patrols strung along the coast looking for Republicans trying to escape across the sea to North Africa. She thought of the shots in the night.

'You have to take care. No one see you.'

When she returned to Almuñecar in the late afternoon she ran into the same two guards as she had the day before. She had been lost in thought and had not seen them until she was almost on top of them.

The one she hated most addressed her. 'So, Señorita Encarnita, where have you been today?'

'To the *campo*. To look for olives.' She opened the sack to show him.

He put in his fat fist and withdrawing one he bit into it, spitting it out a moment later. 'Sour! So you've been stealing, have you?'

'No. The trees are old. They're not tended any more.'

'So you say. Can I trust what you say? Can I trust what you tell me about your precious uncle Rinaldo Benet? He's not hiding out in the *campo*, is he? If you were found to be helping him you could be shot too, you know that, don't you?'

His attention was diverted by the sound of shouts coming from the shore.

'We'd better go and see what's up,' said his companion, making a move.

Encarnita escaped up the hill to Sofia's house.

'Look!' Sofia held up a flounder. 'Juan brought it for us.'

When they were eating she said, 'Juan likes you, you know.'

'He is a good man.'

Sofia glanced at Encarnita. 'You are quiet this evening?'

Encarnita shrugged.

'What troubles you?'

'There is a man in the *campo*,' Encarnita began, then stopped. She should not burden Sofia with it.

'A man? What kind of man? You had better tell me!' After Encarnita had finished Sofia said, 'This is dangerous, Encarnita, you know it is. Just think if you were to be found with him!'

'I have thought. But, Sofia, this man has fought for us! He fought with Pedro and Rinaldo and now he's wounded and a long way from home, with no one but me to help him.'

'He comes from Scotland, you say? His mother must worry very much for him.' Sofia sighed. 'I feel for this woman whom I do not know and will never see. What must she be going through at this very moment? Why do men do this to us, Encarnita!'

1939

The *campo* was out of bounds for Encarnita the following day because of *Guardia Civil* and army manoeuvres. Trucks were parked all along the main road. From her perch up beside the *alcazaba* ruins she could see figures running to and fro into the undergrowth. Their voices carried on the still air. The baker had told her that he'd heard a fugitive had been sighted. She trembled in case it might be the Scotsman.

'I hope it is not,' said Sofia, coming from the cemetery to join her. 'For your sake.'

'He wouldn't tell them about me.'

'You know they can make people talk. They're good at that. He is young, you said?'

'About my age, I think.'

'God help him, that is all I can say.' Sofia sat down on a lump of stone to rest. Her legs were swollen and bothered her greatly. 'Get down, here comes a guard!'

Encarnita slid down the wall to join Sofia. When the guard was a few metres away he stopped.

'What are you two women doing up here?'

'Praying for the dead,' said Sofia. 'We are permitted to visit them.'

'But you, girl, you were up on the wall?'

'I heard noises.'

'Mind your own business, do you hear!' He went lumbering off to join his comrade who had been waiting on the other side of the castle ground. When his back was turned Encarnita stole another quick look over the wall. Activity out in the *campo* had become more feverish. Soldiers were springing out of the trucks parked along the road and running, heading towards the hills, their rifles spearheading their advance.

'I think they might have found someone. I'm going down to see.'

Sofia shook her head. 'Don't go!'

'I must. In case it's him.'

'If it is don't speak to him, for the love of God.' Sofia crossed herself. 'Don't even look at him! Promise me!'

Encarnita nodded. 'It could be Rinaldo,' she said and left Sofia sitting on the wall.

When she reached the *plaza* she saw that a number of people were making their way out towards the main road. Many, like herself, had missing relatives. She joined them. At the road, they stopped and waited in silence.

A few minutes later, a posse of *Guardia Civil* came into sight. Two of them were dragging a man along the ground between them.

'It's Marco!' cried a woman. She was his mother.

Marco had gone with the other men to fight for the Republicans three years before; he had been amongst the *desaparecidos*. His limbs looked slack, as if broken, and blood poured down his face. No one was in any doubt that he would not live long. He was not the first to have been dragged out of the hills.

Encarnita felt a mixture of relief and despair. The sense of relief made her feel guilty, and it did not last long. She had known Marco; he had been a friend of Rinaldo's, a friendly, easy-going man, well liked by everyone. She could not bear to look at his mother's face. The sound of the woman's wailing followed her as she turned and retraced her steps back up the hill to rejoin Sofia.

The two woman sat together, dry-eyed, unable to spill a tear. They stayed there for some time, motionless, not even speaking, until Sofia said, 'Let us go and light a candle.'

'Does it do any good, lighting candles?'

'You must not lose your faith, Encarnita. It is the only thing we have to hold on to when times are bad.'

'At this moment General Franco might be lighting a candle too. Praising God for delivering Marco into his hands!'

'Hush, don't speak about him in that tone of voice. You might be overheard.'

Encarnita went with Sofia to the church, where several women had already gathered, to pray on their knees for the soul of Marco, as if he were already dead. Encarnita knelt beside them and prayed that Marco would die quickly. There was no sign of the priest.

She lay awake in the middle of the night, thinking about the Scottish man lying wounded in her little ruined house, imagining how lonely he must feel, so far away from his homeland and everything that was familiar. When she had not come that day he must have thought that she had abandoned him.

'I don't think you should go to him,' said Sofia in the morning, knowing that Encarnita would go, nevertheless.

'He needs help.'

'So do we all.'

'But he left his home and came all this way to help us. I'm sure Rinaldo would have wanted me to help him.'

Sofia shrugged her shoulders. 'Be careful then, that's all I can say. And come back well before dark, otherwise I shall be worrying about you.'

Encarnita kissed her and went up to Rinaldo's house to fetch a few things. Into her canvas bag she put a cup, another piece of rag, a small bar of hard yellow soap and Don Geraldo's book, *Jack Robinson*, thinking the Scotsman might like to read it, to help pass the time when he was alone. The hours must seem long to him.

Before going she checked out the terrain from the top of the hill to make sure the *Guardia Civil* were not out again today. They might well have been, looking for other fugitives, comrades of Marco. It would depend on whether Marco had given his captors any information or not. 'If they've made him talk we can't blame him,' Sofia had said. It was likely that Marco's friends would be further away by now, up in the higher *sierras*. They would not have hung about or tried to come to his rescue for that would only have ended in a massacre. All seemed quiet in the *campo*, as far as Encarnita could see and hear from the top of the hill.

She decided to risk it.

She met no one except for an elderly goatherd whom she knew a little. His face was thin and stained a deep chestnut-brown from exposure to the sun. He walked from morning till night with his small flock of skinny-flanked brown goats. Some of them belonged to other people; they gave him one or two *pesetas* or an egg to walk them for him. Encarnita had often exchanged a few words with him, enough to know on which side he stood. It would be inconceivable, anyway, that a poor goatherd would support the Nationalists.

He stopped today, wanting to talk, to ask a question. 'Did they get the man yesterday?' She nodded and he swore. 'I saw him running, or trying to. He had a bad leg to start with. I knew he had no chance.'

'Did you see any others with him?'

The goatherd shook his head.

'I keep hoping for news of my uncle Rinaldo Benet.'

'If I hear anything I'll tell you. You come this way often, don't you?'

She was about to move on when she saw that there was something else he wanted to say. She waited.

'I gave the man some milk.'

Her heart skipped a beat. 'The man?'

'In the ruined cottage. He needed food, he was starving.'

'How did you know about the place?'

'I have always known it.'

Of course he would! She had been stupid to think that no one would ever have come across it, especially a goatherd who wandered all over the *campo*.

'But don't worry. I don't think anyone else will know about it, it's so well hidden.'

Encarnita felt uneasy that even he should know. It was not that she did not trust him but, as Sofia had said, the *Guardia Civil* had ways of making people talk, so that the fewer people who knew anything the better.

As if reading her mind, he said, 'No one pays any

attention to me. They think I'm in my dotage and because I do nothing but mind goats that I am an imbecile. I let them think it when they ask me questions.'

'And do they, ask you questions?'

'Sometimes. Have I seen anyone? I pretend to be deaf as well as stupid.'

She put her hand on his ragged sleeve and felt the thinness of his arm. 'Thank you,' she said.

'Be careful,' he responded, before moving off to round up his straying goats. She listened to the tinkling of their bells until they faded into the distance.

She approached the house cautiously, pausing to listen before she covered the last stretch of ground and pushed open the door. He was there, almost in the same position that she had left him in.

'*Hola!*' He lifted his head and smiled. 'I thought I wouldn't see you again.'

She explained why she had been unable to come the day before and he said he'd thought he'd heard shouting in the distance. She spoke of Marco.

'You see, you must not leave the house!'

'I couldn't if I tried.'

She fetched fresh water and gave him a little fruit before setting about cleaning his wounds. He groaned and bit his lip until it bled but he encouraged her to carry on.

'They don't look good, do they?' he muttered. Sweat dripped from his brow. 'A lot of men at the front developed gangrene after they'd been wounded. It was what everyone feared. To lose a leg! And have it sawn off without an anaesthetic.' He told Encarnita that he had served with an ambulance brigade. Hospital facilities had been limited and ambulances had had an impossible task trying to get round the enemy lines.

'Fascist planes were overhead...you could hear their bloody shells whining...there were wounded everywhere. And then they got us. Direct hit. I was one of the lucky ones, I was thrown clear. I felt as if my brains were being blown out.' He said that when he got back to Scotland – *if*, he added – he intended to train as a doctor. He hesitated a moment. 'I don't suppose you could get hold of some iodine?'

'I could try.'

'Don't run any risks because of me. But you're doing that already, aren't you, every time you come here? And I'm grateful, I hope you know that.'

Embarrassed, she looked away. She took Don Geraldo's book from her sack and handed it to him. 'For you, may borrow.'

'Have you read it?'

'Only a little. Too difficult for me. Too many words don't know.' She had read only a sentence here and there but she had enjoyed looking at the book and holding it in her hand and remembering those happy times in Yegen when Don Geraldo had sat beside her and taught her to speak his language. It was something she had tried to hold on to during the three terrible years of the war.

The Scotsman was pleased to have the novel. He admitted that the hours did seem endless at times even though he slept for long stretches. And when he lay awake he worried about his family, especially his mother. 'She'll be going through hell, imagining all sorts of things. Not knowing what has happened is the worst thing of all.'

She nodded. 'For me, with Rinaldo.'

'You are very fond of your uncle?'

'Only family I have.'

'And he's missing! That must be terrible for you. And your mother and father?'

She shook her head.

'I'm sorry. So, do you live alone?'

'No, with good friend, Sofia. But tell me about your family, please.'

He was happy to talk about them and, while he did, he went far away from her, which she understood. When she remembered Yegen and the people she had grown up amongst she felt like that, as if her mind had spirited her away.

The Scotsman – she found it difficult to think of him by his name – had a mother who was herself a doctor, and a father who was a lawyer. So they were not a poor family. His older sister was a talented musician, a pianist, and married to a violinist, and they had a child, with a nanny to look after her when they were busy. They played together, this husband and wife, in an orchestra. Encarnita marvelled at the brilliance of all the things he told her and was reminded of Don Geraldo's friends who had been writers and artists and she wondered if everyone in England and Scotland had such talents. When she asked Conal he laughed.

'Unfortunately not.'

'You live in big house?'

It was so big his mother needed a housekeeper and a cook. They had another house, too, up north, in the mountains. He said that he loved it up there and described the river, telling her how it ran bubbling and golden-brown from the peat when it was in spate and how the hills turned purple in autumn when the heather flowered. He liked to walk in those hills. 'They are not so high as the Spanish *sierras*. And summer is not so hot. Scotland is less extreme than Spain. But I like your country too.'

'But not what my country do to you,' she said sadly.

'No,' he agreed, 'not that.' They fell silent.

She imagined that when he did return to Scotland he would never want to come back. His memories of her country would be too unhappy.

'You're sad, Encarnita.' He put his finger on her cheek and she felt herself blushing.

Soon afterwards, she got up to go, saying she would come the next day as long as neither the army or the *Guardia Civil* were out on patrol. 'And I bring iodine if I can.'

The thought of how to get hold of some preoccupied her on her journey back across the *campo*. It would be too dangerous to ask the doctor. He would want to know why she needed it. She had never had any dealings with him and knew him only by sight. She sought out Sofia in the cemetery and asked her advice, although she could have guessed her reaction beforehand.

'You are asking for trouble! The *Guardia Civil* will be keeping a close watch on the doctor in case he treats wounded Republicans on the sly. I am sure he is far too wary even to think of it.' Sofia shook out her duster. She regarded herself as keeper of all the dead now since many no longer had living relatives. 'You will do this for me, won't you, Encarnita, when I am here?'

'Of course! But that will not be for a long time yet.'

'My legs are not good. The hill is a sore trial for me.'

'Sofia,' said Encarnita, 'you know Marina, don't you?' Marina was the doctor's housekeeper.

'You don't think I'm going to ask her for iodine for this young man, do you!'

'No, of course not.'

Encarnita wandered off down through the village, trying to think of anyone who might have some iodine in their cupboard, but could not. She saw the tricorned hats bobbing along in the distance, coming her way, and ducked inside the church. She talked to her mother but she seemed not to have any ideas of where to procure iodine, either.

It was dusk when she finally went back up the hill. Lamps were lit in the windows. The village looked so peaceful that it was difficult to think it had ever been torn apart by war. As Encarnita approached Sofia's house she smelt fish frying and her mouth watered. Juan must have brought something from his catch.

Sofia was at the stove and about to flip the fish over in the pan. 'It's a big one. Juan is a good lad. You could do worse, Encarnita, I keep telling you that.'

'I don't want a husband.'

'Every woman wants a husband sooner or later.'

'You have managed well without one for many years.'

'I might have managed better if he had lived. If you were to marry Juan we would become family. That would please me, Encarnita.'

Encarnita went over and put an arm round Sofia's shoulder. 'I feel we are family now.'

'But as Juan's wife, we would be family by law. I would leave this house to you and Juan.'

Encarnita's only home now was with Sofia. Rinaldo's house, which he had rented, was about to be repossessed by the owner.

'That is kind of you, Sofia, to offer to do that.'

'You will think it over? Juan asked me to speak to you about it. Now go and fetch the plates from the table.'

Encarnita was about to lift the plates when she saw a small bottle half filled with dark liquid sitting in the middle of the table. She frowned and turned to look questioningly at Sofia, who shrugged. Encarnita picked up the bottle, took out the cork and sniffed.

'Sofia, where did you get this?'

'I went to visit Marina.'

'And what did you tell her?'

'That you had a bad cut on your toe and it was festering. She took it from the doctor's surgery while he was not there.'

'You're wonderful, Sofia!'

Sofia snorted. 'Don't worry, I said nothing about your young man.'

'He is not my young man!'

'I hope he will not be. Do not let yourself get too fond of this Scotsman, Encarnita, for he will bring you nothing but troubles. Now then, bring the plates and let's eat.'

The Scotsman winced as she dabbed the wound and the iodine stung. 'You're a marvel, Encarnita.'

'Sofia got it. She is very good, very kind.'

'Like you.'

She blushed and looked away.

She picked some pieces of dried grass and dead insects from his hair. 'Needs cut,' she said. 'Yes,' he said. 'And washed.' Her hand accidentally brushed his cheek and their eyes met again and she was disturbed. She felt it deep down inside her. It was something she had never felt before. She moved back from him.

Don Geraldo's book was lying open on the ground.

'You enjoy it?'

'Not an awful lot.' When he saw that she frowned he added quickly, 'It's just that I didn't like Jack much, the way he walks out on his mother and stays away for a year and doesn't even let her know if he's alive or dead.'

'You leave your mother.'

'But she knew I was going.'

'And she approve?'

'Not totally. She approved of the cause but she didn't want me to be hurt.'

Encarnita nodded. That was how she had felt when she had watched Rinaldo walk out for the last time, his rucksack on his back. She had wanted to call him back, beg him not to go. But he would have gone anyway, just as the Scotsman would have done had his mother asked him.

She was disappointed, though, that he had not liked Don Geraldo's book. She would like to think that the two men would be friends if they were to meet.

'But you like books?' she pressed. He must, surely he must, since his family was rich.

'Oh yes! I like very much a Scottish writer called Robert Louis Stevenson. He lived in a house just along the road from me. Long before my time.'

'I have his book!' cried Encarnita triumphantly. '*Garden of Verses*.'

'You do?' He went on to recite some of the poems, most of which she knew herself by heart. 'My mother used to read them to me when I went to bed,' he said.

She could imagine such a scene. The land of counterpane. A boy with reddish-blond hair and blue eyes sitting up in bed, propped against fat white, lace-edged pillows, and a lovely lady with a sweet face reading. It was an image she took home with her as she recrossed the *campo*.

That evening, when they were having their meal – another fish from Juan – Sofia asked her what she found to talk about with the Scotsman.

'We talk about books.'

'Books! How many books have *you* read?'

'Some. We like the same poems. It's true!'

'And you can understand what he says, in English?'

'Not all the time. But enough. And he speaks some Spanish. We teach each other.'

Sofia pursed her lips.

A little later, a rap on the door announced the arrival of Juan. He had come to see if Encarnita would like to go for a *paseo* with him along the sea front. It was a fine night, he said. There was a moon. She excused herself, saying she was tired and had a headache. She avoided Sofia's eye.

'I'm sorry,' she said when Juan had gone, wearing an air of dejection.

'You are a fool!' It was seldom that Sofia was angry but tonight she was. She banged a pot lid as she put it on the shelf. 'Why will you not take him? Is he not good enough for you? I have been good enough to take you in and help you when you needed help. Do you think you are so special that you turn down an honest fisherman?'

'You have been good to me, Sofia, and I love you,' said Encarnita in a low voice, 'but I cannot reward you by marrying Juan.'

'I don't want a reward. But I want my nephew to be happy. He would like you for his wife. What is wrong with him?'

'Nothing, Sofia. He is a good man.'

'Well then?'

Encarnita stood with bent head, feeling like a penitent, but unwilling to repent. Her mother had always said she was stubborn and maybe she was being stubborn now but she could not bring herself to marry a man she did not love, or for whom she did not feel some affection. She liked Juan well enough, she thought him kind, but she found his features coarse and he blew his nose between his fingers and spat in the street, like many men did but, still, she did not like it.

'It was that Englishman in Yegen who put ideas in your head, wasn't it? What was his name?'

'Don Geraldo.' It was true that Encarnita had admired his manners and his learning, which perhaps had made her more critical of the Spanish men she met. She could not say so to Sofia, who would only be further offended. Nor could she say that she liked having ideas in her head, things to think about, or even to puzzle over, for Sofia would not understand that, either. Why did everyone think it was so bad to have ideas put into your head? You didn't have to keep them if you didn't want to.

'Well, you won't find a man like him to marry here, so you can forget about that! Like sticks with like in this world. Your Scotsman won't make you his bride, you can take my word for that. He's more likely to end up in the hands of the *Guardia*.'

'Sofia, you wouldn't — !'

'Of course I wouldn't! What do you take me for? Do you think I would betray a man – any man? Even if he had fought on the other side?'

But what if he had killed her Pedro? Encarnita did not ask that question. Some questions were too difficult to ask.

'Don't say anything about him to Juan, please, Sofia!'

'I know when to keep my mouth shut.' Sofia subsided with a sigh. 'I just ask you again, Encarnita, not to make your mind up too quickly about Juan. I will tell him you need time and he should try not to rush you.'

Encarnita was on edge for the next two days because she was unable to go into the *campo*. Continuing army manoeuvres on the main road were making it impossible to leave the *pueblo* without being seen. She could tell that Sofia was secretly pleased even though she was saying nothing. While the older woman was up in the cemetery, Encarnita sat in the house and studied *A Child's Garden of Verses* and when she heard her coming she hid the book under her pallet. It made her happy every time she opened it.

On the third day, the road was quiet again.

'I suppose you are going back to him?' said Sofia.

Encarnita was brushing her hair in front of the pock-marked mirror on the dresser. She brushed it and brushed it with long even strokes, until it glistened. She shook the long dark locks back from her shoulders.

'I can't abandon him now.' She was studying her reflection. Her gaze was level and unblinking. Her life was shifting on its axis, about to change, she felt sure of that.

'How long does he intend to stay out there?'

'Until his wounds have healed and his arm is mended.'

'And do you think he'll manage to get away even then? How will he escape the patrols?' Sofia did not expect an answer and did not get one.

There was no traffic at all on the road today. Encarnita raced across and was soon heading inland. As she neared the house, though, she slowed, wanting to savour the moment of seeing him again, to stretch it out. She felt as if her whole body was tingling with excitement.

But when the house did come into view and she saw that he was standing in the doorway leaning against the lintel, she broke into a run.

'You are leaving?'

'I was considering it. I thought you might be finding it

too difficult to come again and that perhaps I should try to move on.'

'But not strong enough to move?'

'No.' He gave a wry smile. 'My legs feel as if they're filled with sand.'

She led him inside and he dropped like a sack onto the ground. 'You shouldn't have tried to walk!' She fussed over him, changing the dressings and swabbing the sounds, which were looking a little better. 'You need more time to rest.'

'But I'm worried about getting you into trouble, Encarnita.'

'I can take care of me.'

'I couldn't bear it if one of those butchers were to lay a hand on you – you are so lovely! I would want to kill him with my own bare hands.'

Encarnita's heart was racing so madly that she thought he must hear it. 'I am not lovely.'

'You are! You're beautiful.' He slid his hand round the back of her neck and drew her face towards his. Her lips met his. She had known since their first meeting that this moment would come. She thought she might even have willed it.

He began to caress her, to stroke her hair and her body, to murmur into her hair, to kiss her eyes. She had not imagined a man could be so gentle. She offered no resistance. She was ready for him; her passion matched his and as his desire quickened so did hers until they reached such a feverish pitch that their cries would have been heard outside the house should anyone have been passing. Only the goatherd was, and he went on his way, fearful for them.

Afterwards, they lay at peace, entwined together, forgetful of the world that existed beyond the four broken-down walls, aware only of each other.

'Your arm?' she murmured.

'It's fine.' He swivelled his head and kissed her cheek. 'Salt! You've not been crying? I didn't hurt you, did I,

Encarnita?'

She shook her head, so happy that she did not want to speak. He smiled at her and she knew that he understood. She felt he understood everything.

'Say my name, Encarnita. You never have.'

'Conal,' she said. 'Very short. Me, I am Encarnita Pilar Maria.'

'And I am Conal Alexander Roderick MacDonald! Quite a mouthful! After my father and two grandfathers.'

'Tell me the names again.'

He repeated them and she tried to say them after him, making him laugh. 'I like the way you say them. I like everything you say.'

She stayed with him all day and left only when the sun was dropping.

'I wish I can stay with you all night.'

'But you can't,' he said sadly.

'I'll come tomorrow.'

'Don't, if the *Guardia* are around!'

He insisted on coming to the door to watch her go. She looked back at him several times until it was too dark to make out anything but the bare jagged outline of the house. Thick cloud was obscuring the moon.

Her legs were scratched and cut by the time she arrived home. Sofia was sitting at the table.

'Well, come in and shut the door. Don't just stand there.'

'I hope you weren't worried?'

'That wouldn't stop you, would it? So you've lain with him. Don't try to deny it. I can smell him on you.'

'I love him, Sofia,' said Encarnita, her voice quiet and pitched low.

'Love, huh! How many stupid girls have I heard say that! Myself amongst them. And do you think he loves you? He'll be like all men. They want you while they lust after you. They'll lie with any woman who's willing.'

'He's not like that!'

'How do you know what he's like? You've read a few

poems with him, dressed his cuts. Do you think if he was in his own country he would want you?'

'We're not in his country.'

'But he'll go back there. If he lives long enough. I knew this would happen.'

'He's made me happy!'

'Women are stupid,' muttered Sofia. Then she lifted her head. 'There's an egg there for you and some bread. But before you eat maybe you should go and wash. Wash as much of his seed away as you can.'

She said nothing in the morning when she saw Encarnita getting ready to go out, except to warn her to come back before nightfall.

There were a few army trucks on the road but Encarnita lay low in the undergrowth, awaiting her chance, until the road was clear to cross. Nothing would keep her from him today. She flew across the *campo* as if her feet were winged, stopping once only, to pick some wild flowers, anemones, orchids, dianthus, to which she added two flaming poppies even though she knew they would not survive for long. She carried the bouquet in front of her like a torch.

He was waiting for her. He buried his nose in the blooms, then laid them aside to take her into his arms. They made love even before she attended to his wounds.

'They can wait,' he said, 'but I can't.'

It was overcast and the rain came on later but it served to make their hideaway even cosier. The piece of roof that remained kept them dry and their bodies generated heat. They rejoiced in the crackling of the thunder and the flashing of the lightning. They fell asleep in the late afternoon and awoke to find that the storm had passed and it was pitch dark.

'How will you get back?' asked Conal.

'I won't,' said Encarnita, pulling him to her. 'I stay.'

The dawn was quiet, except for the calls of the birds. When she went out to fetch fresh water she thought that she had never seen the *campo* look more beautiful. Back lit by the rising sun, every tree, every blade of grass, rimmed with beads of dew, stood out more clearly than she could ever remember. For a moment she remained quite still.

She returned to Conal, taking him the cool, sweet water. She held the cup to his lips and when she took it away she kissed him. He pulled her to him.

'Don't leave me yet,' he begged.

And so she stayed for another hour or so, or perhaps more. They had ceased to register time passing. She kept saying that she ought to go, the sun was climbing up in the sky, and Sofia would be worrying; and he kept saying that he could not bear the idea of her going, yet he knew that she must. Before she finally did leave she went out again and gathered oranges and olives for him. It was not enough to build a man's strength but the best that she could do. She would come back later and try to bring some cheese and sausage.

Even now, she lingered. This was madness, they agreed. They kissed, parted, came together again, and it was then that he said, 'I love you, Encarnita, I want you to know that,' making it harder for her to leave in one way, yet in another way, not. She could hold the thought of his love inside her while they were apart.

'And you? Do you love me?' he asked.

'Yes,' she said, but he had known that already.

Finally, they separated, knowing that they must. They stood back and looked at each other.

'*Hasta pronto*, Encarnita!' he said. '*Muy pronto!*'

She could feel herself smiling as she made her way back across the *campo*, and at one point she threw back her head and laughed aloud, from sheer happiness. Lost in her reverie, she ran straight into the two guards without a chance of avoiding them. The fat one, the one she hated, seized her arm, pulling her to a halt.

'So, Señorita, what have you got to be laughing about?'

No longer laughing, she concentrated on keeping her voice steady. 'It's a lovely day.'

'What do you do out there in the *campo*?'

'I like being out in the country. I don't like the town.'

'You steal fruit, don't you?'

'Only the ones on the ground. They'd go rotten if I didn't lift them.'

'That's still stealing.'

'No one owns them now. They would go to waste. It is wicked to waste food.'

Unable to think of anything else, he pushed her away. As soon as she was out of their sight she began to run. The encounter had unnerved her. Did they suspect her of meeting someone? But if they did they would have followed her, wouldn't they? She thought – hoped – that they had been merely idling around and that the fat one liked to amuse himself by tormenting her.

Sofia was in the cemetery. 'So you managed to tear yourself away?'

'We could hardly bear it.'

'*We?*'

'Yes, him too. Sofia, I could never have imagined anything to be so wonderful.'

'You do have a good imagination, I can say that.'

'We love each other.'

Sofia sighed. 'It's not new. How many times have I heard it! Sometimes the ending is good, often bad.'

'You look too much on the dark side, Sofia.'

'That's what life has done to me.'

'I'm going back to him later.'

'What am I to say if someone asks where you are?'

'No one comes to the house in the evening, except Juan. And he might not come for a while, since he's annoyed with me.'

'What if he does?'

'Couldn't you tell him I'm asleep?'

'You want me to lie for you now?'

'Oh, Sofia, it would only be a little lie!' Encarnita put her arms round her. 'I'm sorry I'm upsetting you but I can't help it!'

'That's what they all say,' muttered Sofia.

Encarnita washed her body and her hair and put on clean clothes. She spent a few *pesetas* in the shop buying cheese, sausage and half a loaf of bread. She would gather oranges on the way. They would have a feast.

She waited until late afternoon to set out again.

Sofia issued her usual warning to take care and keep her wits about her. 'Your head's in a whirl.'

Near the burnt-out house where Encarnita picked oranges, the two guards were lying in wait.

The fat one seized her bag and looked inside. 'And who would all this food be for?'

'I was going to have a picnic.'

'A picnic, eh? Who was going to share it? It's a lot of food for one.'

'I thought I'd give some to the goatherd.'

'Oh, you did, did you? What would you give a man like him food for?'

'He's so thin. He looks starved.'

'What a kind *chica* you are! Trouble is I don't think you're telling the truth.' Suddenly he lifted his hand and slapped her across the face.

She stepped back, putting her hand to her cheek.

'Now tell me who the food was for? Your uncle?'

'No one.'

He hit her again, this time across the mouth. 'Who?'

She gulped, tasting blood. She shook her head and he lifted his hand again but his companion said, 'Let her go. We'll talk to her later. We haven't got time, we'd better catch up with the others.'

Go home, they told her, stay in the house and don't dare to leave it.

She stumbled as she went, blinded by tears, but when she heard goat bells she sniffed and dried her eyes on the back of her hand. The flock came into view, their keeper close behind.

He stopped beside a bush and motioned to her to join him. He scanned the landscape before he spoke.

'They're everywhere, the rats. You've come across them, I see. I overheard them talking earlier. They were saying that a man had been sighted near a ruined house.'

'*No!*'

'They weren't sure where it was exactly but they've called up more forces. I managed to get there before them.'

'You think they've found *my house?*'

'Yes, but I was there first. I told the man to leave with me straightaway.' The goatherd said that he had shown him how to reach a cave further up the hill.

'How do I get there?' asked Encarnita.

'You can't go just now.'

'I must!'

'Not with all the patrols around.'

'I could try.'

'Don't! It would be too dangerous. You might even lead them to him.'

Encarnita was silent now, recognising the truth of what he had said.

The goatherd added, 'They may be looking for you after they search the house.'

'Why?'

'He remembered he'd left something. We couldn't go back. It was too late.'

'What was it?'

'A book.'

'*No!*'

'He was worried because it had your name in it.'

'It does!' Don Geraldo had inscribed on the fly-leaf, 'To my good friend Encarnita.'

'He also asked me to give you his love.'

Encarnita thanked the goatherd. He had taken a considerable risk himself, though he waived aside her praises.

When she arrived home she told Sofia everything. The older woman wasted no time in recriminations. She bathed

Encarnita's lip, put some clean clothes and a food in a bag and rolled up a blanket, then told her to come with her. She knew a safe house, a place where Republicans on the run had been able to lie low until escaping by boat. Encarnita added to the bag her books and the drawing done by Don Geraldo's friend Carrington.

They made their way safely through the dark streets until they reached a house with shuttered windows. Sofia glanced around before knocking on the door. After a moment a voice behind it asked who was there.

'It's me, Sofia. And a friend. We need help.'

An elderly man let them in, bolting the door behind them, and took them along a passage to a kitchen at the back where his wife sat knitting. No introductions were made and the elderly couple asked no questions, requiring only to know that Encarnita must lie low for a while.

'Until we decide where she can go,' said Sofia and Encarnita realised then that she would never be able to go back to Sofia's house.

'I hope they won't give you a bad time,' she said anxiously. The *Guardia Civil* were bound to question Sofia.

'Don't worry. I will tell them that you ran off into the *campo* and I have not seen you since. They'll get nothing more out of me.'

They kissed and the older woman left without another word.

Above the kitchen, there was a space under the roof, high enough for someone to sit up in, though not to stand. It was ventilated by an opening in the gable-end wall. The man brought a ladder and climbing up, he dislodged two wooden planks in the ceiling, making a hole for Encarnita to crawl through.

'You can spend some time here in the kitchen with us,' said the woman. 'We are quiet people. We are seldom disturbed.'

Encarnita was exhausted and ready to retreat to her warm eyrie, which smelt of woodsmoke from the stove in the kitchen. She felt stunned. Everything had happened so quickly. She lay on top of Sofia's blanket and listened to the murmuring of the old couple's voices below and she thought of Conal. She could not stop thinking about him. She felt deeply afraid for him and imagined him in the hands of the army or the *Guardia Civil*. When she heard a shot she jerked upright and sat there in the dark, listening to the thudding of her heart. It was a long time before she slept.

She wakened when she heard the floor boards being shifted and sat up, once again, in alarm. A balding white head bobbed into the space.

'It's only me. Nothing to worry about. We thought you might like some breakfast and to relieve yourself perhaps.'

She relieved herself in the yard while the wife kept watch, then she sat with them at the table and shared their bread and coffee. There was little they could talk about, but when the husband said that he had taken a stroll along the front earlier Encarnita asked if he had seen any sign of the *Guardia Civil* patrols. He had not but had met a man who'd told him that they'd been searching the *campo* the day before for a fugitive.

'Did he know if they'd found anyone?'

'He didn't think so and he's a man who hears most things.'

That was a relief, if only a partial one. Encarnita felt desperate to go out and track down the goatherd but she knew it was not possible. She found it unbearable to be so confined and helpless.

'Patience, child,' advised the wife. 'I'm afraid it's the only answer.'

Was that the only answer now for all of them, to sit, resigned and quiet, and wait until some miracle happened and General Franco was brought down? Encarnita did not voice her thoughts as she would have done had she been with Sofia. Sofia would have told her to hush and pray to Our Lady. She missed her friend. She missed even her

scolding and their arguments. Her hosts here were kind,
but passive. She would not get to know them no matter
how long she stayed. Perhaps that was how they had managed to hide fugitives; they had contained their curiosity, or
perhaps had had none, so that the people they had hidden
had come and gone and left few traces for them to erase.

The wife taught her to knit socks, which helped to pass
some of the time, and Encarnita read her book until each
word was lodged deep in her brain. She lived day and night
with the boy in the land of counterpane who in her dreams
turned into a man with red-gold hair and penetrating blue
eyes. When she lay awake in the night she talked to him in
her head, telling him that she had not forgotten him, that
she would come and find him. During the day she sat for
short spells out in the enclosed yard to breathe the air but
her lungs felt deprived and her legs restricted. Once when
she complained of feeling restless, her elderly host said quietly, 'Imagine what it must be like for our men in prison,'
and she felt ashamed. But what pained her more than anything else was her separation from Conal and not knowing
what had happened to him. At times she thought she would
go mad, shut up in such a tight space, and she would come
down into the kitchen ready to tell her hosts that she must
leave, but when she saw their patient faces she had known
that she must bear it, for a while yet.

A week passed, and then another. After four weeks, one
evening, after dark, Sofia came. Encarnita fell on her and
held her in a tight embrace, reluctant to let go.

'Any news?'

Sofia shook her head. She had heard nothing, which
might mean he had got away.

'Have they been looking for me?' asked Encarnita.

'Of course. They had the book. I told them you hadn't
come back that day. They probably think you went with
him.'

'Good.' Encarnita wished that she had. She wished that
she had risked going to find him in the cave but then she

might have risked his life.

'You have to leave Almuñecar, Encarnita. I got word to my sister Arrieta in Nerja, and she has agreed that you can go there. The two guards who knew you have been moved up to Jaén so it's safer now for you to make a move. I've arranged for you to get a lift tomorrow morning with Miguel.' Miguel was a second cousin of Sofia's. He delivered vegetables and various other commodities along the coast in an old van. 'He will be outside at seven o'clock.'

'I wish you could come with me, Sofia!'

'You know I can't.'

They took a sorrowful farewell of each other and when the door had closed behind Sofia Encarnita wondered how many more people she would have say goodbye to. Her heart felt like a stone in her chest.

She rose in the morning before first light and made her way into the dark *campo*. She thought the goatherd would be out with his beasts while the dew was still on the ground. Dawn was breaking when she caught up with them.

'He's gone,' he told her. 'He left two weeks ago, heading west, for Gibraltar. He said to tell you he would come back for you.'

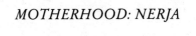

MOTHERHOOD: NERJA

Concepción's head descended into the light on the first day of the new year. Encarnita thought it no coincidence that her child was being born on this day; it was the date not only of her own birth but also that on which her mother had left the world.

Arrieta, sister of Sofia, exclaimed as she helped ease out the baby's head. 'Its going to be fair!' When the child's head had been cleaned they saw that the blond hair was shot through with reddish tints. Arrieta looked at Encarnita, with her black hair and eyes and olive skin. 'She doesn't look at all like you. Her skin is as pale as milk.'

The new young mother nodded. She felt sure, too, that when the baby got round to opening her eyes they would be revealed to be a deep turquoise blue.

'The man, then, was a stranger in these parts,' observed Arrieta. When Sofia had sent Encarnita to her back in the summer she had simply been told that the girl had to leave Almuñecar. After a while, once it had become obvious that Encarnita was pregnant, Arrieta had thought that possibly the father was a local Almuñecar man with a wife. But Encarnita had said no, he was unmarried, and had added that he was in the war. Arrieta had sensed that there was something more to the affair than this, but had not asked.

When the priest had accosted Arrieta in the street, asking about the young woman she was harbouring, she had told him that Encarnita's husband had fought in the war and not returned. It was not an uncommon story. Had she told him that Encarnita was unmarried he might have tried to turn her out of the parish. He had done it before, with the help of the *Guardia Civil*, just as he'd helped parents to force their pregnant daughters into marriage. The men were similarly coerced, in that, if they refused to marry, they could be jailed. Arrieta had no problem about telling this lie to the priest. She had no more faith in the confessional than

Encarnita. Why should she confess to such a man? He was just a man, one who helped to make women's lives miserable, encouraging them to breed more and more children, and deepen their poverty. She preferred to talk directly to God or to Mary without his interference.

'She is a very pretty baby,' she said. 'What will you call her?'

'Concepción Alexandra.'

'Concepción will be enough for such a small thing.' Arrieta wrapped the new baby in a piece of frayed but clean blanket and put her to her mother's breast.

'People will wonder, of course. About her colouring. It is not often that men with such hair and fine skin are seen around here.' She could not recall having seen any.

'That is true,' agreed Encarnita.

As far as she knew, there had been no sighting of any reddish-fair-haired men in the area since she had come to Nerja. Conal, like her uncle Rinaldo, would appear to have vanished into the air except that she sensed he had reached safety, whereas, with her uncle, she did not. Her unease about him was deep and troubling. His spirit, wherever he was, was not at peace.

Sometimes she fancied Conal to be still up in the mountains and that one day he would come down and take her and his child away, to his own country, the land of counterpane where they would be safe from Franco's *Guardia Civil*. She dreamed it in her sleep and woke over and over again to face the pain of disappointment. She still trembled when she saw a civil guard and averted her eyes automatically as she was passing. But then most people did, she had noticed, whether young or old, male or female. The sympathies of the inhabitants of Nerja, who earned a poor living by fishing or working in the local sugar factory, had lain for the most part on the Republican side.

Arrieta's husband had died fighting with the Republican army. In private life, he had been a fisherman. From her house perched on the cliff top his widow could still see his old, weathered boat lying abandoned on the beach below. When he had returned in the mornings she would go down and help him and his brother – killed, also, in the war – bring in their feeble catch. They had named the boat after her, even though it had not legally belonged to them, but to a local landowner, the owner of a number of boats. The one manned by the two brothers had been in poor shape for a long time before their death and afterwards was allowed to rot where it lay. Few fishermen could afford to buy their own boats, which meant that by the time they gave the pro-prietors their cut not a great deal remained to share out from the sale of their daily catch. Arrieta said it was no wonder that fishing families were poor.

Her name was still visible on the side of the boat, just. But in time it would be eroded and the boat itself would fall apart and lie in pieces on the sand. After the death of her husband, their only daughter had married a member of the *Guardia Civil*, something that would have made him spit had he been around to see it, and which Arrieta herself had found difficult to stomach. Indeed, following the wedding, she had begun to suffer from intermittent bouts of gastro-enteritis. The only saving grace in the whole affair was that Angelita and her husband had been sent up north, to Burgos, too far away for them to come back on visits, even if they would have wished to. Arrieta did not speak any more of her daughter. She said that God had sent Encarnita to take her place and for that she gave thanks. And now he had given her a grandchild also.

'We must have her christened soon,' she said.

'I hope the priest won't ask any more questions about her father.'

'He can't make you answer. He's not the *Guardia*.'

'I would tell you about her father, Arrieta, except I think maybe it's better not. I don't want you to have to lie if you're questioned.'

'You may tell me what you wish to tell me in all good time. As it is, I have my own ideas, and if they are right they're dangerous. If you're asked you must say her father was a Spaniard. I'm sure it must be possible for some Spaniards to have such colouring. In the north, perhaps.' To Arrieta, the north of Spain was almost as distant as France or England. 'It's a pity, though, that she couldn't have been born with dark hair and eyes.'

'It's not a pity at all! I am pleased she is as she is.'

'Nevertheless, I think she would look good in a little cap. I have an old one of Angelita's in the chest.' Arrieta ferreted out a cotton, lace-trimmed bonnet, with a ribbon that fastened under the chin. It covered the baby's red gold hair perfectly. 'There! That will help keep her out of trouble.'

Encarnita loved the late evenings when she was awake and Arrieta asleep, and the house was so quiet that only the rhythmic pulsing of the sea could be heard. She would sit by the dying fire and, removing the little bonnet, rejoice in her little girl's glorious hair. The sight and feel of it brought her closer to Conal. She talked to him inside her head, letting him know that she was reading *A Child's Garden of Verses* to his child. Just as his mother had to him.

'One day, Concepción Alexandra,' she told her, 'you and I will go to a country far away called Scotland and we will find your papa, Conal Alexander Roderick MacDonald.' She had always known that some day she would make a journey across the sea, but now she knew where it would take her.

Not long after coming to live with Arrieta, Encarnita had crossed the boulder-strewn, grey volcanic plain that lay between Nerja and the hills and penetrated a little way into the *campo*, hoping that she might stumble across Conal, or even find traces of him. He would have had to pass that way when making for Gibraltar. She had looked inside two burnt-out cottages but seen no signs of recent habitation and then gone up into the white hill *pueblo* of Frigiliana. She had wandered up and down its steep, narrow streets, stopping to talk to anyone prepared to be friendly, old women in black mostly who leant in their doorways or sat outside on hard, upright chairs letting nothing escape them. They had been suspicious at first of Encarnita but after the first few minutes they had softened and allowed themselves to be engaged in limited conversation. From what they had said, no foreigners had come to the village since the early months of the war.

Afterwards, venturing a little higher into rockier terrain, she had come across the remnants of a barricade, stones piled high, with slots for guns, and, close by, a cairn. A marker for the dead? Rinaldo might have been buried there. How would she ever know? She had picked a few pink and purple wild flowers and laid them on top, for whoever might lie beneath. She had moved around cautiously, knowing that bandits as well as Anti-Franco guerrillas were operating throughout the region. She was much less afraid of them than of the *Guardia Civil,* so that when she had caught sight of two men a little way off she had stood still and waved her arms in the air and shouted, *'Hola!'* They had come slowly towards her, their hands on the pistols at their sides, but as they had drawn closer they had dropped them. They were obviously not Franco men. These were men who lived rough in the hills. They were long-haired and bearded and their faces were weathered. She had decided it would be safe to speak.

'Have you seen a man with reddish-fair hair? He's a Scotsman. He fought with the International Brigades.'

They had been sympathetic but unable to help. They had passed a few minutes together and they had said that one day, in the not-too-distant future, Franco would be defeated and the Republicans back in power. They would not give up the struggle.

On the way back down to the coast, keeping by the dried-up river bed, she had come across a gypsy family encamped in a cave. She had seen the sparks from their fire and heard their singing from a little way off. They were singing a lilting *copla,* one that she had heard sung before, in Yegen. It told, as many did, of lost love. Her mother had told her that it was a song her father had sung.

The gypsies had met a foreigner with light-coloured hair and for a moment Encarnita had become excited, until she had realised that the details did not match Conal. The other man had been small and spoken a language different from English. German, they had thought.

A gust of wind rattled the window shutter. The fire was at its last gasp. It was time to join Arrieta in the bed.

'I expect your father will be at home in his bed in Edinburgh, Concepción.' Encarnita got up carefully so that she would not waken her sleeping child. 'It is a fine city, he told me, with a castle sitting on a high rock. One day we shall see that and the house where the man who wrote our book lived as a boy. I promise you that.'

Encarnita lay down beside Arrieta, keeping the baby against her shoulder. She was a contented child who had thriven since the day of her birth. She was rosy-cheeked alongside some of the puny babies in the street. Arrieta said she was obviously of good stock.

When Concepción was two weeks old, the priest called. He had heard of the new arrival and would have come earlier had he not been suffering from a bout of colic.

'I can sympathise, Father,' said Arrieta. 'I, too, suffer with my stomach. It is God's will.'

The priest did not seem to like that idea too much; it might hint at retribution for a sin committed. 'I ate something,' he said. He was quick, however, to tell the villagers that it was the will of God whenever they complained of ills or injustices and that they should examine their consciences.

'You have a delicate stomach,' suggested Arrieta.

He turned his attention to the child in the house, the reason, after all, for his visit. He had not come to discuss the state of his stomach, or his soul.

'You will want the child baptised?'

'We do,' said Arrieta.

'Do you have your marriage papers?' he asked Encarnita,

who was smoothing the brow of her child, which had become ruffled with the arrival of the black-suited man into the house.

Again, Arrieta spoke for her. 'So many things were lost in the war, Father.'

'I take it she has not been born out of wedlock?' he asked sharply. 'Was she? Are you a married woman, Encarnita?'

'Father,' said Arrieta, 'it was all most unfortunate. They were about to marry when her young man was called up. He had to go and fight for our dear leader General Franco. He could not refuse to do that, could he? It is only on account of the war that they did not marry.'

'But she lay with him when she was not married to him.'

'Things happen in the heat of the moment, Father, especially in such terrible times.'

There was a knock on the outside door.

'You go and see who it is, Encarnita,' said Arrieta. 'I will take Concepción.' She held out her arms to receive the baby. 'You must admit, Father, that it is a fine Christian name, Concepción?'

Encarnita went to the door to find two women clad in black from head to foot standing on the pavement. From their necks hung little black cloth bags bearing a label that said *For the Dead*. Encarnita could hear the tolling of the funeral bell in the background. The sight of these women always gave her the shivers but Arrieta said bad luck would not come to you as long as you gave them something. Also, if you did not help to give someone a proper burial you might not get one yourself when your time came.

'One moment,' said Encarnita and she went back into the room to fetch an offering.

'That day will suit us very well, Father,' Arrieta was saying.

Encarnita found a few centimos and took them back to the women, who asked God to bless her. She closed the door.

'It is all arranged,' said Arrieta, when Encarnita rejoined

them.

'It is a shame that this child will never know her earthly father,' said the priest. 'But she will be blessed by knowing her heavenly one when she is received into the church.'

'*We* are happy to know that, are we not, Encarnita?'

'What unusual eyes she has!' The priest leaned forward to look into her face. Concepción was staring steadily at him, without blinking. 'I can't recall ever having seen such blue eyes.'

'My grandmother had blue eyes,' said Arrieta, which, indeed, was true. They had been a dark bluish-brown, but had definitely held a glint of blue in them.

'Is that so? Ah well, let us hope that the little Concepción has a good life in front of her in spite of her unfortunate beginning. At least we have peace in our country now, praise be to God and our leader for that!'

The women murmured.

'But look at what's happening in the rest of Europe!' The priest shook his head. 'It saddens me that men have to go on fighting each other and will not follow the example of our Saviour.'

Encarnita and Arrieta were aware that some kind of war was being waged in Europe but they knew little about it and were not even sure who was fighting whom.

'There have been heavy air raids on London,' sighed the priest. 'Many lives have been lost.'

'London!' repeated Encarnita.

Arrieta gave her a warning look and engaged the priest's attention. 'You are interested in the news of the world?'

'I hear it on the radio.'

'Who was bombing London?' asked Encarnita.

'The Germans, of course, who else?

'Hitler?' she said, remembering Jacobo and their conversation about being a Jew in Germany.

The priest nodded.

'Is he not a friend of our own leader?' put in Arrieta, a little smile making the corner of her mouth twitch. 'Along with his other friend Señor Mussolini of Italy?' They knew Mussolini. He had sent planes to bomb Málaga in the early stages of their Civil War.

'Indeed.' The priest looked as if he was about to go.

'So Germany is fighting England?' said Encarnita, her voice urgent. 'And Scotland? What about Scotland?'

'It is a part of England,' said the priest, 'so I expect it must be involved too.'

She was about to ask if he had heard anything about the city of Edinburgh being bombed but stopped herself in time.

After the priest had gone, Arrieta said, 'You must watch your mouth, girl! Sometimes it opens too wide.'

'I don't think he suspected.'

'What? That the father was a foreigner? Which he was, wasn't he? But, thank God, our baby is going to be baptised. I couldn't rest easily in my bed if she was not.'

'How did you persuade him?'

'I gave him a little something.' Arrieta rubbed her index finger against her thumb. 'For the church.'

'Not your savings, Arrieta!'

'Not all of it. What does the money matter? It is more important that our child should be baptised.'

Concepción went to the church in her bonnet and a well-worn christening robe borrowed from a neighbour and did not cry when the priest daubed water on her forehead. She stared up at him with her unblinking turquoise blue eyes. Promises that she would be reared in the Christian faith were made by her godmother, Arrieta, and she came home – as far as her mother was concerned – neither the better nor the worse for wear for the experience.

'How can you say that, Encarnita?' demanded Arrieta.

Encarnita shrugged. 'It's just that the church has let such terrible things happen. Well, God doesn't stop Franco stamping on us and treating us like animals, does he? And then he goes and prays as if he is the holiest of holies!' Men were still being executed in the *campo*. They'd heard shots again only the night before. Every time Encarnita heard them she felt sick. *Please* God, she would mumble to herself, *don't let it be Conal or Rinaldo*. And then she would wonder why she was asking God to do anything when she knew that He would not, could not. He appeared to be as powerless to change things as they were.

'Hush, child. Don't speak so loudly. Besides, you must give God the benefit of the doubt.'

'I do!' Encarnita smiled. Arrieta often said things that made her smile. She would not have wanted to admit it but she was pleased that her child had been baptised. Beliefs were not so easy to cast aside. When she lit a candle in church for Pilar she heard her mother's voice telling her so.

She held Concepción in her arms whenever she talked to her mother so that they were all three joined together in communion. Sitting in the dark church in the early evening, with only the flickering candles giving light, she remembered their life together in the little mountain village of Yegen. She remembered, too, her English friend Don Geraldo and wondered if he had been caught up in the war with Germany. Her childhood friend Luisa also came into her mind and she resolved to write to her. During the war they had lost contact.

When Encarnita left the church she walked out onto the Balcón. The Balcón de Europa. The name had been given to it by King Alfonso XIII when he had come on a visit to Nerja after it had suffered an earthquake. The piece of land jutted out into the sea like a balcony and somewhere, on the other side, lay North Africa. The waves were high tonight and dashing against the rocks below in a great fury, sending spray flying in all directions. Encarnita loved living within the sound and sight of the sea. It made her think of voyages and links to other places and other people. It made her think of Scotland. A scattering of small lights blinked in the darkness. Fishermen. It was a wild night for them to be out. Arrieta said her husband had enjoyed being on the sea at night, away from the shore and noise and people, with the width of the sky over his head. Encarnita understood the peace of it. She rocked the baby in her arms, feeling the warmth of the little body against her own on a cool January night.

A soft curtain of rain swept over them and she turned back for home. The fronds of the palms trees were fluttering in the wind. A storm was brewing. Three or four small children scurried bare-footed across the road in front of them, heading, too, for the shelter of their houses. Lights gleamed at windows. Arrieta's street was only a few steps from the Balcón. As Encarnita turned into the narrow street, inhabited mostly by fishermen and their families, she realised that she felt at home here now. In spite of it being an unpaved and not overly clean street, where people struggled to survive, she felt that it was a place where she could bring up her child. In daytime, it buzzed with life; children played in the gutters while their elders hung about in doorways ready to chat. Encarnita knew that she had little option, anyway, but to stay. She was not so foolish as to think that she could find the money to enable Concepción and herself to sail across the sea in the near future. But, some day, she would. First, however, she would have to find a way to work and earn and save money.

The war that had been raging in the rest of Europe had finally ended. Encarnita heard the news from an old man sitting in a doorway. Half the men in Nerja sat in doorways, out of the way of their womenfolk. Señor Quintana was missing a leg. He sat there, most days, from early morning until sundown, enjoying the air, with his trouser leg pinned back and a book in his lap. He was not the only man in Nerja to be missing a limb.

Encarnita had found employment as a servant in the house of a small landowner on the outskirts of Nerja. On her way home from work she would often stop to pass the time of day with Señor Quintana, who lived with his daughter in a slightly-better off street at the eastern end of the town. He had been a school teacher in days gone by. She liked talking to him. They talked about the world that existed beyond Nerja, and he lent her books, some for herself and some for her child. He said it was never too early for the young to start, which Encarnita knew herself. She had already begun to teach Concepción to read a few words. She did not want her father to be ashamed of her when they met. Señor Quintana freely expressed the opinion that children needed books other than those they were given in school, which were based on religious texts and proscribed by the state. The ones he favoured were works of the imagination.

'Yes, I heard the news about the war on the radio this morning,' he said. 'There are to be big celebrations in Paris and London and other cities. Not Madrid, of course,' he added with a chuckle. 'I don't suppose our general will be rejoicing now that his old friends have been beaten!'

'So the English have defeated the Germans?'

'The British have, along with the Americans and their other allies. They still have Japan to deal with but that doesn't seem to be too big a problem, from what they're saying.'

'So Europe is a safe place now?'

'As safe as any place can be until someone decides to start another war. No doubt somebody will. It seems the world can't get on without them.'

'The British – that means Scotland too?'

'It does. You're interested in Scotland, Encarnita, aren't you?'

'It seems a nice country,' she said, trying to sound off-hand. 'They have mountains there as well, like us,' she added limply, remembering Arrieta's warning about not opening her mouth too much, even when she felt she could trust someone.

'Was that Scotland you were speaking of?' asked the man's daughter, coming from within the house, drying her hands on her black apron. Josefina was a woman of fifty and some years, and had never been married. She broke off when she saw the book on her father's knee. 'You shouldn't be reading that out in the street!'

He held the book up for all the world to see. 'Federico García Lorca'. He enunciated the name clearly.

'Papa!' She glanced up the street. 'You know very well —'

'That they have not only murdered our greatest poet but they are doing their best to kill his work too by banning it. Well, our house is one in which it will continue to live. *Viva Lorca!*'

'Hush, Papa, *por favor*! You'll get us arrested.'

'Don't worry, Josefina! They would only take me.'

'And do you think that would not affect me?'

'Of course. I'm only teasing you.' He put the book back, face down on his lap. 'Let us go back to talking about Scotland. That is a less dangerous topic.'

'You remember the Scotsman who came here before the war, Papa?' said Josefina, sounding wistful. Encarnita wondered if she had loved this Scotsman. Looking at her, it was difficult to believe that she might have done. She seemed too prudish, the kind of woman who spent much time on her knees in church and nagged at her father, who seldom went himself, using his disability as an excuse. But perhaps she had become like that because she had been disappointed in love.

'He told us that he sometimes wore a kilt when he was at home,' said Señor Quintana. 'For special occasions. Like weddings. He was an agreeable fellow and he could speak Spanish tolerably well. He visited our house several times. Perhaps visitors from abroad will start coming again now that it will be easier for them to travel.'

Encarnita thought about that as she walked down Calle Cristo. Conal had told the goatherd that he would come back for her. But how would he find her? He had not known where she lived in Almuñecar, except that it was with a woman called Sofia, whose son had been killed by the Nationalists. The goatherd had not known much more but he might not even be alive by now; the blood in his veins might have dried up. Encarnita did not allow herself to consider the idea that Conal might not have survived the clutches of the *Guardia Civil*, or the warfare that had come to his own land. She presumed that, like young men here, he would have been conscripted into the army and expected to fight for his country.

She carried on to the *plaza* to see if the man selling loquats would be there. He was. The small yellow fruits were set out temptingly on a tray of cactus leaves while beside them stood a pot of red toffee kept warm by a flame. Encarnita was going to allow herself to be tempted today. She stopped and bought three, one each for Concepción, Arrieta and herself. The man snagged them with a toothpick and then dipped them into the bright red toffee.

On the way back to her own street she saw two members of the *Guardia Civil* standing on the corner, their hands resting slackly on the pistols at their waists, their rifles slung in the usual cross-wise fashion over their chests. One of them engaged Encarnita's eye. She looked away at once. She had never seen this guard before. Most she knew by sight. There were about thirty guards in all in the *pueblo* and they patrolled the streets and beaches ceaselessly, by day and night. As a result, there was little crime, little ordinary kinds of crime, that was, such as theft, which could be punished by a few days in prison, even if the stolen goods amounted to no more than a couple of bunches of grapes from a stall in the market. Smuggling, however, did go on along the coast. Most of the men in the village, *Guardia Civil* included, smoked contraband tobacco.

'Got a lollipop for us?' asked the guard who had eyed her and he made a slurping sound.

Averting her eyes, she forced herself to walk past them, annoyed that they had the power to spoil even the small pleasure that buying the loquats had given her. As she entered the house, she heard a familiar voice. They had a visitor.

'Sofia!' She put down the loquats and went forward to embrace her. She had seen Sofia only rarely since leaving Almuñecar. She had come to visit them shortly after Concepción's birth and two or three other times since. 'Your legs, how are they?'

'They don't look good but they're still bearing me up. I thought it was time I saw your child again. Miguel gave me a lift. Arrieta tells me the little Concepción is well?'

'She is! Where is she now, Arrieta?'

'Down on the beach below the Balcón, with the other children.'

'I have a letter for you, Encarnita,' said Sofia, taking it out of her bag. 'It came to my house a little while ago but I thought I'd wait and bring it to you. '

'That's odd,' said Arrieta, lifting an envelope from the dresser. 'You had one in the post this morning too.'

'Two letters!' Encarnita took them both into her hands. One bore a Spanish stamp, the other a British one. Her heart was racing so fast that she had to put a hand to it to try to still it.

'Open them, then!' said Sofia. The sisters never received letters themselves, since neither could read nor write.

Encarnita slit open the British one first and lifted out a sheet of thick white paper. Her eye went straight to the signature. It was not from Conal.

'Bad news?' asked Arrieta.

'I don't know.' Encarnita frowned.

'Who is it from?'

Encarnita looked at the signature. 'Frank Osborne,' she said, trying the unfamiliar name on her tongue. 'It's in English.' She read the letter slowly, translating it haltingly into Spanish as she went along. Frank Osborne said that he was writing to all the friends of his aunt, Miss Hermione Osborne, listed in her address book, to inform them of her death. She had been caught in an air raid on London and after some time had died of her injuries.

'Poor Miss Osborne!'

'May God keep her!' said Sofia, crossing herself. 'She was good to you in the hotel, wasn't she?'

Encarnita nodded. It had always been part of her plan to go to London first on her journey, and visit Miss Osborne. But that was not to be. She opened the other letter. It was from her friend Luisa. They had exchanged a couple of letters since Encarnita had come to Nerja.

Luisa was still living in the *campo* outside Yegen, in her childhood home. She was married to a man called Diego, whom Encarnita had known to see in passing, a surly looking fellow, or so she had always thought. The couple inhabited the house with their two young sons, as well as three of Luisa's siblings and her mother.

Luisa wrote that her mother's health was poor and Diego had hurt his leg and could not work so she herself was working in the fields. Two of her brothers were causing trouble, getting drunk and into brawls. Luisa feared that they would end badly. Like their father, thought Encarnita. She hoped that Diego was not like him, too.

'Your friend is well?' asked Arrieta.

'Her life is not easy.'

'Which woman's life is?' asked Sofia.

'Mine is easier than Luisa's,' said Encarnita, smiling and touching Arrieta on the shoulder.

At the end of Luisa's letter there was news of the sisters Maria and Rosario, the housekeepers of Don Geraldo. They had stayed on in Churriana. Antonio, Rosario's husband, had been entrusted to rent out the house as best he could and to use the rent money to pay taxes and keep what was left over for his own family. They were hoping that Don Geraldo and Doña Gamel would return once the war in Europe was over.

'The war's over now.' Encarnita folded up the letter. 'Señor Quintana told me.'

The older women were not much interested. They had had enough of wars and that particular one had not touched them, for which they were thankful.

'Go and find your daughter!' said Sofia. 'I want to see her! Tell her I've made a little doll for her.'

Encarnita went down to the beach to fetch Concepción. When Encarnita herself was a child she had played amongst trees and flowers where multi-coloured butterflies had whirred and insects buzzed. Her feet had kicked up dirt and enjoyed the softness of damp grass. She had picked wild flowers though she had never let her fingers even graze the paper-thin red poppies. She had drunk in the smells of lavender, rosemary and thyme and watched lizards snaking over stones and birds soaring overhead. Her daughter's childhood was different: Concepción played on gritty sand and in the waters of the Mediterranean sea and knew nothing of plants that grew in the earth. She was running now, in and out of the waves, her shift clinging to her slim body, her red-gold hair shining in the sunlight. Until she was three years old she had worn bonnets fashioned by Arrieta but now she refused to have her head covered and tossed her curls so that they floated freely in the air. Their neighbours, used to her different colouring, scarcely noticed it. In summer, her mother worried about the paleness of her skin which burned easily in the fierce rays of the sun.

Encarnita plunged into the sea to join her daughter, enjoying the cool freshness of the water as it broke over her body. She did not venture far from the shore since she could not swim. Most of the children were able to float with ease on their backs or else they floundered around on their stomachs, thrashing their arms about, showing no trace of fear. They shrieked and laughed. The older boys swam far out, their lithe brown bodies twisting and turning as they dived into the waves and resurfaced, moments later, shaking the drops from their sleek heads.

'We have a visitor,' Encarnita shouted to her daughter above the sound of the sea. 'Sofia, Arrieta's sister. She has brought you a present.' She held out her hand for Concepción to take.

They were almost dry by the time they made their way up the steep steps from the beach and across the Balcón. The streets were busy now with carts and donkeys coming back in from the *campo*. An ox-cart cart had overturned and dumped its load on the ground at the entrance of Calle Generalissimo Franco, causing a furore and much shouting on behalf of other carters who were unable to pass. A municipal guard was trying to sort the problem out. The *Guardia Municipal* was under the control of the mayor instead of the state and was not feared in the same way as the *Guardia Civil.* Encarnita knew this guard, Eduardo. She was friendly with his wife, who had a crippled leg and struggled to look after their seven children.

The two civil guards she'd seen earlier were still around and she would have to pass them again. The guard she'd taken an instant dislike to was looking at Concepción and frowning. A stab of fear pierced her heart. He was leaving his companion and coming towards them.

'Can I see your papers?' He lifted the hand from his pistol and held it out.

'I have them in our house.'

'You don't carry them?'

'I was bathing in the sea and didn't want to get them wet.'

'Where do you live?'

'Calle Carabeo. Just round the corner.'

'Right, let's go!'

'What is it, Mama?' asked Concepción.

'Nothing, love,' said Encarnita, taking a firm hold of her hand and leading her along the street, with their bodyguard following on behind. When they reached Arrieta's house she told Concepción to go inside, but the guard intervened.

'No, let her be. I want to see her papers, too. You go in and fetch them.'

Encarnita briefly told the sisters what was happening, then she took their papers from a drawer and returned to the street. Concepción was standing by the door looking frightened.

Encarnita handed over the papers.

'So you were born in Yegen? A God-forsaken place that is. I was once there.'

Encarnita said nothing.

'And the child, she was born in Nerja, I see?'

'In this house.'

'It does not state who her father is.'

'No.' Encarnita felt the heat creeping up her face into the very roots of her hair.

'It was like that, was it? Father unknown?' The officer sniggered. 'Where do you work? In the street?'

'No. I work for Señor and Señora Portales.'

That caused him more amusement. 'I see. Friendly with the señor, are you?' He studied the top of Concepción's head. 'Don't see many children round here with that colour hair.'

'I think it is more common in the north.'

'What, the Asturias? Galicia?'

She raised a shoulder in a half-shrug.

'You have the look of the gypsy in you. Half of them up in the Alpujarra are, aren't they? Live in caves like animals.'

Again, Encarnita made no response.

He shoved the papers back at her, wheeled about and

marched off down the street.

'Why do I not have a papa?' asked Concepción.

'You do. But I can't tell you anything about him now. One day I will.'

'When we go on our journey?'

'Yes, that will be the time.' Encarnita put away a few *pesetas* weekly from her paltry earnings. Concepción loved to help count it and each time would ask how much more would they need to have before they could go. 'Come on,' said her mother, 'let's go inside. Sofia is eager to see you.'

'Is everything all right?' asked Arrieta anxiously, as they came in. Encarnita closed the door behind them even though it was hot in the room, with the fire blazing. Arrieta was cooking *patatas a lo pobre*. The smell was mouth-watering.

'Everything's fine,' said Encarnita.

Concepción, who scarcely remembered Arrieta's sister, stood back shyly, but when Sofia opened her arms she went into them.

'Come, little one, sit on my lap. See what I have for you!' From her pocket Sofia produced a rag doll with yellow wool hair and a red and white striped dress. Concepción was delighted.

'What a lucky girl,' said Arrieta.

Encarnita found it difficult to fall asleep that night. It was very hot with four of them in the bed. She and Concepción were lying head to toe with the two sisters, both of whom were on their backs and snoring. After a while she got up and went out into the garden. The night air was welcome after the heavy atmosphere inside the house. Somewhere, close by, a jasmine tree was sending out its powerful scent, and an almost-full moon was lighting up the sea, highlighting the ripples. She thought she saw a boat out there. Yes, she was sure there was one, just faintly discernible. Her eyes were sharp. Her mother used to say she was born with eyes that could see to the other end of the world. The boat was showing no lights. Smugglers, probably. As she watched she saw something dark come cutting through the waves towards the shore. A dog. The smugglers used dogs to bring in their contraband; they strapped it in water-proof pouches on their backs.

She went to the edge of the garden and looked down into the beach, immediately drawing her head back. Two civil guards were passing below. Their headgear was unmistakable. Being high up, she had a better vantage point than they did. They might not be able to see the dog who, having spotted them, was lying low in the shallows. As soon as they had gone the dog streaked out of the water and raced off down the beach in the opposite direction. Encarnita smiled.

'*Mama*!' The cry came more as a scream. '*Mama! Where are you, Mama?*'

Encarnita hurried back into the house. The two women were awake and Arrieta was trying to comfort Concepción, who wanted only her mother. Encarnita gathered her up and carried her out into the fresh air.

'It's all right, my love,' she said, rocking her as she had done when she was a baby. 'Everything is all right. Mama would never leave you, you know that. Whatever happens, you and I will always be together.'

Encarnita was excited. She was about to make her first visit back to Yegen since leaving sixteen years before. She was taking Concepción with her and they were to stay with Luisa. Now that both Luisa's mother and husband were dead, and her three siblings gone, there would be room for them in her house, with only herself and her four sons left. They would share the bedroom with her. The boys, who ranged in age from seventeen to five years, slept in the living room. Encarnita was not clear what had happened to their father, other than that there had been some kind of accident. The men in that family did not die natural deaths.

Over the years Encarnita had at times thought about going back to Yegen, half-wanting to go, half not, lest she stir up difficult memories, but Luisa's letter had made up her mind. She had written to say that Don Geraldo and Doña Gamel were coming on a visit and would stay with Enrique, the brother of Maria and Rosario.

Their bag packed, the travellers were ready to go.

'It's a pity you can't come with us, Arrieta,' said Encarnita.

'The journey would be too much for me. It's a long way! Besides, you want to be with your friend.'

'Come on, Mama, we'll miss the bus!' urged Concepción.

They were to go by bus to Almuñecar where Miguel would meet them and take them up to Órgiva.

'Have you got the flowers for Sofia?' asked Arrieta.

Encarnita nodded. She kissed Arrieta, told her to take care of herself while they were away and not to exert herself too much. She was having trouble with her heart.

On the way up the street they passed the house where Concepción was employed as a seamstress, something which pleased Encarnita, who regarded it as more delicate and suitable work for her daughter than scrubbing other people's floors. The window was open and they could hear the whir of the sewing machine. There was only one machine – it was an object much admired in the village – and half a dozen girls. One used the machine while the others sewed by hand, chattering away as they did so. Concepción loved the work; she had proved to be nimble-fingered and her stitching was neat. She put her head into the window now to say '*Hola*!' and the girls chorused in return, saying how lucky she was to have a holiday! The señora who employed them had agreed after a little persuasion from Encarnita. She was a good-natured woman who chatted and laughed with her girls and was especially fond of Concepción. 'She has such dainty hands,' she had said to Encarnita. 'She is a real treasure.' She always gave Concepción the more delicate work to do, like trimming the underwear for a bride's trousseau. Girls, even from poor families, would save for years to buy their wedding linen. Engagements tended to be long-lasting and any magic that had existed between the couple had often worn off well before the wedding day arrived.

They stopped at one of the little shops set up in the front room of a woman's house to buy a loaf of bread, a lump of cheese and a piece of *chorizo*.

'We're going on a journey,' Encarnita told the woman. 'Up to Yegen, in the Alpujarra.'

'You're always talking about going on a journey. So now you are actually going on one!'

'One day we'll go further, won't we, Concepción?'

Concepción shrugged. She was not as interested in the idea of travelling as Encarnita had been at her age. She was happy enough in Nerja; she liked her work and she had lots of friends and admirers. Encarnita was watchful of the admirers and made sure that when Concepción went out on the *paseo* she walked only in the company of other girls. They flirted, of course, with words, but, as far as her mother knew, there was no physical contact except that hands might perhaps brush lightly as they passed. She was determined that her daughter should not throw herself away on an impoverished fisherman or clumsy factory worker. With her beauty and intelligence, Concepción could do much better than that. Her writing was as skilful and neat as her needlework and she had read more books than all her friends put together.

The bus was busy but Encarnita and Concepción had arrived early and managed to get a seat at the front so that they would have a good view. Men in wide-brimmed straw hats were at work in the fields outside the village, cutting swathes through the rippling fronds of sugar cane. It was strenuous labour, hard on the hands. Some of the workers looked up at the bus and waved. Encarnita waved back, Concepción did not.

'Francisco has managed to get a permit to work in the factory this year,' she said. A steady procession of mules and donkeys was moving steadily westward in the direction of the sugar factory. 'He will make good money.'

Francisco was a young fisherman who lived further along their street. He worked on a boat with his father and three brothers.

'Only for three months,' Encarnita pointed out. 'It's a short season.'

'But better than nothing.'

Encarnita enjoyed the trip to Almuñecar. The road hugged the narrow strip of coastline, snaking around sharp bends, some so perilous that the travellers, fearing that they were about to be tipped over the edge, cried out in alarm and pleaded with the driver to take more care. He paid no attention. He went on singing. Below them, on their right-hand side, lay the sparkling, azure-coloured sea. On their left-hand side, the *sierras* rose steeply.

It was warm by now in the bus. Women clutching bags and baskets were headed for the market in Almuñecar. One man had a box on his knee from which a live chicken kept trying to escape. A dog belonging to another passenger was showing interest in the chicken. Encarnita's flowers were drooping.

They arrived in La Herradura, set around the horseshoe-shaped bay which gave the *pueblo* its name.

'Isn't it beautiful, Concepción!' exclaimed Encarnita. 'Don't you think the Mediterranean Sea must be one of the most beautiful seas in the whole world?'

But Concepción was still lost in her own thoughts. Her mother did not ask what they were, knowing that she would not get an answer or, if she did, it was unlikely to be a particularly truthful one. She feared the girl was spending too much time thinking about Francisco.

More people squashed into the bus until finally the driver held up his hand. The chicken was now squawking and the dog barking and everyone was complaining about the heat. In Almuñecar they tumbled gratefully out into the open air and Encarnita led the way down to the shore.

'Look,' she said, 'there's the old hotel Mediterráneo still in business. I worked there as a girl.'

'I know you did,' said Concepción. 'You told me the last time we came here.'

Encarnita lingered for a moment, remembering those days, happy days on the whole, until the war started, and wondering what had become of Jacobo and Lorenzo. She hummed *Rio Rita* as they moved on up the hill towards the ruined fortress. On reaching the house at the top of the street Encarnita stopped again. She could hear children's voices. It must house a family now. She refrained from saying that that was where she used to live with her uncle Rinaldo. She felt sad when she thought about him. She had never found out what happened to him and thought that now she never would. No doubt his bones rested in some mass grave. Like many others, he seemed destined to stay a *desaparecido*.

They climbed up into the cemetery. The last time they had come had been to inter Sofia. At rest here, too, was the elderly couple who had sheltered Encarnita before she had left for Nerja sixteen years ago. She took a rag out of her bag and began to dust the fronts of the niches which held the remains of her dear old friend Sofia and her son Pedro.

'It was a terrible war,' sighed Encarnita. 'Poor Pedro died so young. And for what?'

'It all happened a long time ago, Mama,' said Concepción, a trifle impatiently. She hated stories about the war and Encarnita could not blame her. The young did not want to think of that as their heritage.

Encarnita laid the flowers on the ground where they would soon wilt and then she stood for a while thinking about her old friends. Concepción was leaning against the wall, with her eyes closed against the sun. She looked so like her father that his image had remained sharp and clear for Encarnita over the years.

Concepción opened her eyes. 'Shall we go now?'

Down at the shore, Miguel was waiting for them. His van was loaded, he was ready to take off.

Concepción sniffed. 'Are those *goats* you've got in the back, Miguel?'

'I'm afraid so,' he said cheerfully. 'They don't smell too sweet but there's nothing I can do about that.'

Concepción looked appealingly at her mother, who shrugged. It was either a van filled with goats or a very long walk.

The two passengers crammed into the front beside the driver, Encarnita allowing her daughter to take the seat by the window. Behind them, the goats stamped and bleated and released their pungent odours. Encarnita did not look at her daughter who had her head half hanging out of the window; she chatted to Miguel to take her mind off the smell and the jolting which she could feel travelling right up her spine into the base of her neck. Miguel drove in jaunty fashion with a cigarette hanging from the corner of his mouth. When the jolting got bad or the van swung too violently the goats became agitated. Encarnita felt anxious for the beasts but Miguel, she knew, would be unconcerned. This was his business. Some days he carried goats; on others, vegetables, which smelt better and were less trouble.

He would not understand someone like herself who had regarded her goats as her companions and missed them still when she went walking in the *campo*.

'I thought I was going to be sick,' said Concepción, the moment she set her foot on the ground in Órgiva. 'What must we smell like?' She tugged a strand of her hair across her nose and sniffed it.

'By the time we walk to Yegen the smell will have gone,' her mother retorted, turning to thank Miguel and put a few *pesetas* into his hand. He said he could give them a lift back to Almuñecar in four days' time, if that would be of any use? He had to bring up another delivery. Encarnita accepted gratefully.

'I hope it won't be goats next time,' said Concepción, when they had waved him off. 'I'm starving, Mama.'

They found a wall to sit on and ate some bread and sausage.

'Is it far to Yegen?' asked Concepción.

'A good walk.' Encarnita could not have said how many kilometers exactly but she did know it would take some hours to reach it by foot and the day was getting on. Also, her daughter was not as good at walking the *campo* as she had been as a girl, and still was. Whenever she felt restless she would turn inland from Nerja and go for a long walk.

'Are there no buses?' asked Concepción.

Encarnita thought that if there were they would not be frequent.

'Couldn't we get a lift?'

'I don't know anyone in Órgiva.'

'You don't need to know anyone. See that man over there who's been pumping up his tyre? He looks ready to leave. I'm going to go and ask him.'

'Concepción, come back!'

But Concepción was half way across the road, dodging an ox-cart, and was now on the other side talking to the man who stood beside a rusted grey van. It looked in even worse condition than Miguel's but that was not what was worrying Encarnita.

Concepción returned to say they could have a lift, part way. The man was going to some place called Bubión but he could drop them on the road before he turned off.

'We can't take a lift from some man we don't know.'

'Of course we can. He doesn't mind.'

Concepción was already on her way back to him. Encarnita could only follow.

They sat three abreast in the front again, but this time Concepción sat in the middle. It seemed to Encarnita that the man's leg was resting disturbingly near her daughter's but it was cramped in the van and she did not have a clear view and since there was nothing she could do about it anyway she allowed herself to enjoy the scenery. The road climbed up and up, leaving behind the wide swathes of countryside planted with fruit and olive trees; on the mountainside sprawled white houses, forming little *pueblos*. It all felt so familiar. Encarnita felt she was going home.

At the turn-off for Bubión and the other high villages of Pampaneira and Capileira, the driver pulled up. He glanced sideways at Concepción, who smiled at him. When she smiled her whole face lit up.

'I could take you the rest of the way if you'd like,' he offered. 'I've got time.'

'We can walk from here.' Encarnita tugged at the door handle.

'Mama, it's kind of Alfonso.'

'No trouble,' said Alfonso, revving up the engine.

He took them all the way to their destination, by-passing Yegen, which lay below on the lower road. Encarnita had to make do with a glimpse of the roofs. Tomorrow, she would go and see her village.

When they arrived at Luisa's house, Encarnita jumped out straightaway and ran to meet her friend. They held each other in a long embrace. *You look just the same! You haven't changed.* They said the things that old friends do after a long separation. But Luisa had changed, physically; she looked like a woman in her mid- to late-forties, ten years older than she really was. In spite of that, it was as if the years between had not existed. Their reunion was proving to be easy; they would be able to talk to each other as they could not with anyone else. Encarnita knew she was going to tell Luisa about Concepción's father, and that she could trust her.

'You must meet my daughter,' she said, looking round for her.

Concepción and Alfonso were standing together, a little way off, facing each other, with not much space between them. He was looking into her face as if he would like to devour her, reminding her of the way Don Geraldo had looked at Juliana in the beginning. Alfonso had the face of a wolf, thought Encarnita.

'Concepción!' she shouted, breaking the couple's trance.

'I'm just coming, Mama!' Still the girl lingered, until Encarnita made a move in her direction. Concepción murmured something to Alfonso, then drifted over to join her mother and Luisa. Encarnita wanted to tell her to walk properly and stop that silly act.

'What a beautiful girl you have, Encarnita!' said Luisa.

Too beautiful for her own good at times, Encarnita thought. Later, when they had a moment alone, she said to her daughter, 'You should not encourage men the way you were doing with Alfonso.'

'I was only flirting, Mama. There's no harm in that. All girls like to flirt a little.'

Concepción had four more young men here with whom she could flirt. Luisa's sons, ranging in age from seventeen down to five, buzzed about her like bees round a honeycomb. Encarnita felt there must be protection in numbers; each boy was making sure that the others did not steal a march on him and go off with her on their own.

Luisa was amused by it. 'Wouldn't it be wonderful if Jaime and Concepción were to marry? That would join our families together.'

'They are very young.' Encarnita changed the subject. 'Have Don Geraldo and Doña Gamel arrived yet?'

'I heard they came up from Úgijar this morning. He walked, she rode a mule. It's their first visit back since they left Yegen. Like you.'

Don Geraldo and Doña Gamel were receiving a steady stream of visitors, old friends he had known way back from his early days in Yegen, many of whom were now white-haired and stooped. He himself was almost bald. Doña Gamel had aged but not changed greatly, in Encarnita's opinion. She still had her rather dreamy, faraway smile.

Don Geraldo was pleased to see Encarnita and hugged her warmly. He remembered her, of course he did. How could he not! He remembered their talks about books, sitting up on the hill, and how he had started to teach her English. 'Can you still speak some?'

'A little. I still read the *Garden of Verses*.' She did not tell him what had befallen his book about Jack Robinson.

'That's good. And did you ever manage to go on a journey?'

'Only as far as Nerja.' Over the years, at intervals, she had considered it, but every time she had scraped almost enough money together there would be some other use for it. She had paid for Sofia to have a proper funeral. Then there had been Concepción's confirmation dress to buy and medicine for Arrieta.

Don Geraldo laughed. 'Never mind. You've got time yet. What age are you now, Encarnita? I remember you as a baby in your mother's arms.'

'Thirty-five.'

'I wish I could be thirty-five again! That's young, you know.'

To her, it did not seem so very young.

She asked if he still went on journeys himself and he told her not so much as before. 'Gamel and I are very entrenched in our Churriana house these days. We're not inclined to leave it too often.'

'But you've come back to Yegen?'

He had come to take photographs for a book he had written, based on life in Yegen as he had known it. It was to be called *South From Granada*. The villagers were amazed that they were about to make an appearance in a book and some wondered uneasily what he might have to say about them. It was to be published first in English and, later, he hoped it would be translated into Spanish.

'And Miranda, your daughter,' asked Encarnita, 'how is Miranda?'

'She's well. She's married to a French doctor and they live in Paris and they have two beautiful children, a son of three called Stefane and a daughter, Marina, born just recently, in January.'

Encarnita listened in wonder. Imagine a daughter of Juliana having such a life! She did not ask if he had seen or heard of Juliana, who was living in Granada with her ex-civil guard husband. She felt sorry for her not being able to see her daughter and beautiful grandchildren.

Don Geraldo glanced past Encarnita and saw Concepción. Luisa, who had come with them, saw how his face changed. His eyes had lit up. 'Is this your daughter, Encarnita?' he asked. 'She's a real beauty.'

Encarnita introduced them and Concepción lowered her eyes as he took her hand. He held on to it. '*Que bonita!* You will break many hearts, I fear, little one.'

But Concepción, not being so enthralled with him as he was with her – he was an old man, about sixty years old – shortly removed her hand and wandered off to rejoin Luisa's sons, who were larking about in the street.

Don Geraldo put his back to the room. 'Your daughter – where did you get her from? Is her father Spanish?' When Encarnita did not answer he said, 'I rather think he can't be. Does he know he has this child? If he did I'm sure he'd want to give her a better chance in life. Have you never thought of that?'

'Yes, but it's not been possible.' She knew that nothing

would have persuaded her to part with Concepción, even if it had.

'Some people didn't approve of me taking Miranda to England but she's pleased now that I did it. Think what her life would have been if she'd stayed with Juliana!'

When Encarnita repeated this to Luisa, her friend said, 'I don't know if Miranda's life is all that happy. From what we've heard, she's been depressed since the last baby was born. And it seems that's not new. She's been depressed for a long time. Imagine being taken away from your mother when you're three years old to live in a country where you can't understand what they're saying! She must have spent half her life wondering about her mother. I know you've always admired Don Geraldo, Encarnita, but you can't admire some of the things he's done.'

'That's the same with everybody.'

'But he still likes young girls. It can't be very nice for a lady like Doña Gamel to be married to an old man with wandering eyes. You must have seen the way he eyed your Concepción. He could hardly keep his hands off her.'

Encarnita was tempted to say that Luisa's sons could hardly keep their hands off Concepción, either, but did not. She knew that was different: they were young, the lads, in the springtime of their lives, with the sap rising. It was natural that they would be drawn to a young and pretty girl. She could not decide whether it was unnatural for an old man to be tempted also. She had known plenty that were. It was true that she did not like that aspect of Don Geraldo's character, but he had opened up new worlds for her, given her books, taught her his language, put the possibility of travelling into her head, and she was grateful for all of that. She might not have travelled much yet but she had made many journeys inside her head.

Now she wanted to explore the village, to poke into every corner, meet up with her old neighbours. The houses had been whitewashed and looked neater and cleaner than before and people appeared to be a little better off, though not a great deal. Many of those she had known had gone. Black Maria was dead, having gone mad. Don Geraldo's friend Paco, too, had died, a few months before, in Argentina. And Luisa said that quite a lot of the young people were going down to the coast to look for work.

'Jaime would like to go. Would there be anything for him in Nerja?'

Encarnita shook her head. 'There's only the fishing – and you have to be born into a fishing family for that – and part-time work in the sugar cane. Like here, the *cortijos* round about are too small to employ people.'

Don Geraldo had said that hotels and apartments for tourists were starting to be built along the coast near where they lived on the outskirts of Málaga, in fishing villages like Torremolinos and Fuengirola. He did not care much for this new development, but locals were finding jobs there, so he supposed that was one benefit, as long as it did not get out of hand.

'Not too many tourists come to Nerja,' Encarnita had said.

'Wait and see! People who live in northern countries crave the sun.'

Encarnita felt at home in the village, yet she could not imagine coming back to live here again. It would hold nothing for her, except her memories and her friendship with Luisa. In Nerja, she had work, as did Concepción, and, what was even more important, they had Arrieta, who was like a mother and grandmother to them.

She went walking again, on her own, along old familiar paths, and afterwards went into the graveyard but stayed only briefly for the broken-down walls and sad looking mounds, one of which covered her mother, disturbed her. The church was more calming. She lit a candle for Pilar and said a prayer.

She spent hours, too, talking to Luisa. She told her about her Scotsman and swore her to secrecy, not that it might matter so much now, with the Civil War sixteen years behind them. In return, Luisa talked about her feelings for her father. She spoke bitterly of him. 'I was glad when he died. The priest said it was a terrible sin that I should feel that way, but my father had committed worse sins himself.'

Encarnita did not tell Luisa about her father's visit to her in the night; there was no point in it now. She had left it behind. Too much had happened in her life since then for it to be important any longer.

The young ones roamed the countryside and, although Encarnita had other preoccupations, she noticed that Concepción and Jaime were often managing to lose the three younger boys. Concepción's laughter could be heard like the song of a lark rising. Luisa said not to worry about them, they were just young and high-spirited, and Jaime was a good lad who would know not to go too far.

On the last evening of their visit, Encarnita went outside to smell the air and look at the stars. She heard noises coming from the shed. She crossed the grass noiselessly and pushed open the door to see the bodies of Concepción and Jaime locked together on the straw-strewn floor. The family goat stood behind them, showing no interest.

Luisa had come to visit her grandchildren. Encarnita thought her lucky that she saw them only for twice-yearly visits after which she could go home to the peace and quiet of her own house in the Alpujarra. All her sons had left home, and the two who had married were living with their wives' families. It was one benefit of having sons. Daughters tended to stay close to their mothers. Perhaps Concepción would benefit eventually once her sons were grown. There were five of them, ranging from fourteen years down to fifteen months. Mario, the youngest, and eight-year old Felipe had their mother's colouring and were finer-boned; they stood out from the rest. Shy, sensitive Felipe was his grandmother's favourite. He liked books and was quick to learn. The two eldest, Juan and Antonio, ran wild. They stayed away from school, stole cigarettes and lounged down on the beach smoking them. Their father, who was fond enough of the boys, did little to control them but, then, he was no better himself, so what could you expect? Concepción had fulfilled her mother's worst fears: she had thrown herself well and truly away.

Encarnita could not understand why her daughter had not been able to do something about the constant stream of babies – there had been two miscarriages as well. She had said so each time Concepción had become pregnant and Concepción had always been indignant and demanded to know what was she supposed to have done. Jaime was like a charging bull when he came home after he'd been drinking; fighting him off was not in her power. And contraception was illegal. There were ways of getting it, said her mother. 'Try persuading Jaime to use it,' Concepción had retorted, 'when he's in a mood like that.'

Jaime, unfortunately, had turned out to be cast in the same mould as his father and grandfather and Encarnita could not argue with what her daughter said. When he drank he did so copiously and then he became aggressive and got into fights. *Nada cambia*. Nothing changes. Encarnita could only sigh and help her daughter in whatever way she could. It pained her to see how her lovely daughter had changed; her body had become slack with childbearing and her fine, pale skin was beginning to show lines. Even the colour of her hair had faded.

They were all crammed into Arrieta's house. Arrieta, who was now eighty years old, and Encarnita slept in the living room, so that Concepción, her husband and children could sleep in the two remaining rooms. They had no other choice. Jaime found work only occasionally and Concepción was too busy bearing children, which left Encarnita to earn the daily bread for the household.

She had a job in a tourist urbanización called Capistrano Village, on the eastern outskirts of the town, which were steadily being pushed further and further out into the *campo*. It was a lovely place, with little self-catering villas and apartments set in beautiful gardens where gardeners tended the flowers and watered the grass with sprinklers in dry weather and maintenance men kept the pathways neat and clean and sorted out plumbing problems for the guests. There was even a swimming pool. Encarnita loved going there. She loved the order of it, the trees and flowers, and the spaciousness. She dreamed about living in one of the villas, with bougainvillaea climbing up the wall, and a proper kitchen, fully equipped, as they described it in the tourist brochures, and a tiled bathroom fitted with one's choice of either a bath or a shower.

She dreamed about it as she gathered up the soiled sheets and scrubbed the baths and toilets until they gleamed. She took pride in her work. It disturbed her when she found burn marks where people had laid smouldering cigarettes. She could not understand why they would want to mess up such nice things.

'Because some of them are pigs, that's why,' one of the guests, a very forthright young woman, told her. She said she believed in calling a spade a spade. Her name was Morna and she had told Encarnita to call her that, though Encarnita, finding the idea a bit embarrassing, tended not to call her anything. Morna could speak Spanish, having studied it at university, and was keen to have some practice. She was interested, too, in Encarnita's life and when she heard that Encarnita could speak a little English she offered to give her an opportunity to practise some in return.

'We can do intercambio,' she said with a smile. She gave Encarnita a Pocket Spanish-English dictionary.

'To keep?'

'To keep.'

Encarnita tucked it into her apron pocket.

She thought Morna must be not much more than twenty years old and was surprised to find that she was thirty-one, a year older than Concepción, who looked by far the elder. Encarnita was even more surprised when she discovered that the lady was Scottish.

'I live in Edinburgh,' said Morna, as if that would be the most common thing in the world to do.

'Edinburgh,' repeated Encarnita, her heart giving a leap.

'Do you know it?'

'No. But I would like very much to visit it one day.'

'You must! Before I go I'll leave you my address. We'll keep in touch.'

First, though, Encarnita had to save and that was proving even more difficult than before, with so many in the family. Whenever she did manage to put away a few *pesetas* a child would need medicine or a pair of shoes and she would have to go to her box. Morna suggested selling Carrington's drawing, which Encarnita had brought to show her, when she had shown interest in Gerald Brenan and his friends.

'It might be worth a bit,' said Morna. 'Not huge amounts – it's not as if she's Picasso. But I think she's reasonably well known, with her being on the fringes of the Bloomsbury Group and a friend of Lytton Strachey.'

'*Sell* my picture?' Encarnita was horrified at the suggestion. It was akin to asking her to sell a part of her life. She had saved up until she could buy a decent frame with glass to protect it from the dust. Nerja was full of dust from all the building work that was going on and then there was the sand which snaked its way up from the beach and was impossible to keep out. The picture hung on her bedroom wall where she could see it every morning when she wakened.

During her fifteen-minute walk home Encarnita considered asking Morna to make enquiries about Conal. But she was reluctant to do that. It was too private an affair. She did not like the idea of someone – especially someone who liked to call a spade a spade – confronting Conal. She could imagine Morna doing that. No, some day she would go with Concepción and try to find him. Right now it would be impossible for Concepción to go anywhere.

While she was waiting at the kerb for the lights to change a car with a GB plate came past. She looked at the driver, she always did when she saw a GB plate. He bore no resemblance to her Scotsman. Although she had not seen him for more than twenty-one years she was certain she would still recognise him. There had not been a day in which she had not thought about him. The lights changed and she was about to step out when a motor cycle came screeching round the corner. Motor cycles ridden by youths were the bane of their lives, especially since the owners neutralised the silencers to enhance the noise. This machine was tilted dangerously to the right as it rounded the curve, and clinging to the back was Diego, her eldest grandson. He was desperate to have a bike himself but Encarnita had told him that she was not going to give him money so that he could go and kill himself.

She arrived home to find that Luisa had the fire going and was cooking a stew, comprising mostly of beans, with a few chunks of *chorizo* thrown in to give it flavour. The males in the house all had huge appetites. Since Encarnita had been working full-time the family had been able to eat better but, even so, the boys had to fill up with masses of potatoes and bread. Sometimes the guests at Capistrano Village would give Encarnita bits and pieces that they had left over when their holiday was finished: lumps of cheese, a quarter bottle of olive oil, half a packet of rice, a lump of butter – a real luxury – and maybe even a few rashers of bacon. All offerings were gratefully received and put to good use. Better than being wasted, the guests would say, who thought it possible that the maids would not be all that well paid. Often, too, there were tips, given in money, which would be even more appreciated. Encarnita did well there for she took more trouble than some of the younger cleaners and she had a friendly disposition. If someone wanted an extra pillow she would make sure that they got it. It mattered to her that the visitors would go home having thought well of their stay in Nerja.

She also brought home discarded English newspapers and magazines: her special treats, which she saved for when there was peace in the house. While she read, taking her time, often managing only two or three paragraphs at a time, she would think that perhaps Conal might be reading these same papers and magazines.

She sat down now on the opposite side of the fire from Luisa, glad to rest her feet for a while. She was on them all day. Arrieta was dozing in her chair and the younger children had gone out with their mother. The older ones were seldom at home, except to eat. This was a good time of day to be in the house.

'So what is new in Yegen?' asked Encarnita.

Luisa shrugged. 'Not much.'

'What about Don Geraldo? Have you heard how he is?'

'Not recently.'

'But the English girl, Lynda, is she still with him?'

'Oh yes, indeed.'

Doña Gamel had died two years previously of cancer, after much suffering.

It had been a terrible time for Don Geraldo, as well as, of course, for her, but he had rallied when yet another young girl had come into his life. She had moved into his house only weeks after his wife's death.

'But he must have known her before?' insisted Encarnita.

'I would think so,' Luisa assented.

He had brought Lynda with him on a visit to Yegen in the autumn of 1968. Luisa had told the story to Encarnita before, but they enjoyed turning over the details, so mystified were they by this turn of events. Don Geraldo would never cease to be a topic of interest for them. How could he, when he had been a part of their lives over a period of some fourteen years? Also, it was comforting, in a way, to go over old gossip. Each had their own questions and responses and it did not matter that they had been rehearsed before.

'You say she was twenty-four?'

'When they came two years ago, she was. So she would be twenty-six now.'

'And him?'

'Fifty years older.'

'And she isn't ugly or anything like that?'

'Not at all! The opposite. The men's heads turned as she walked down the street. She was a lovely looking, girl, tall and slim, and she had long brown hair down to her shoulders. I liked her when Don Geraldo introduced us. She had such a nice voice and good manners.'

'So she could have other men if she wanted them?'

'Maybe she doesn't want them?'

'But why would a pretty girl of twenty-four come to live with a man aged *seventy*-four? He is not *so* rich, is he?'

'Not so very. She likes to read books. They both like to read books.'

Encarnita nodded. She was beginning to see a possibility: it might be that the girl liked the company of Don Geraldo in the way that she herself had, learning from him, benefiting from his knowledge. She might be greedy for that.

'We've heard that her health is not good,' said Luisa, stirring the pot so that the stew would not stick. 'It seems she has a bad back and weak lungs. Doña Gamel wasn't strong, either, of course. And Don Geraldo's never all that well himself – all those colds and flu he keeps getting – so they can look after each other. Maybe Don Geraldo is a kind of father for her.'

But they knew that he had never seen young girls in that light.

'He might now that he is older,' suggested Luisa, but neither felt convinced.

It would have to remain a mystery to them, but Encarnita felt sure that, regardless of how Lynda would feel about Don Geraldo, he would have fallen in love with her. The subject was one that they would return to many times.

The door blew open, jerking Arrieta out of sleep, and in came the children, boisterous, hungry, impatient. Concepción snapped at them, telling them to stop shoving and pushing, they were going to knock the table over. They had already bumped Arrieta's chair. Encarnita could not blame Concepción for snapping when she had five such demanding boys to cope with but she regretted that her daughter's once-soft voice had become high-pitched and shrill. Concepción's life as a mother was not at all like the tranquil one that she herself had had with a young child. But boys were not like girls, willing to go and pick flowers in the *campo*.

The children were set down at the table to eat first. Their mother berated them, telling them not to grab, gobble, or gulp, nor to shake the table or kick each other underneath it.

'They are just boys,' said Luisa, who, having had four herself, was more used to such chaos and clamour. None of hers had turned out well though Encarnita held back from saying so.

When she had said it to Concepción on one fraught occasion, her daughter had turned on her. 'If you hadn't taken me to their house I wouldn't be married to Jaime now! My life could have been different.'

'So you're blaming me?'

'Luisa was *your* friend.'

'Was it my fault that he got you pregnant? I warned you not to give yourself too easily to a man. And certainly not unless you were in love with him.'

'I was in love with him! Well, I thought I was. How could I know whether I was or not? I was fifteen. He was good looking. He liked me very much.'

'He turned your head.'

'He was nice to me. What was wrong with that? But he changed.'

'Once you were married. I suppose it's not unusual. You changed too, didn't you?'

'Well, so what? How about yourself? You were sure that you were in love with my father, were you?'

'Yes, I was sure,' Encarnita had said simply, finishing the conversation. 'He was a fine man.'

No one, not even his mother, could claim that for Jaime.

After the children had eaten they were sent out to play in the street, the older boys instructed to look after Mario and not to dare let him out of their sight. The four women then sat down at the table and ate their meal.

'Have you left some for Jaime?' Concepción asked her mother-in-law. There was no sign of him.

'Of course,' said Luisa. As if she would not! She knew how quickly her son could lose his temper, though when he did she took it calmly, saying that men tended to be like that and the best way to cope with it was to wait for the storm to blow over. She spoke from much experience. And she had survived, after all. Sometimes Encarnita thought her friend was wise; at others, she questioned it. She felt that she herself would not have been prepared to endure such tempests.

'He's late,' said Concepción. 'Later than usual,' she added, drumming her fingers on the table.

On occasions Jaime had not come back until morning and, when challenged by his wife, had admitted to being with another woman. 'Go and live with her then if you want to,' Concepción had screamed at him and Encarnita had devoutly wished that he would, even offering up a short prayer to that effect, but he had had no intention of doing so. The woman in question had several children of her own and no money.

'I've put the lid on the pot to keep the stew warm,' said Luisa.

Jaime would be ravenous when he came in from his drinking. Encarnita did not know where he got the money from but she did not ask. He pestered her at times to give him a few *pesetas* and was abusive when she said she had nothing left from her wages, calling her a mean old woman, but when she looked him in the eye he would mutter and back off. She had always done her best to keep control of the money she earned and put it away in various hiding places. Sometimes, inevitably, he had found it. Or else one of his sons had. Now she had an account in a bank. On the day that she had opened it she had hardly been able to believe it. That she should have an account in a bank! What would Pilar have thought of that?

A scream reached them from the street.

'Sounds like Mario.' Arrieta was concerned and made to rise from her seat.

'It's all right, I'm going,' groaned Concepción. 'You can never get a minute's peace round here.' She went to see what was happening, returning after a couple of minutes to say it had been about nothing. 'Somebody pushed him over, that's all.'

'He's too small to be out there with the older boys,' said Arrieta.

'Felipe looks after him.'

'Felipe's too young to have the responsibility.'

'All the kids play out.'

'The little ones should be in bed.' The clock on the shelf

showed that it was almost eleven. Not that many children in the street went to bed before that.

'You know they won't go until the rest do!'

'No sign of Jaime when you were out?' asked Encarnita in an attempt to defuse the situation. Concepción was edgy tonight and Arrieta tended to be even more critical than usual of the children's behaviour when Luisa was visiting. Encarnita thought that Arrieta, even though she would deny it if challenged, partially blamed Luisa for her son's behaviour and treatment of his wife. If only Luisa had been more particular about how she'd brought up those sons of hers!

'God knows where he is!' said Concepción, going out into the garden.

She had gone to have a cigarette. She had picked up the habit from Jaime.

A little while later, the door burst open and Juan came in shouting, 'It's the *Guardia*!'

'The *Guardia*?' Encarnita got up. 'Looking for us?'

'They want Mama.'

'Concepción,' called Encarnita, 'you'd better come.'

Encarnita went to the door with her daughter. Two civil guards were standing in the street surrounded by a gaggle of children, all of whom were quiet now.

'We've come about your husband.'

'So what's he done this time?' asked Concepción.

'Can we come in?'

She let them pass and told the children to stay outside. Encarnita scooped Mario up into her arms and carried him in. He'd been sitting, half-asleep, his head slumped against the wall. She pushed the door shut behind them. Luisa was on her feet by the fire looking anxious.

'I'm sorry to bring you bad news,' said the guard who was the spokesman.

'Just tell me!' said Concepción.

'He got into a fight.'

'What a surprise!'

'This time I'm afraid, Señora, it's been more serious.'

'Don't tell me he's killed somebody!'

He had. He'd been in a fight on the Balcón and pushed the other man over the rail. The man had been dashed against the rocks below and was found to be dead when they went down to pick him up. Luisa began to wail. Concepción was silent. Her face was paler than her mother could ever remember seeing it. Encarnita rocked Mario, who had dropped off to sleep.

'What a father I picked for my children,' muttered Concepción.

'I'm sure he wouldn't have meant to do it,' cried Luisa. 'It would have been an accident.'

It had probably not been intentional, the guard agreed, and so he might have a chance of getting off with a sentence of twenty years or so.

'Twenty years,' moaned Luisa.

Jaime was now in custody, here in Nerja, said the guard, but he would be moved to Málaga the next day. They left and Encarnita brought the children in so that they could break the news to them before they would hear it in the street.

The children took it calmly; they were stunned and could not quite take in the fact that their father was in prison. Concepción did not say that he had killed a man, only that a man had been killed during the fight.

'The other guy might have been trying to push Papa over,' said Juan, beginning to be angry. 'I bet it wasn't his fault!'

This was the line that he and Antonio would follow and when other boys called their father a murderer they would defend him with these words as well as their fists.

In the morning, they found out that the man who had been killed had been involved with the same woman as Jaime. The fight had been over her.

'That's me finished with him now,' said Concepción. 'He can rot in jail for all I care!'

Luisa left for Yegen after being allowed a brief visit to her son. Encarnita and Arrieta sat down together and tried to work out how best to keep the family together. They decided that it would be better for Concepción – as well as the family – if she were to find a job. Arrieta would look after the younger children, which she did most of the time anyway. Encarnita thought she should be able to get Concepción a job alongside her.

Her daughter was not taken by the idea. 'I don't want to clean up other people's mess. I've enough of that here.' She seldom did do much to keep the house clean but her mother held her tongue on that point. But she was determined to force Concepción to do something to improve herself. She had let herself sag into a constant slouch and often her hair would be tangled and her dress stained. If she were to go out to work each day, Encarnita reasoned, she would have to smarten herself up.

'Look at yourself!' said Encarnita. 'Look in the mirror! You're only thirty years old. It's not that old.'

Concepción grimaced at herself in the mirror and straightened herself up. 'You're right, Mama, I look a fright!' She agreed to let her mother go ahead and try to obtain a place for her at Capistrano Village. Encarnita gave her money to go to the market to buy a new dress and to the hairdresser's to have her hair cut.

Concepción did not settle into the job as easily as her mother had. She worked well and the supervisor was pleased with her but, every morning, as they trudged out to the urbanización, she would complain.

'Do something about it then!' retorted Encarnita, losing patience. 'Find yourself another job. You can read and write and speak a little English.' Concepción had shown a facility for picking up English and she could even manage a few phrases in German. Her handwriting, also, was neat. Her teacher had said that Concepción was intelligent enough to go to college and train to be a teacher herself, but there had been no question of that. Apart from the fact that she was pregnant by then, Encarnita could not have afforded it.

On her day off, Concepción put on her new dress, made up her face, skilfully using lipstick, eye shadow and liner, and went round the town asking at hotels, shops and offices. She came back in the evening to announce that she had a job, with more money than she earned cleaning. She was to work in a haulier's office as a clerk-receptionist. To celebrate, she had brought in a bottle of brandy and a packet of Chesterfield cigarettes. Juan eyed the latter but was told to keep his hands off them.

He remained a problem. He had left school but there was nothing for him to do. He hung about the streets, chucked stones at foreign cars and got into fights.

'He's going to end up like his father,' said Arrieta. 'There's rotten blood in that family.'

'If he could just get a job,' said Encarnita.

'What could he do?'

'He's interested in cars and engines.'

'But who'd take him on? Everybody knows what these boys are like.'

'It's terrible they should be damned before they get a chance.' Encarnita sighed. Felipe would be different; she felt sure about that. And Concepción was doing well. She liked her new job; she was efficient, good on the telephone and face to face with the customers. Her employer sang her praises when Encarnita called at the office.

Emilio was a small, stocky man about the same age as Encarnita, twenty years older than Concepción. He was bald and could not have been called handsome but he had a vitality that made him attractive. He was a successful business man; he'd started out with one small rusty van and now had three large trucks with ambitions to expand even further.

It was obvious to Encarnita on the first meeting that Emilio was smitten by her daughter, who had recovered some of her earlier prettiness.

'She's an angel, your daughter,' he enthused. 'The last one

got the books into a terrible muddle and snapped at customers on the phone. I had to get rid of her.'

Emilio was a widower, with no children. He had a smooth manner and knew how to talk to women, though not in an oily way. Encarnita found him likeable. He took the trouble to flatter her, which she appreciated, even while she knew it was flattery. He had a good sense of humour too, another point in his favour.

After Concepción had been working for him for a week he invited her out to dinner on the Saturday night.

'We're going to a new restaurant down the coast, just opened,' she said, as she brushed her light eyelashes with black mascara. She spoke as if she were used to going out to restaurants. The children watched, fascinated by this new vision of their mother. She had bought a gold lamé blouse with her earnings and gold earrings to match, which swung against her neck as she moved. 'It's owned by a friend of his. Its speciality is seafood.'

He came to call for her in his car, a Volkswagen, brand new. Made in Germany, Concepción informed Encarnita, who already knew that. The younger children clambered over the bonnet while they waited for their mother to emerge in her finery and high heels; the two older ones asked to look in the engine. Emilio was pleased to have the opportunity to be pleasant to her children. When Concepción came out he opened the passenger door and ushered her in with a small bow, like a perfect gentleman.

'I think he is a gentleman,' said Encarnita.

'We'll have to see,' sniffed Arrieta. 'I just hope he doesn't get her pregnant.'

'She's older now,' Encarnita retaliated sharply. She was quick to criticise her daughter herself but still felt defensive when others, even Arrieta, did. Nevertheless, she was on tenterhooks and did not sleep until her daughter came in, which she did at half past midnight.

'You didn't go back to his house?'

'No, I did not, Mama.' Concepción came to kiss her.

'He's an honourable man. We had a wonderful evening. The *gambas* just melted in your mouth.'

Encarnita raised an eyebrow but said nothing. Concepción had found an old pile of women's magazines left behind in her office by its previous incumbent and was picking up their language. At mealtimes she would read out recipes and reviews of restaurants in cities like Madrid and Barcelona. She was also interested in beauty tips and had bought an auburn rinse for her hair, to give the colour a lift. Encarnita was not sure about the result but, once more, she said nothing. She sometimes thought that one of the most important things you could have as a mother was the ability to hold your tongue.

Emilio took Concepción out the following Saturday, and the next again. This time she did not come home until morning.

'What did I tell you?' demanded Arrieta.

'I hope you know what you're doing,' Encarnita said to her daughter, for there was a time to speak as well as to stay silent. She had seen Concepción make one big mistake in her life. In fact, two. The first had been getting pregnant by Jaime, and the second, marrying him. Encarnita had advised her against it at the time but Concepción would not listen. She had been in love.

'Mama, I am not a child!' she said now.

'We don't need any more in the family.'

'There are not going to be any. Emilio is very careful, he takes precautions.'

'I hope so.'

'Mama, I'm having fun, for the first time in my life.'

Encarnita could not grudge her that.

Two months later, Concepción announced that she was moving in with Emilio. He had a very nice modern house in the *campo* on the way to Frigiliana. It had three bedrooms, a modern kitchen and bathroom, and a small, kidney-shaped swimming pool.

'He's obviously not short of money,' said Arrieta.

'I'm not going with him for his money!' said Concepción.

'What about the children?' asked Encarnita.

'He says I can bring the little ones, Roberto and Mario, with me, but the older ones might be better staying with you.'

'Better for whom?' asked Arrieta.

'They wouldn't fit in,' said Concepción.

Encarnita had changed jobs and now went to work by bus. She enjoyed her daily ride, which took her from the west end of town, through the centre streets, out to the suburbs on the eastern side. She was constantly amazed by how much Nerja had changed, was changing, like all the other old fishing villages along the coast. Buildings were shooting up in all directions, creeping further and further into the *campo*. The grinding of road drills and the whir of cement mixers mingled with the roar of the ever increasing traffic. That did not bother her too much. She took each new development in life as it came, having realised a long time ago that there was no point in kicking against it.

Her life was easier now than it had ever been; it had levelled out onto a plain, with fewer bumps to disrupt it. After all the difficult, up-and-down years of looking after Concepción's three older boys, she lived alone with Arrieta who, at ninety-three, was semi-blind, but still in possession of her other senses. Arrieta spent the day in a rocking chair, inside the house when it was cold, and in warm weather, outside, in the garden, where she could listen to the sound of the sea and the cry of the birds. She seldom complained. Neighbours dropped in to visit her while Encarnita was at work and brought her soup. With only a few teeth left, she could eat little else. When Encarnita was at home they were content with each other's company; they reminisced about old times, discussed the doings of the neighbours as well as Concepción and her children. On fine evenings Encarnita would push Arrieta out in a wheelchair lent to them by social services.

Encarnita was feeling especially pleased this morning. In her bag she had three letters: one from her Scottish friend Morna, who wrote regularly; one from Luisa, who did not; and the third from Felipe, who wrote once a month. It was the first time in her life that she had ever received three let-

ters in a week, let alone all at once! They'd been left the day
before by the postman with a neighbour who had forgotten
to hand them in.

The bus stopped at Capistrano Village, her former place
of work, to drop people off, pick some more up. The
tourists were dressed in skimpy shorts and tops and their
sandalled feet were bare, in spite of the day being cool, in
Encarnita's reckoning. She was wearing a ribbed jersey with
a polo neck and a black leather jacket, and on her feet a pair
of soft, supple leather shoes made in Italy. Shoes were her
weakness. She saved up until she could afford a decent pair.
When she arrived at work she would change them for a pair
of *alpargatas*. The jacket was a present from Emilio. She had
been overwhelmed when he had presented it to her on her
sixty-fifth birthday. That *she* should have a leather jacket!
She had seen the prices of them in the shops. Her daughter
had two, one black, and one honey-coloured, with trousers
to match. Concepción's wardrobe was packed with expensive clothes which she wore when she and Emilio went on
expensive holidays to Tenerife, Acapulco and Florida.
Recently they had been going on cruises, round the Greek
islands and to the Caribbean. Emilio was always saying that
Encarnita must come on a trip with them – he knew how
much she wanted to travel – but she said she could not leave
Arrieta. Sometime then, he said, meaning when Arrieta
would no longer be there, which Encarnita did not wish to
think about. They had been living together for forty-five
years.

Emilio's fortunes had increased in keeping with the
housing boom. Encarnita had lost track of how many
removal vans he had on the road. He had built a new house
further into the *campo*, with five bedrooms, two bathrooms
and a shower room, an enormous wrap-around terrace from
which you could see the sea and the mountains, and a bigger swimming pool than they'd had before. The house was
visible from many kilometers around, sitting up in such a
prominent position. Concepción had a car of her own and

sometimes she would come down to take her mother and Arrieta out for a run though neither were very happy at being driven by her on the narrow, twisting roads where the edges were unprotected and the drops sheer. They thought she clipped the corners too closely and were relieved when they were returned home safely.

After its stop the bus carried on to the *urbanización* of Capistrano Oasis and, finally, to that of Capistrano Playa, where Encarnita alighted to walk the short distance to her place of work. The house was large, detached, and surrounded by a high wall, but it had an elevated situation so that it looked right over the sea. She rang the bell, waited until Jorge answered, then she spoke into the intercom, and the high, electronic gates swung open to let her enter, closing immediately behind her.

Jorge came down the path to meet her. She told him about her letters straightaway.

'Anything from Felipe?'

She nodded. Jorge knew her grandson and was always interested in his progress. She opened that one first while they drank their morning coffee.

'Doing well still, is he?'

'Very well.' Encarnita offered Jorge a *churro*. She had bought half a dozen, newly fried and hot, on her way to the bus. 'He's a good boy.'

'How long now till he qualifies?'

'Another year.'

'And then you'll have a lawyer in the family!'

Encarnita smiled.

'You've done well by him.'

'He's done well by himself. He's worked hard for it.'

'But you put the money up, you and Emilio, so that he could go to university.'

Felipe had earned some of it himself, Encarnita reminded Jorge; he had taken whatever job he could lay hands on during the vacations, whether it was running pedaloes on the beach or working on building sites. She had contributed the money that she'd put aside each week for her journey, without telling Felipe why she had been saving it. He had not wanted to take it, but she had insisted, and he had said that he would pay back every centimo. It had been obvious from his early years that he was highly intelligent. His teachers had declared him to be brilliant, one of the best students they'd ever had, and they'd said it would be a shame if, somehow, he could not be given the opportunity to continue his education. They had understood that that might not be easy; any grant he might qualify for would not be enough. Encarnita had conferred with Emilio, who had immediately agreed to help and had approved of Felipe's choice of law as a subject to study.

'It's always handy to have a lawyer in the family,' he'd said. 'You never know when you might need one.'

'Don't suppose Felipe will come back to Nerja, do you, when he finishes?' said Jorge, helping himself to another *churro*. 'Wouldn't be much here for him. He might decide to stay in Granada.'

'He might,' agreed Encarnita. 'It's a lovely city.' She had visited it twice, both times to see Felipe. He had taken her to see the gardens of the Alhambra, and she had been enchanted.

'I'm sure he'll look after you in your old age.'

'I don't expect anything from him,' she said, although she knew she would always be able to rely on Felipe for any kind of help she might need. She liked to think he was made in the same mould as his grandfather, an honourable man. She folded up the letter and put it in its envelope. There was nothing new in it – he always reassured her that he was eating well and studying hard – but she would read it again later. She read all her letters several times, savouring each tiny piece of news. And she would reply to all of them, writing slowly and carefully, taking more than one evening for each.

'No news of the other two, Juan and Antonio?'

Encarnita shook her head. There had been no news from

them for three years but she had stopped worrying. They were grown men, getting on for thirty years old, and had to look after their own lives. The last they'd heard they'd been in Badahoz and hoping to go to Madrid to look for work. The next two grandchildren in line were doing better. Roberto, who was nineteen, was working as a car mechanic, while sixteen-year-old Mario was still at school. His grandmother hoped that Emilio might put up the money for him to go to university to study engineering. Both boys lived at home with their mother and stepfather, and their half-sisters, Paulina and Angelina. The girls had been born following the death of Jaime in prison, which had allowed Concepción and Emilio to marry. The children had been his idea, not hers. Before their marriage Emilio, who was a devout churchgoer, had been against bringing illegitimate children into the world.

'That family is doing all right, anyway,' commented Jorge. 'No need to worry about them. Oh, I forgot! Thinking of families, Mrs Pilkington phoned this morning to say that Hubert is coming tomorrow with some friends.' He got up. 'I'd better get a move on and do a bit of work. The place is in good shape, though.'

'Certainly in good enough shape for Hubert,' said Encarnita dismissively. Hubert was the son of the Pilkingtons, their employers. The parents were very reasonable, courteous people who believed in treating both their house and their staff well. Hubert brought friends who drank too much and picked up girls on the beach and regarded Encarnita and Jorge as servants who should be at their beck and call at the snap of their fingers. Encarnita had been tempted more than once to speak to Mr and Mrs Pilkington about them but, remembering the behaviour of her grandsons Juan and Antonio when young, had decided not to. Hubert would grow out of it, she told Jorge, who had never been married or had children and grumbled about them more than she did. Hubert's visits were the only tiny drawback in their otherwise agreeable jobs.

'How many of them are coming?' asked Encarnita. 'And for how long?'

Jorge had no idea. He went out to finish watering the garden. Encarnita decided to sit on for a few minutes and read her letters. She opened Luisa's first.

Since Jaime had been sent to jail Luisa had come seldom to Nerja and Encarnita had gone back only once to Yegen after her visit there in 1955 so that their main contact was by letter. Luisa's contained news about mutual friends and acquaintances, nothing else. Her life did not change from day to day.

'Did you hear about Don Geraldo and his pneumonia?' she began.

She always began with Don Geraldo. Encarnita had heard about it on the television news. Gerald Brenan had a high profile in Andalucía now, as a well-respected Hispanist. There had been regular bulletins until he had recovered sufficiently to leave hospital in Málaga and return to his home in Alhaurin el Grande, where he lived with attendants. His young friend Lynda had married a Swedish painter and for a while they had all lived together, but in the previous year, Lynda, her husband and children had gone to live in the Alpujarra.

'I hear he is looking very old and frail,' Luisa went on. He was bound to be, since he must be nearly ninety years old and his health had never been good, although, considering that, he had fared well, better than his wife and daughter. Miranda had died of cancer in 1980, the same year as her mother, Juliana, whose closing years had been sad since for the last seven she had been blind. It was said that she had never got over the pain of losing her one and only daughter. In an earlier letter, Luisa had relayed a rumour she'd heard, which claimed that, some years before Juliana went blind, Don Geraldo had taken her to visit Miranda when she was on holiday in Granada with her French husband. There had been one condition: that Juliana would not reveal that she was Miranda's mother. Don Geraldo had introduced her as his former maid from when he'd lived in Yegen. Could it be true? Could Don Geraldo have been so heartless? Encarnita had been upset after reading Luisa's letter.

She then opened the letter with the British queen's head on the stamp. Morna wrote in Spanish, which was fortunate since she wrote immensely long letters. She liked to record her daily life in detail, almost like a diary. And at Christmas she sent a long typed screed which she called a 'Round Robin'. Through all of this Encarnita was gradually building up a picture of the city of Edinburgh and its activities. She knew about Marks and Spencers, whose underwear Morna favoured, and Jenners department store, unique in the land, the Portrait Gallery where you could get good wholefood lunches, and Henderson's vegetarian restaurant where you could sit for hours with friends, eat salad and drink wine and listen to people playing the guitar and the banjo. Not to mention the art galleries on something called The Mound, and the Botanic Garden which Morna frequented when she felt in need of peace and green grass under her feet. The views of the city from there were mind-blowing and never failed to inspire her. Encarnita kept all the letters; they were packed with information that would be helpful when she came to make her visit.

Morna wanted to know when she was going to come. 'You can't put it off for ever. Is that what you are trying to do?' Encarnita paused to consider. Was she? She had to admit that part of her was reluctant. She had her memory of Conal well preserved. Did she want it disturbed now, at this stage in her life? And yet. And yet... The feeling that fate would draw her there at some point had never left her. Otherwise, something would be left unfinished. 'I know you don't like the idea of leaving Arrieta but could your daughter not look after her for a couple of weeks?' Morna's letter went on. 'Or some other relation?'

There was no other relation. Besides, Encarnita would not go without Concepción, who, by making late additions to her family, had delayed their journey. It might be possible to persuade Emilio to look after the children for a few weeks once they were a little older.

'Don't leave it too long,' wrote Morna.

Encarnita read no more for now she must go and make up beds for Hubert and his guests. She had just taken the sheets out of the cupboard when she heard the electric gates whirring. Going out into the porch, she saw a car nosing its way into the drive, followed closely by another. Hubert knew the code so he would have opened the gates himself. The doors were flung open on either side and out tumbled Hubert and his friends, making a noise already.

'Jorge!' yelled Hubert. He was a tall, good-looking young man with thick blond hair that fell over his forehead and which he kept flicking back with a toss of his head. 'Where art thou, good Jorge?'

Jorge appeared from round the side of the garage with a rake in his hands. Small, and with a weathered, nut-brown face, he presented a strong contrast to the young Englishman.

'Bring in the luggage, there's a good chap!' Hubert spoke his own language. Jorge knew only a few basic words of English but he understood the order. The Pilkington seniors had a reasonable command of Spanish and believed in using it. Mrs Pilkington had told Encarnita that she thought it inexcusable the way the English refused even to try to speak other people's languages. She despaired of Hubert on that front and, perhaps, too, on others.

Encarnita met the guests in the hall.

'Ah, Encarnita, *buenos dias! Qué tal*?' Hubert was showing off now but that was the extent of his repertoire. He gave Encarnita a smile that was intended to charm and that she had seen charm many young women.

'*Muy bien*,' she answered. '*Y tú*?'

'We're absolutely starving, Encarnita. We got an early flight. Can you be a dear and run up some breakfast for us? The food on the plane was absolutely dire.'

'Not much food in house.'

'She speaks English,' said one of the girls who was wearing enormous sunglasses that covered half her face.

'What a wonderful name,' giggled another girl who was ready for the sun in a pair of bubble-gum pink shorts that barely covered her crotch. 'Encarnita! I love it.'

'They often have funny names, like Ascensión or Epifanía. A Spanish girl at our school was called Maria-Jésus. And, would you believe it, her brother was called Jésus-Maria!'

That caused them to fold over and emit shrieks of amusement.

Encarnita stared at them unblinkingly.

'How do you mean, there's not much food in the house, Encarnita?' Hubert's handsome face was drawn into a frown. 'You knew we were coming. Mother must have phoned?'

'Phone only this morning. Say you come tomorrow.'

'We had a change of plan. Can't you go and get something at the supermarket? There is some kind of supermarket here now, isn't there?"

'I ask Jorge to take me.'

'Get some bacon, can you?' He pulled a wad of notes from his trouser pocket and put some into her hand without counting them. 'And eggs! Nothing like a plate of bacon and egg after a hard night. We had a bit of a booze-up.'

Encarnita went to the supermarket on the back of Jorge's motor bike. She was used to riding pillion; Jorge usually gave her a lift home after work and sometimes he took her down the coast in the evening to have a drink at one of the *chiringuitos* – beachfront restaurants and bars – at La Herradura. They liked watching the sun go down over the bay until the pink and orange streaks would gradually bleed from the water leaving it the colour of milk. It was a very calming thing to see.

They kept company quite often, the two of them, and Jorge had asked her to marry him, but she had said that she could not leave Arrieta. She preferred, anyway, to keep their friendship as it was.

They did their shopping and on their return Encarnita set about frying bacon and eggs. The girls sat around the kitchen table smoking and drinking coffee, saying they did-n't normally eat breakfast but they would today. The smell of the bacon was getting to them, as it was to the cook her-self. She would put aside a couple of rashers for a sandwich for Jorge and herself later. The boys were in the pool, splashing about. Their voices carried. In some ways, thought Encarnita, as she cracked an egg against the side of the pan and dropped it in, it was quite nice to have young life about the house. That's what houses were for, after all. If only they didn't leave such a mess behind them!

Encarnita and Jorge had a busier day than usual so did not get away until eight o'clock. It was not part of Encarnita's duties to cook an evening meal for Hubert, a point that had been established, by her, on a previous visit. He was going out to a restaurant with his friends and after-wards they would go drinking in bars. She knew that when she came in in the morning she would find them snoring in their beds and the house upside down with odd pieces of clothing and shoes strewn about and wet towels on the floors of all three bathrooms.

'Shall we go for a drink?' asked Jorge. 'We need it today.'

'A quick one. Arrieta will be waiting for me.' Arrieta would not fuss; she accepted that Encarnita often finished work at different times and on occasions had a drink with Jorge.

They went to a bar near the Balcón and had a brandy. They talked about the young English people.

'I expect young Spanish ones with money are no better,' said Encarnita.

'I hope Concepción's girls don't grow up with any fancy ideas.'

'They've got them already. They think money grows on trees. Put your hand out of the window and pick it. Emilio is talking about sending them to an International School. As if the local one isn't good enough for them!'

Encarnita did not stay long. She kissed Jorge on both cheeks and left him to sit on in the bar. Some of his friends would come in later.

She felt tired as she turned into her street. She was getting on in years so it was not surprising that she should be after a day's work. Felipe was always telling her that it was time she retired. As she approached the door she heard children's voices. They sounded extremely like Paulina's and Angelina's, querulous and complaining. Their grandmother hesitated a moment, tempted to turn and go back to rejoin Jorge.

Bracing herself, she opened the door and went in. All the members of Concepción's family were gathered, except for Emilio.

'I didn't know you were coming. Is there anything wrong?'

'Anything wrong?' Concepción sprang up from the sofa. She was wearing her honey-coloured leather trousers and jacket and gold, high-heeled shoes. Encarnita noticed that the girls were dressed in their Sunday best, in puffed-out dresses with two layers of stiff white underskirts below, white tights and buckled, black patent leather shoes. They were each clutching a life-size doll decked out in similar clothes to their own. The boys wore their normal jeans and were slumped on the floor.

'What's happened?'

'We've been locked out of the house!' Concepción almost choked on the words.

'By Emilio?'

'No, the *Guardia Civil.*'

Encarnita thought she had better sit down. She advised her daughter to do the same and tell her, taking her time, what was going on.

'They want Emilio for drug-running,' said Roberto, before his mother could speak.

'It's all a terrible mistake,' she cried.

'But is it true that the *Guardia* want him?' asked Encarnita.

'Seems he's been running drugs up and down the coast in his trucks,' Roberto went on. 'The hard stuff. Well, according to the two guards that came to the house. They've impounded everything belonging to him. The business, the lot.'

'*And* our house.' Concepción dried her eyes. 'They let us leave with only what we were standing up in.' She admitted that she had managed to slip into the bedroom and change her clothes – she had been wearing jeans when the guards arrived – and to cram some of her jewellery down the front of her jacket. 'They've sealed the whole place up. They wouldn't even let me take my car. It's *my* car, I told them.'

'But it was registered in Emilio's name,' said Roberto.

'Everything is,' said Concepción. 'We had to walk all the way to Frigiliana and get a taxi. You know what the road's like. I think I've sprained my ankle.'

'You shouldn't have worn those shoes,' said Roberto. 'I told you not to.'

'Did you think I was going to leave them behind? They cost a fortune. Emilio bought them for me last time we were in Madrid.' Concepción began to cry again, and so, too, did Angelina. Arrieta invited the child to come and sit on her knee but she did not want to.

'And where's Emilio now?' asked Encarnita.

'He's taken off,' said Roberto. 'Can't really blame him. If he'd hung about they'd have got him.'

'I can't believe Emilio would do a bad thing like that,' said Arrieta. 'Deal in drugs.'

Encarnita could, though.

'So he just went off without a word?' asked Arrieta.

Concepción blew her nose. 'Actually, he left me a note.'

'You never said!' said Mario.

'I didn't want to let the guards see it.' Concepción took a piece of paper from her pocket and read out the message.

'Sorry, *cariña*. I'll send for you and the girls when I can.' She folded it. 'I knew he wouldn't run out on me if he didn't have to.'

'But, Mama, would you want to go with a drug-runner?' asked Mario.

'He's still Emilio, isn't he? And he's been good to you, hasn't he? I don't want to hear a word against him.'

'Have you any idea where he might have gone?' asked Encarnita.

Concepción shrugged, then said quietly, glancing round to make sure the door was closed, 'Could be Uruguay.'

'Uruguay? What makes you think that?'

'He's been talking about it recently. He's got a friend there.'

'Probably another drug-runner,' put in Mario.

'Oh, shut up, Mario!' said his mother.

'In the meantime,' Encarnita began, and said no more. What was the point? For the last five years she and Arrieta had been able to live in peace and quiet, with sufficient space to breathe, but that she could see was about to come to an end.

'I'm sorry, Mama,' said Concepción. 'I hate doing this to you but there's nowhere else we could go. We've got no money. It won't be for long, I promise you. Emilio will send for us as soon as he gets settled. You know what he's like, he gets on with things.'

The trouble with her daughter, thought Encarnita, was that she didn't think things through to the end of the line. *If* Emilio did manage to send for them and she was to pack up and take off with the girls, the *Guardia Civil* would be on their tail, to see where they were heading.

'You don't think he will send for us, do you?' said Concepción, aggression creeping into her voice.

'I'm sure he means to.'

'But circumstances may not permit it?' suggested Mario.

'Shut up, Mario!' snapped his mother again. 'You're too smart at times!'

'Did he leave any money behind?' asked Encarnita.

'None that we could get our hands on. But we'll manage somehow. Roberto's working, thank God for that, at least.'

'I don't earn enough to keep everybody!' he objected.

Concepción turned back to her mother. Her voice softened, becoming almost wheedling. 'You shouldn't have to give money to Felipe, Mama. Not at his age. He's been at university long enough. He must be able to get a decent job with what he's done already.'

'He's going to finish,' declared Encarnita.

'He won't want to take your money once he knows how things are here.'

'Don't worry, I'll make him take it! There's only one thing for it, Concepción, and you know it!'

'All right, all right, I'm going to get a job, so don't start going on at me! But I don't see how I can earn enough to support myself and the girls. They're used to better things.'

'They'll just have to get unused to them then, won't they?'

'Then there's Mario.' Concepción looked at him. 'Mario, you might have —'

Encarnita cut across her. 'No, he won't. He's going to stay on at school. And then we'll see. He deserves his chances, too.'

'You're terribly bossy,' grumbled Concepción.

'Somebody's got to be in this family or we'd all starve. You'd better start looking for a job tomorrow. There's always cleaning to be had.'

'I'm sure I can get something better than that!'

'I want to go home,' wailed Angelina.

Encarnita and Concepción were spending the day in Málaga, having come in on an early morning bus. They had had lunch on a café terrace overlooking the Plaza de la Constitución with Angelina, who was living in the city with her interior-designer boyfriend. She had a job in the cosmetic department of El Corte Ingles, which she enjoyed. She was a cheerful girl and had the air of being happy with life. Encarnita thought she had the temperament of her father, Emilio.

After their lunch Concepción had done some shopping and she was now carrying several carrier bags in each hand and complaining about their weight, especially since she was having to carry them all the way along the Paseo del Parque. Her mother was making no comment. Her only purchase had been two bars of almond and camomile soap. Good soap gave her pleasure, like good shoes.

'I don't know what you want to go to an old cemetery for,' grumbled Concepción. 'It's not as if you're going to *see* him. It's a bit late for that. Walking about among the dead gives me goose flesh.'

'British cemeteries are different from ours. Morna told me.'

'Morna tells you everything.' Concepcion did not get on too well with her. The Scotswoman disapproved of her rather flashy clothes and although she did not ever make a remark about them, it was obvious. Morna herself dressed soberly, favouring grey flannel skirts and walking boots in cool weather and loose khaki shorts in the heat. They knew that not all Scottish women dressed like her; the tourists frequenting Nerja were evidence of that.

'Not everything,' Encarnita rejoined. 'But she did tell me that they don't put their bodies into niches. They either burn them or bury them in the ground, in coffins, in proper graves, and they plant trees around them.'

They passed the bullring and, shortly afterwards, on the other side of the road, they came to the English Cemetery. The high, black wrought-iron gate was locked. There would be no possibility of climbing over it.

Encarnita went up to it and rattled the bars and peered through but there was no one around to call out to for help. Nothing was to be seen but a drive that rose upward and vanished into trees. A notice informed them that this was the location of the English church was but that was not visible, either.

'You should have known it might be closed,' said Concepción, who was half-annoyed and half-pleased. She put down her bags and lit a cigarette.

'Maybe there's another way in.' Encarnita led the way round the corner. An alley climbed up the side of the cemetery. Feral cats, who had been feeding out of little aluminium trays put down for them by cat-feeders, scampered off as the women mounted the steps. The lane stank of cat pee and rotting food.

Halfway up, Encarnita stopped and put her face to the railings. Here, it was possible to see into the cemetery.

'It's a ruin,' she wailed.

Concepción joined her. 'Could do with a clean up,' she agreed.

Headstones inclined, half-toppled over and broken, weeds grew between the graves.

'Maybe there are no relatives left to look after it,' said Concepción. 'It's not used any more, is it?'

'It's a disgrace. To think of a man like Don Geraldo lying in there! And his wife Doña Gamel. She was a lovely lady. They deserve better.'

'They don't know though, do they? It won't be bothering them. After all, he let them have his body for medical research, didn't he? So he can't have cared what they did to him.'

Gerald Brenan, having died in 1988 at the age of ninety-two, had been interred here only the previous year.

Encarnita sighed, her indignation giving way to sadness. 'Life goes so fast. And then look what happens to us.'

It was at that moment, as she gazed into the neglected garden where lay the remains of the British dead from times past, amongst them her old friend, who had taught her many things, who had given her ideas to keep her mind alive, that Encarnita finally made her mind. 'Concepción, we are going to Scotland.'

'Now look, Mama, do you think that's a good idea? After so many years. Sixty, isn't it, since you've seen him?'

'Sixty-two, getting on for sixty-three. It was the summer of 1939.'

'It's like a lifetime away. It *is* a lifetime. What if he is still alive and I meet him what am I going to say to him? *Hola*, Papa! Here I am and I'm *sixty-two* years old. I can't believe it! Sixty-two! He'll be a stranger. To you, too.'

'I would know him.'

'He might not know you.'

Encarnita shrugged.

'He might not be pleased to see us.'

'He might not.'

'He might be dead.'

'He might. But I want to find out what happened to him. I don't even know if he got back to Scotland. The time has come for our journey, Concepción, and I have the money for the flights in the bank.'

'I'd rather go to Lanzarote.'

Concepción had gone a couple of times with a man who was no longer in her life, to her mother's relief. He was a drifter, in and out of work, and when he was out he had sponged on Concepción. Since Emilio's departure she had been involved with various men, most of them unreliable. She had heard only once from Emilio, two years after his departure. A postcard had come from Bolivia saying, 'Hope you and the children are OK. Will send for you when I have the money.' It was signed only with 'E' and there was no return address. Encarnita had said straightaway that he wouldn't get the money together so Concepción should not live in hopes of it. Besides, would she want to go to Bolivia? It was one of the poorest and most primitive countries in South America. As far as they were aware, Emilio had not been tracked down by the *Guardia Civil*, who had ceased calling on them once he'd been gone for a few months.

'We're going to Edinburgh,' declared Encarnita. 'We're free now that we're both retired.' She had given up work seven years ago, when she was seventy-five, at Felipe's insistence. Concepción had retired only recently and had done so reluctantly, but her boss had wanted to put in a younger woman to manage his leather goods shop. Concepción's pride had been wounded and her mother thought that was why she had embarked on this hectic shopping spree, blowing all of her last week's wages. 'There's nothing to stop us,' Encarnita went on. 'The family are all settled.'

'I don't know about Paulina. She and Carlos aren't getting on too well.' Carlos was a fisherman and Paulina had a job on a supermarket check-out. They lived in Nerja with their two children in a rented apartment on the N-340. 'Paulina was telling me last night. She says he's drinking too much. And he's not bringing in much money. Catches are low.'

All the more reason to go soon, thought Encarnita. Paulina would have to get on and sort out her own mess.

Felipe was doing well. He had become a partner in a firm of lawyers in Granada and had married the daughter of the senior partner, a beautiful young woman called Elena, who was herself a doctor, a gynaecologist. Encarnita and Concepción were somewhat in awe of her and although she was very nice to them and invited them up for a week-end every now and then they were unable to feel totally at ease in her company. Felipe and Elena had a splendid house, with views over to the Alhambra, and two pretty children, a boy and a girl, both with hair the colour of their father's, and of their grandmother's, when she was young. She dyed hers blond now, to cover the invading strands of grey.

Felipe never forgot them. He drove down to Nerja in his Mercedes once or twice a month, sometimes bringing the children, but seldom Elena, whose life, they realised, was very busy. He gave them regular amounts of money, maintaining that he was only returning what they had given to him; and the previous year he had paid for them to have a holiday in Morocco in a four-star hotel. They'd crossed by boat from Algeciras, Encarnita preferring that option to flying. She was prepared, however, to fly in order to get to Scotland. Having studied a map of Europe she had realised how long and difficult would be the journey by train and boat.

'I shall write to Morna tonight.' She had not written for a while and owed her Scottish friend a letter.

Her other correspondent, Luisa, did not write often nowadays and when she did it would be not be much more than a sentence or two in a shaky hand. She had high blood pressure and arthritis as well as a few other more minor ailments, which meant that she kept close to home. A visit into Yegen, even, had come to be an expedition. Too many hills, she said. Encarnita had visited her a couple of years ago but had found the days long, closeted with her old friend, who could speak of nothing but her grandchildren and their failings. Especially their failings. Encarnita had gone for two or three long walks into the *campo* by herself. On her return Luisa, a little piqued, had told her she was lucky to be so strong and in such good health. But in spite of everything, they had parted fondly from each other.

Encarnita composed the letter to Morna in her head on the journey back to Nerja. *We are coming, at last we are coming...*

They disembarked at the bus station, which did not, in fact, exist, even though it was so-called; it was merely a few bus stances on the N-340.

Paulina's apartment was close by.

'I think I'll pop up and see how she's doing,' said

Concepción.

'That could be a mistake,' said Encarnita.

'You couldn't take a couple of bags for me, could you?'

'I suppose so. As long as they're not too heavy.'

With a bag in either hand, Encarnita crossed the road, avoiding being mown down by a motor cycle ridden by a man with his small daughter on the back and a dog perched on the handlebars, and cut down Calle Granada to the Balcón. It was busy, as usual, with tourists, but she scarcely registered them. Her mind was full of their journey.

As soon as she went into the house she took her pale blue, lined writing pad from the drawer and sat down to compose her letter. She did not say very much, only that they were coming and she hoped it would still be all right for them to stay. Morna had said many times that she would love to have them and show them her city. Encarnita put the letter into its matching envelope but did not close it. In the morning she would go to a travel agency and book their flights and then add a note giving Morna the date and time of their arrival.

She had just put the pad and remaining envelopes back in the drawer when she heard them arriving, Concepción, Paulina, and Paulina's children.

'Mama, Paulina's been having a terrible time! Look at her eye! Carlos hit her last night.' One of the children began to cry.

Encarnita was concerned for her granddaughter. 'You should make a complaint to the police the next time he does it.' The Spanish courts had been cracking down on domestic violence after years of more or less ignoring it.

'There won't be a next time,' said Concepción. 'Mama, they've got to stay here with us. We can't put them out.'

They had their luggage with them. It consisted of much more than what Concepción's brood had brought with them when they'd moved in fifteen years ago. Paulina might always be short of money but the children had more bagfuls of toys than they could carry. Dolls, dolls' clothes and other accessories, teddy bears, furry squirrels, dogs, cats and koala bears, toy cars, tractors and aeroplanes, jigsaw puzzles, colouring books, and even story books, the latter bought by their grandmother. The children let them spill out all over the floor.

'I'm going out,' announced Encarnita, lifting her helmet from the shelf and stepping over the display of goods littering the floor. She pulled the door shut behind her and paused to take a breath of air. It was a fine evening to be out, mild, with no wind.

She found Jorge in the little bar he frequented. 'Let's go down to La Herradura,' she said. 'Let's go and have something to eat and drink. I'll pay.'

They got a seat outside a *chiringuito* where they had an uninterrupted view of the sea and the setting sun. The sea was dead calm, with scarcely a ripple to disturb it. A little way out, a man was fishing from a rowboat; his wife was rowing.

Encarnita sipped her brandy and told Jorge her plans. He did not show much enthusiasm.

'What's the point in going to see this man after all those years?'

'I'd always planned to.'

'I know.' He shifted restlessly on his seat. 'How are you going to find him?'

'It's not a big country, Scotland.'

'Even so.'

'Morna will help me. She knows how to do things. She's been a social worker.'

Jorge was quiet. He gazed out to sea.

Encarnita put a hand on his arm. 'I'm not going for ever, you know.'

'How long are you going for?'

'I don't know.'

'But you'll have to know before you buy your ticket.'

'I thought I'd just buy singles. Well, we've no idea how long it'll take to find him.'

'This is a mad idea, Encarnita, if ever I heard one.' He sighed. 'But when your mind's made up you never change it, do you?'

'Let's have another brandy!' Encarnita signalled to the waiter. 'Don't let's be sad, not tonight.'

They had a good evening and Jorge deposited her, replete with brandy, grilled sole and *patatas fritas,* at the end of her street. The house was quiet when she opened the door. The children were asleep, Concepción was watching television – bought by Felipe – and Paulina had gone out.

'Mama, I don't know how I can leave her.'

'Of course you can! She's perfectly capable of looking after the children on her own. In the morning I go to the travel agent.'

Encarnita was there when the shop opened. 'I want to go to Edinburgh,' she informed the young man, who looked as if he had just risen from his bed. 'Two tickets, one way only.'

'When do you want to go?' He couldn't stop yawning. He had enlarged tonsils.

'As soon as possible.'

'I'll have a look.'

She sat patiently while he fiddled with his machine. Eventually he looked up at her and asked, 'What about Saturday? Couple of seats left.'

Encarnita pondered. Today was Wednesday. Three days to get ready; that should be enough. As far as she was concerned, she could be ready to go tonight. Not Concepción, however. 'Saturday will be fine,' she said.

'You have an up-to-date passport?'

She nodded. She had acquired one when going to Morocco.

'Shall I just go ahead?' asked the young man.

Again, she nodded. He took all her details, and Concepción's, and she paid with a cheque, amazed that it was all proving so easy. He told her to come back and collect the tickets on Friday morning and gave her a pen with the agency's name printed on it as a gift for booking with them.

'Don't forget you'll need to change your money into sterling!' he called after her as she made for the door.

'Of course not!' she retorted though, in fact, it had not occurred to her. Walking back down the street she felt slightly unsteady and had to stop for a moment to get her breath back before going into the bank. The teller told her the rate of exchange, which meant nothing to her, she signed a cheque, and he slid a bundle of notes bearing the head of the queen of England over to her. No, not just the queen of England, she told herself. Great Britain. She must not make that mistake in Scotland. She remembered Conal telling her how it annoyed the Scots. She was beginning to remember more of the things he had said to her. It was as if a time slip was happening inside her head.

She found Jorge in the pensioners' recreation club at the end of Calle Diputación. Sometimes they came evenings when there was dancing and they had a few turns on the floor together. Jorge was not much of a dancer but she managed to steer him around. The villagers in Yegen had loved dances, especially those that Don Geraldo had held in his house. Encarnita often wished she had learned to dance *flamenco*; the music always stirred her. When Morna came she took her to the Cultural Centre in Calle Granada to performances of genuine *flamenco* song and dance, which were quite different from those put on in hotels. Morna was scornful of those; she called them chocolate box-*flamenco*. Morna was much in her mind also this morning.

Jorge was drinking coffee and reading the paper. Encarnita collapsed into a chair beside him.

'I've done it! We go on Saturday.'

'Saturday! That's quick, isn't it?'

That was also Concepción's reaction when she heard. 'How am I to get ready in time? I must go to the hairdresser's, I need my roots done. I can't go like this! And what about my clothes?'

'You've got all those new ones you bought in Málaga.'

'They wouldn't be enough.'

'Better start washing and ironing, then.'

At nine o'clock in the evening, when Felipe should be home from work, Encarnita went out to a phone booth and rang him. Elena answered. Yes, Felipe was home, just this very minute. He'd had a hard day at the office and was having a small whisky, but she'd call him. First, though, how was Encarnita? Elena hoped there was nothing wrong?

'No, nothing,' said Encarnita, unwilling to give the news first to Elena. 'We're all fine.'

'I'm pleased to hear that. You must come up for a visit soon with Concepción. You've not been to see us for ages. Would you like us to fix a date now? Our diary tends to get filled up well ahead.'

'We're going away for a while. We don't know when we'll be back.'

'Oh, I see.' Elena waited to find out if she was to be enlightened further, but when she realised that she was not, she said, 'Hang on a minute, I'll fetch Felipe.'

Felipe said, 'Elena says you're going away somewhere. Where to?'

'Scotland.'

'Good for you! What can I do to help?'

It was arranged that he would come down to Nerja early on Saturday morning, bringing two suitcases equipped with wheels, and then he would drive them to Málaga airport.

'*Hasta luego*!' Encarnita put down the receiver.

In the street, she bumped into Paulina's Carlos, who was looking gloomy but sober.

'I didn't mean to hit her,' he said. 'But she was going on and on at me about not bringing in enough money – as if it's my fault that the fish are low! – and I'd had a few *marcs* and I lost my temper. I want her and the kids back.'

'I've a feeling she'd like to go back. She and her mother are at each other's throats. But she's too proud to do it without being asked. Why don't you go round and say you're sorry? And maybe stop drinking so much?'

'I'll try, Encarnita, really I will.'

'Try hard,' she said to his retreating back.

To give him time to make his plea she dropped in on Jorge in the bar. He, too, was looking gloomy.

'You'd think I was going to my doom,' said Encarnita cheerfully.

'I can't help worrying about the two of you going off to a strange city like that.'

'Morna will look after us.'

Jorge asked if he could go with them to the airport. 'There'll be a spare seat in Felipe's car, won't there?'

'There should be, unless he brings the children.'

Felipe arrived on his own. Elena was taking the children to visit her parents. They had been invited to lunch with some very old friends of the family who were visiting from Madrid. No doubt Felipe had been expected also. Encarnita wondered if Elena would tell her parents that her husband was taking his grandmother to the airport so that she could go in search of an old lover, his own grandfather.

The women packed the suitcases Felipe had brought, Concepción taking up part of the space in her mother's. Even then, she had to leave some items out and sit on the case to close it.

'What marvellous things,' said Encarnita, pushing her case too and fro and remembering how she'd carried all her possessions on her back from Yegen to Almuñecar. If Pilar were to return to this world now she would not recognise her own country.

Felipe put their suitcases in the boot and they set off for the airport, Concepción riding in front, and Encarnita behind with Jorge. The two in the front chatted, the two in the back said little. The car purred smoothly along the motorway and in less than an hour they were approaching the airport. Jorge reached for Encarnita's hand. She was beginning to feel a little sick in her stomach. What *was* she doing? They were in a lane for airport departures now and

Felipe was looking for a suitable space to park.

The two men escorted the travellers into the airport building, waited with them until they had stood in a long queue and checked in and then walked them to the point where their paths must part.

'*Buen viaje!*' said Felipe. '*Y buena suerte!*' Good journey. Good luck.

'*Buen viaje!*' echoed Jorge.

The women embraced the men.

'Let's go!' said Encarnita, unable to stand another minute of this torture. If she had to, she might turn back.

She took Concepción's arm and they passed through to the area where only *bona fide* travellers were permitted to enter.

At last, Encarnita's journey had begun.

THE LAST STAGE: EDINBURGH

'Welcome to Edinburgh,' said the captain. 'We hope you have enjoyed your flight with us today and we look forward to welcoming you on board another time. The temperature in Edinburgh is currently ten degrees.'

Encarnita let out her breath in a long sigh. She felt as if she had been holding it ever since they had taken off from Málaga. That had been the worst part. When she had peered out of the small window to see the world lying tilted below she had wanted to be released. It had seemed unnatural, to be hanging up there in the sky, higher than the birds who had always been intended to fly. Relax, Concepción had told her. She had tried to and once the plane had straightened itself out she had found the panorama of mountain tops astounding. They had looked so rugged and unconquerable that they were awe-inspiring. She had only ever seen them from below, where – strangely, perhaps – they had seemed more approachable. The roads, the few that there were, were like thin lines cutting through them and the *pueblos* clinging to their sides, splashes of white. As for man, he was too small to be visible from such a height.

Once they had landed, Concepción took charge. Their normal roles reversed, with Concepción knowing so much more than her mother about airports, from her travels with Emilio. She wasted no time in finding them a trolley and expertly hauled their suitcases off the carousel while Encarnita stood by feeling bewildered. It was all too hectic for her.

'Let's go!' said Concepción, setting off as if she were running a race, steering their trolley in front of her like a battering ram. Encarnita struggled to keep up.

When they came into the main area of the airport they slowed and looked about, studying the clusters of people awaiting new arrivals. Some were holding placards aloft and although they did not expect to find their name they scrutinised them, nevertheless. There was no sign either of their name or of Morna, not as far as they could see, but, then, the airport was crowded.

'She's often late,' said Encarnita, peering into the crowd.

Concepción leaned on the handles of the trolley, straightening herself up to sigh when Encarnita announced that she needed to go to the toilet. She had refused to go on the plane, being reluctant to get up once she had been seated and strapped in. Also, a neighbour had told her about a woman who had got sucked on to a toilet seat in a plane and was stuck there until they landed.

'All right, Mama, you go and I'll stay with the luggage.'

It was fortunate that toilets had universal symbols to guide passengers for Encarnita did not feel confident enough at the moment to try out her use of English. She found one easily. It was peaceful in here. She was tempted to linger. She rinsed her hands and face and combed her hair and allowed herself a brief glance in the mirror, not much liking what she saw. Lines left by the passage of eighty-two years. He would not know her. She shrugged. What was done was done. She went out to rejoin her daughter.

'You took your time!' said Concepción. 'There's still no sign of her.' The crowd had thinned around the arrival area. 'When did you write the letter to her?'

'I posted it on Wednesday.' Encarnita faltered. Three days ago. Not long for a letter to come all the way from the south of Spain to Scotland. Not long enough, perhaps.

'She won't have got it yet!'

'No, possibly not.'

'Possibly not? So what are we doing standing here waiting for somebody who doesn't even know we're here? I always said this journey of yours was a stupid idea.'

'Calm down, Concepción! People are looking at you.'

'They won't know what I'm saying.'

'How do you know? Lots of people in Edinburgh might speak Spanish. Besides, you're shouting.'

A new wave of arrivals was already coming flooding in,

threatening to swamp them. They seemed to be standing in the middle of a traffic lane. They moved to the side.

'Now what?' demanded Concepción.

'I've got Morna's address here.' Encarnita dug in her bag until she found the piece of paper. 'St Stephen Street,' she read out. 'Morna says it's an interesting street. It's got lots of bars and hairdressers and second-hand shops, things like that. Morna said you might find some nice dresses at a reasonable price.'

'Not second-hand!'

'Morna buys second-hand.'

'Morna! She looks as if she's come out of a ragbag.'

'She says the world needs to recycle.'

'She says! Where is she now?'

'How would I know? We'll just have to find her street ourselves.'

'Just!' Grumbling, as was her habit, Concepción said she supposed they could ask at Information. The woman behind the counter did not speak Spanish, which surprised them, but Encarnita was able to muster enough English to explain their dilemma. The address was in central Edinburgh, the woman told them, and she recommended that they take either a taxi or a bus. She pointed in the direction in which they should go.

Encarnita thought a taxi would be expensive since, according to Morna, everything was much dearer in Edinburgh than in Nerja. 'We have to watch our money.'

'If we took the bus what would we do after that? I'm not going to stand here arguing. We're taking a taxi! Or else I'm getting on the next plane back to Málaga.' Concepción looked thoughtful.

'Let's find a taxi,' said her mother hurriedly.

A short wait in a queue, and then they were bowling along the road from the airport into the city centre. Rain lashed the taxi's windows and wind buffeted its sides.

'It doesn't always do this,' said the driver. 'The weather was brilliant until yesterday.'

As they neared the city centre the traffic thickened and their progress was reduced to a crawl. Rush hour, said the driver, yawning. Every light turned to red as they approached. They lurched from one to the other, with stops and starts. Encarnita watched the lit-up figures in the fare box mounting. Entering Princes Street they caught a brief glimpse of Edinburgh's famous castle sitting high up on its rock before the driver turned off. They speeded up a little now and rattled over cobbles, past imposing squares and dripping green gardens guarded by black, wrought-iron railings until, finally, they entered a small narrow grey street. It was choked with cars, reminding them of the streets in Nerja. That was the only similarity between the two towns that Encarnita could see.

'Well, this is it, ladies,' announced the driver cheerfully, managing to find a space to squeeze into at the kerb.

They could not decide if the fare was high or low without translating it into *euros* and they had too many other things to concern them. They gazed around. The street was grey, the pavement was grey, the buildings were grey, and so was the sky.

'It will look better when the sun comes out,' said Encarnita.

'It would look better with some whitewash.'

When they found Morna's number Encarnita was greatly relieved. Standing in the airport she had begun to wonder if her Scottish friend existed. There was her name beside one of the bells at the side of the door. Encarnita put her thumb squarely on it and held her head close to the speaking grill. Nothing happened. She pressed again, this time holding it down for a few seconds.

'It seems she's not in,' remarked Concepción, sounding almost pleased, so her mother thought. 'Meanwhile, we're getting wet standing here.'

Encarnita tried twice more before conceding that her daughter must be right, on both counts. Concepción suggested they try one of the other names. They studied them and Encarnita chose *crazyclean.com*.

'What kind of a name is that?' asked Concepción.

A voice answered and Encarnita, putting her mouth to the grill, said, 'Morna's friends. Can we speak?'

'Come up.'

The door buzzed, ready to be opened, and they went in, bumping their suitcases up the three dark flights of stairs to *crazyclean.com*, pausing, on the way, at the door of Morna's flat on the second landing to try the bell there, even though they realised that there would probably be no answer. There was not. They squinted through the letter box and looked into darkness.

A young woman with a ring through each nostril was waiting for them on the top landing.

'We look for Morna,' said Encarnita, puffing from the climb.

'Morna! She's gone to visit her cousin in Canada.'

'Canada,' echoed the two visitors.

The young woman, whose name was Flick, brought them into her flat, from where she ran her cleaning business. Hence the name on her bell, she explained to them and, as regards the business, she was it. 'I clean like crazy! It's good money. Women are desperate in the inner city. They'll pay anything.' She talked in a high, fast voice so that her visitors were not always able to follow, although they were listening hard. She said she had thought of calling the business *squeakyclean* but, in the end, she had gone for crazy.

'What do you think?' she asked.

'Squeaky?' Encarnita frowned. 'Noise of mouse?'

'No, no.' Flick laughed. Her laugh was also high-pitched. 'Hair.' She rubbed a few strands of her own together.

Encarnita was even more mystified. 'You work alone?' she asked. She had not been sure if that was what Flick had meant when she had said she was it. It was all very well knowing some English words and phrases but understanding everything that was being said was another matter. How easy it would be to misunderstand.

Flick said that she had employed other women, at times, but they had always let her down in the end, either by not turning up or messing up the job, breaking valuables and so forth. Everyone who ran cleaning businesses found the same thing. Encarnita, who had been involved in it for many years herself, was interested, though the situation was different in Nerja, where women were glad of the work.

Flick was kind, however. She invited them to take off their wet coats and sit on her furry black and white sofa striped like a zebra and she made them coffee and listened sympathetically to their story. Encarnita did not tell the whole story, only that they had intended to come to Edinburgh for a long time to stay with their friend Morna and that they had bought tickets on the spur of the moment and, well, here they were.

'So here you are!' said Flick brightly, and what a pity Morna was not! Flick was sorry that she couldn't invite them to stay with her but the flat, as they could see, was small and she shared it with her partner, who would be home shortly. She glanced at her watch. The best thing would be for them to go to a B&B. Bed and breakfast, she explained. Good value for money, unlike the hotels. She knew of one only ten minutes' walk away that she could recommend.

Encarnita said that the bed would be enough since they did not eat much breakfast, but Flick explained that the two went together. A good Scottish breakfast would set them up for the day. Encarnita knew about those from her association with her former employers, the Pilkingtons. They still kept in touch with her; they sent a card at Christmas and when they came out to Spain they called to see how she was doing and bring her a present, chocolates or special biscuits from an expensive shop in London. Concepción had seen Harrods mentioned in a magazine. Even Hubert came bearing gifts. He was a successful stockbroker, married, with two children.

Flick scribbled the B&B address on a slip of paper, along

with the name of the landlady, a Mrs Mack, and drew a few squiggly lines for a map, while rattling off a list of instructions which they could not follow. After they had finished their coffee they thanked her and set out. Concepción did not speak as they dragged their suitcases through the wet streets, humping them over kerbs and puddled gutters. They got lost only twice and each time Encarnita managed to ask a woman on the street, by showing the piece of paper.

The B&B proved to be chilly. The heating did not come on until after six o'clock, Mrs Mack informed them. Guests did not normally come back before then. There was a kettle on the dresser and they were welcome to make themselves a cup of tea, which they did as soon as they had divested themselves of their wet outer layers and kicked off their shoes.

'Mama, this is crazy,' said Concepción, as they sat on the edge of the bed sipping their tea and contemplating the colourless room. One light bulb glowed weakly above their heads. Beyond the net-curtained window daylight was waning. 'It's past six o'clock,' Concepción went on, putting her hand on the radiator. 'You can barely feel it.'

'Sometimes life is crazy,' agreed Encarnita, staring into her cup of tea. 'Other times, sad. Or it can be both.' She was thinking of her Uncle Rinaldo and how he had fought to save his country from the forces of General Franco and given his life. In vain, most people would say. About that, she had never been able to decide. They hadn't managed to liberate themselves from Franco until he died. Since then, Spain had flourished. 'We can't give up now, Concepción.'

Her daughter sighed. Above the bed was a large sign saying NO SMOKING. She was desperate for a cigarette. She was about to indulge in a grumble about it when she looked up and caught her mother's eye. They both laughed. After that, they felt better.

Arm-in-arm, they set forth to look for somewhere to eat, ending up in an Italian restaurant where the waiter wielded an enormously long pepper mill and the prices astounded them. They each had a pizza and a glass of red wine.

'At this rate,' said Encarnita, gazing at the figure at the bottom of the bill, 'we cannot last long.'

For once, her daughter did not argue. She was in a happier frame of mind now that she had been able to smoke. To her mother's annoyance, she had insisted on sitting in the smoking area.

In the breakfast room of the B&B there was another large NO SMOKING sign propped on the mantelpiece. Those signs must be big business here, commented Concepción. They were much less frequently to be seen in Andalucía.

The women sat down to cornflakes, bacon, sausage, black pudding, fried tomatoes, mushrooms and egg, plus toast with marmalade, all of which they consumed, along with several cups of strong tea. They left not a scrap of anything edible on the table.

'You have good appetites,' observed Mrs Mack, collecting the empty plates. She had told them that she was renowned for her breakfasts. She'd been mentioned in a guide book. 'You'll be going out for the day?'

'Can you tell us please the street of writer man Robert Louis Stevenson?' asked Encarnita.

'You know about him?' The landlady showed her surprise.

'I have his book.'

'He wrote more than one, you know!' The woman's tone was nippy. Softening a little, she offered to show them where it was on the map. 'No. 17 Heriot Row. It's not far, just ten minutes up the street, in the New Town. The *Georgian* New Town,' she added, emphasising the word Georgian. Encarnita knew that Jorge's name meant George in English and was puzzled. There was much to learn when travelling in a strange country. Another thing she could not understand was why Mrs Mack was called a landlady. She owned no land, not even a yard.

Mrs Mack lent them the map, asking them to be careful not to fold it the wrong ways to avoid extra creases.

Concepción lit a cigarette as soon as they turned the corner. Encarnita kept her distance. As the landlady had promised, ten minutes walk uphill took them to Heriot Row.

'Doesn't look very new to me,' commented Concepción.

It was a fine, wide street with a garden on one side, edged with the kind of black wrought-iron railings they had noted on their taxi ride. The terraced houses had an unassailable look. They were grand and obviously expensive. The day was bright and crisp with a few wispy white clouds trailing across an otherwise blue sky. Encarnita pointed out that the taxi man had been right, the weather could be quite good.

Concepción sniffed. She had the collar of her leather jacket pulled up to her ears.

'Your father lived in this street, too, when he was a child,' said her mother.

'So he didn't come from a poor family?'

'Certainly not. Your grandfather was a lawyer, and your grandmother a doctor.'

'Like Felipe and his wife.'

'That is true!'

They came to No.17 and stopped to read the brass plaque attached to the railings. Under the initials RLS were inscribed the words: *'For we are very lucky with a lamp before the door.'* Encarnita spoke the familiar words aloud. 'That's from his poem about Leerie the Lamplighter. One of your father's favourites.' Whenever she thought of the boy who lived in the land of counterpane she saw him with reddish-gold hair and blue eyes. He had become inseparable from Conal.

'I suppose no one round here would remember him now?' Concepción glanced about as if someone might pop up to say that they did.

They wondered if some members of his family might still be living here. After all, Encarnita had lived in the house in Nerja for more than sixty years, and Arrieta had done for more than ninety. In their experience people did not move unless they had to.

'Let's give it a try,' said Encarnita.

Leaving the writer's house in peace, they moved a few doors along the street. They mounted the steps and Encarnita rang the bell. The door was opened by a woman in an overall with a yellow duster in her hand.

'We look for Conal Alexander Roderick MacDonald,' stated Encarnita.

'Excuse me?' The woman frowned. 'What did you say his name was?'

Encarnita repeated it.

'Sorry, hen. No one of that name here.'

They went next door. This time a woman wearing well-cut tweed trousers and a soft heather-coloured sweater came out onto the step. She also frowned as Encarnita went through the names.

'I'm terribly sorry. I don't think I can be of any help. We don't really know many people in the street. We've only lived here for five years.' She smiled at them before closing the door.

'We can't try every house,' said Concepción.

They wandered back down the hill to Morna's street. They thought they might ask Flick if she knew when Morna would be returning but Flick was not at home. She must be out crazycleaning. They went back to try Morna's bell, thinking she might have returned from Canada, but she had not. They were standing outside when a woman in black Spandex shorts came sprinting along the pavement to press Morna's bell.

'Gone to Canada,' said Encarnita.

'Really? I didn't know. Are you friends?'

Encarnita went through her usual explanation.

'But how terrible for you! Look, come home with me and I'll make you some coffee. Any friend of Morna's is a friend of mine. We help each other out. I live just along the street.'

This woman was called Effie, and she lived alone. Like Morna, she was a social worker, though younger, perhaps about forty years old. 'I'm a counsellor, really.' She was vigorous and energetic and she liked to hear the story of other people's lives. Before long she had managed to draw out the whole of Encarnita's story. She found it thrilling.

'You actually *met* Virginia Woolf? Wow!'

'Mother only three years old at time,' put in Concepción.

'I remember her very well,' said Encarnita, annoyed at her daughter's intervention. 'She wear very soft button shoes.'

'I'm sure you would remember her!' said Effie. 'Who would not? She must have had quite a presence. Imagine, arriving on the back of a mule! How wonderful.'

'In those days everyone come on mule. No road.'

'How fascinating!'

'I have book of hers. About a lighthouse.'

'*To the Lighthouse*? Don't tell me you've actually read it!'

'Bits.'

'Small bits,' added Concepción, earning another frown for herself from her mother.

'This is all absolutely amazing! Morna told me she had a Spanish friend out there – a wonderful woman, an example to us all! – but she didn't tell me you'd known Virginia Woolf. Or that you had had a Scottish lover.'

Encarnita shifted uncomfortably on her seat, wondering if she had been wise to tell this woman so much. But what was done was done. It had become her motto of late.

'So now we must set about finding this man of yours. Concepción's father!' Effie gave Concepción a smile, which was not returned. 'What did you say his name was again?'

'Conal Alexander Roderick MacDonald,' said Encarnita.

'Quite a mouthful. Amazing that you've remembered all those years.'

Encarnita stared at her. How would she not have remembered the name of her child's father? 'Is possible to find him, you think?'

'Everything is possible,' declared Effie with relish. 'Never say die! The first port of call must be the telephone book.'

The problem was that there were too many MacDonalds listed. It was a fairly common name in Scotland, Effie warned them, so it might not be easy. Also, some people were ex-directory.

Humming softly, she ran her finger down the columns, speaking a name aloud here and there. Alistair. Bruce. Colin. Damn it, no Conal. She went through the entire list without finding any Christian names or sets of initials that would match their subject. She was not deterred, however. There were sure to be other ways forward.

'Leave it with me,' she said.

TWENTY-TWO

They heard nothing from Effie for three days. While they waited, they did the tourist route around Edinburgh; they went for a ride on an open-topped bus and froze, visited the castle and Holyrood Palace and poked around the knick-knack shops in the Royal Mile, with Encarnita restraining Concepción from spending too much money on MacDonald tartan gifts for the children. They also walked up and down Princes Street and visited Marks and Spencers and Jenners. Encarnita thought that Morna would have been pleased with them.

She was becoming worried about money. The B&B, although it had been described as 'reasonable' by Flick, was costing them sixty pounds a night. They had discovered fish and chips, however, a cheaper meal than the one they'd had in the Italian restaurant. When they had tried to bring them into the B&B the landlady had objected. No food in the bedrooms: that was one of her rules. It attracted mice. But, apart from that, fish and chips left a lingering smell behind them and she had other boarders to consider, not that there were any in the house at the moment. The women were forced to eat their supper in the street, which they did not mind overly much. In fact, they rather enjoyed it, not that Concepción would have readily admitted it.

'I suppose we could always get some work,' said Encarnita, as they wandered down Broughton Street with their fish and chip bags. This was more of a workaday street than posh Heriot Row, with a butcher and a fishmonger, as well as cafés and restaurants, pubs, Pakistani grocers and second-hand shops, a street where one could eat fish and chips without people looking at you.

'Doing what?' Concepción popped another chip into her mouth.

'Cleaning, of course. What else? We could ask Flick.' Encarnita licked her salty fingers. 'That was good,' she said, scrunching up the bag and dumping it in a waste bin. She liked the brown sauce the man spattered liberally over the chips. 'Salt and sauce?' he asked each evening, while holding the salt shaker suspended over the bag.

'Mama, you can't go cleaning houses at your age!'

'Why not?'

Mrs Mack met them in the hall when they came in. Her long thin nose twitched slightly. 'Your friend called.'

'She leave a message?'

'She said she had some news for you. She thought she had a lead. Whatever that would mean?'

Encarnita did not enlighten her. Instead, she said to Concepción, 'We must go to see Effie straightaway!'

'Will you be back late?' asked the landlady, but they were already on their way.

They were breathless by the time they reached Effie's street and climbed the stairs to her flat. Concepción had a stitch in her side. Encarnita rang the bell. Effie answered straightaway and brought them in.

'Tell us the news, please!' said Encarnita.

'I think a little drink would be a good idea first.' Effie poured them each a glass of sherry and raised hers, saying, '*Salud*!'

Concepción drank, Encarnita did not. She had her eyes fixed on Effie's face. She had the feeling the Scottish woman was trying to avoid eye contact.

'Now please, you tell!'

'Well, a friend suggested trying Registrar House. That's where they record births, marriages and deaths. They're terribly helpful —'

Encarnita cut across. 'You find something?'

'As a matter of fact, I did. I found, first of all, the record of his birth.' Effie picked up a notebook that was lying on the table. 'Conal Alexander Roderick MacDonald, that sounds like him, doesn't it?'

'Yes, yes!'

'Born Edinburgh, the first of May, 1918.'

'That seem right.' Encarnita sat back. Now they had to believe that this man existed. 'He two years more than me. In 1939, I nineteen, he twenty-one.'

Effie hesitated before going on. 'I also found the record of his marriage, I'm afraid.'

Encarnita shrugged. She had expected that he would have married at some point during all those years.

'He married Margaret Edwina Cecilia Simpson in 1948. They had two children, a son, Edwin, and a daughter, Celia.'

'You have a brother and a sister,' Encarnita informed Concepción, who was looking slightly alarmed at the prospect.

'His wife died in 1995,' Effie continued.

'So she dead,' said Encarnita.

There was a pause. Effie had something further to say but was hesitating.

'More sherry?' she invited, splashing some into Concepción's glass and her own. Encarnita had not touched hers. She was staring into space, seeing far beyond the room into another one where wild flowers sprouted through cracks in the walls and part of the roof lay open to the brilliance of the sky. She looked back at Effie.

'He dead too?' she said.

Effie nodded. 'I'm really very sorry.'

'Not your fault. Not worry. I was ready. Last autumn I had a dream.'

'You foresaw his death? Perhaps you have the second sight?'

Encarnita frowned. 'My eyes good. No need glasses.'

'Mama, why we come?' Concepción burst out.

'To find out.'

'What good is that for us now?'

'I not want to die not knowing.'

'You not near to die so not say so!'

'That true.'

'You look extremely well for a woman of your age!' put in Effie.

'When he die?' asked Encarnita.

'Seven months or so ago.'

'Only seven months,' wailed Concepción. 'Oh, Mama!'

'I would like to go to his grave,' said her mother.

Effie was looking apologetic again. She explained that most people in Scotland tended to be cremated. 'I must warn you that there may not be a grave.'

'There is nowhere to talk to your dead?'

'Except in your head, I suppose,' said Effie uncomfortably. 'But there may be a grave, of course. I'm not saying there isn't. He died in Inverness-shire, not Edinburgh. And at home, not in a hospital.'

'We go there then and find out. Where is this place?'

Effie brought out a map of Scotland and showed them the county of Inverness-shire. 'You see, it's up north, and quite mountainous.' She indicated the brown-shaded parts. 'That is the village there, where he lived.'

'I am used to mountains,' said Encarnita. 'I grew up with them. He like mountains too. How do we go there?'

In the morning, they said goodbye to Mrs Mack, who wished them a good holiday in the Highlands and hoped to see them again.

'I think she got used to us,' said Encarnita, as they dragged their suitcases up the hill to the bus station.

'Got used to our money, you mean. Perhaps we should start a B&B in Nerja.'

'Our house isn't big enough. And we don't have an *en-suite* bathroom to offer.'

The landlady had been proud of her *en-suite*, in spite of the fact that they had only been able to get a dribble of hot water out of the shower, which was housed in a kind of cupboard. They had not complained. They were not sure what to expect when travelling in this country. Concepción spoke of sumptuous bathrooms with marble floors and gold taps when she had travelled with Emilio in Lanzarote and Mexico, but her mother did not believe half of it.

They found the bus station for Inverness. Effie had

written the name down on a piece of paper, as well as that of the village where they were to disembark. 'Ask the driver to let you off at Kincraig,' she had instructed them. She had said that, if it were not for her work, she would have gone with them, but they were glad she could not. This part of the journey they wished to undertake on their own.

They were first in the queue and thus able to procure a seat at the front. The bus was comfortable and the driver friendly. He called them 'ladies' and told them not to worry, to sit back and relax, and he would see that they got off at the right place. They settled down to enjoy the ride.

It was a beautiful journey, even Concepción admitted that, especially once they reached the mountains. They were not as high or as bare as their *sierras*, nor did they present such formidable chains cutting across the landscape, but they were impressive, nevertheless. This countryside was softer than the Andalusian *campo*, the colours more muted. The deciduous trees were sprouting fresh green leaves, in contrast to the dark colour of the pines.

The bus took them through various small grey towns, with names like Pitlochry and Blair Atholl, which they found difficult to pronounce. Concepción eyed the gift shops in Pitlochry longingly as they travelled up the main street. They were both enchanted by the sight of Blair Castle, which looked like a black and white castle in a fairy tale. The driver told them little bits about the history of the various places. Scotland's history was a pretty bloody one, he said cheerfully. Folk were always killing each other, trying to grab each other's land.

'Bloody in Spain too,' said Encarnita.

'The world over,' said the driver.

Concepción unwrapped the sandwiches the landlady had provided for their journey, at a small cost. They were ready for something to eat despite having had a full Scottish breakfast earlier. Encarnita thought perhaps it was the climate that had sharpened their appetites.

'I always knew I would like Scotland,' she said, as she bit

into a cheddar cheese and brown pickle sandwich. 'It's good that you do, too, Concepción, since you are half-Scottish. Perhaps that's why you're so fond of tartan.'

'I suppose it is true,' said Concepción slowly, 'that I am half-Scottish. I have never thought of myself in that way before.' She was quiet as they crossed the moors.

'Kingussie coming up,' called out the driver. 'Next stop after that will be Kincraig, ladies.'

When they left the village of Kingussie behind they saw snow-capped mountains on their right-hand side which Encarnita thought, from consulting Effie's notes, must be the Cairngorms. Effie had drawn a map and written detailed notes for them. And there was the loch with a little tree-clad island in its centre. Small sailboats bobbed near the far shore.

Concepción was up on her feet, struggling with her suitcase. 'Mama, we have to get off in a minute.' The bus was slowing.

'Kincraig,' called the driver, pulling up. 'Village is just down there to the right, ladies. Have a good day!'

They alighted and waved goodbye to him. He had come to seem like a friend and after the bus had gone they could not help feeling a little lonely. They stood by the side of the road for a moment to reorientate themselves, before setting off down the hill. Their suitcase wheels were making an awful noise on the road but there was nothing they could do about it.

This was a pretty village, they realised straightaway. It was not stretched out in a long straight line like many of the others they passed through. The road curved, with a side street branching off it, and each of the houses looked different from its neighbour. They passed a hotel sitting up high, went under a railway bridge and shortly afterwards saw the loch on their right. At the foot of the hill there was a general store-cum-post office with cheerful red and white striped awnings. They went in. Effie had said to ask at the shop.

The woman behind the counter smiled and asked if she could help them. Encarnita cleared her throat.

'Is there graveyard in village?'

The woman frowned as if she had not quite understood. 'You are looking for a graveyard? Would it be the one at Loch Insh church?'

'Could be. Where is that place?'

'I'll show you.' She escorted them to the door and pointed across the loch. 'You see some white showing through the trees, up on that knoll? That's it. You go over the bridge and follow the road round by the loch until you see the sign for the church.' She looked at their suitcases. 'Would you like to leave those? I could put them behind the counter. It would save you dragging them all the way there.' They were thankful to be rid of them for a little while.

They followed her instructions and when they saw the blue notice board with CHURCH OF SCOTLAND, INSH CHURCH, written in white letters, they unlatched the low wooden gate and went inside. Encarnita felt herself quicken with excitement. She sensed that she was drawing closer to him. They took the path that wound its way up the hill until it led them to the little white church. It was a simple building and standing in this high, yet secluded place, overlooking over the loch, it had an air of great tranquillity. Encarnita could not imagine a more peaceful place than this to be buried.

Close by the church lay old graves, their upstanding headstones grey and weathered. Others were in the form of tablets set into the ground. In many cases the inscriptions were indecipherable. They made out some names. Grant. Kennedy. MacPherson. Encarnita was beginning to feel a little anxious. But he must be here, somewhere!

'He wouldn't be amongst these, would he?' Concepción pointed out. 'They're all from too long ago.'

They walked on, up to the top of the slope, went through another gate and found a new cemetery sited at the foot of the hill.

After that, they found the grave quite quickly. The very sight of his name engraved in stone – CONAL ALEXANDER RODERICK MACDONALD – gave Encarnita a shock. It felt almost as if a bolt of electricity had been shot through her.

'Are you all right, Mama?' Concepción slipped a hand into hers and they locked fingers.

'I am fine,' said Encarnita, taking a deep breath. She was calm enough now to read the rest. 'Beloved husband of the late Margaret Edwina Cecilia MacDonald.' And the dates of his birth and death. 1 May 1918. 1 September 2001. They stood together listening to the sigh of the wind and the cries of the birds in the tall trees. 'He is at peace, your father. He wants us to be at peace too, Concepción.'

'How do you know what he wants, Mama? How do you know he ever gave you another thought after he left you?'

'I know. From the beginning I know him.'

'But you know what men are like!'

Your men, Encarnita wanted to say, but did not.

'My feet are frozen.' Concepción was stamping her feet.

'I told you to put on warmer socks. Go and sit in the church and say a prayer for your father's soul. I'll join you in a minute. I want to talk to him alone for a few minutes.'

Concepción trekked back up the hill, while Encarnita stayed by the grave, able to spend some time at last with Conal. She talked to him, but there was so much to say that it almost tied her tongue. She bent and tidied the plot a little, pulling out a weed here and there. To do this comforted her. Tomorrow, before they returned to Edinburgh, she would bring flowers for him.

She then went to join Concepción in the church. The interior was as simple and as peaceful as its exterior, with its white walls and mahogany-coloured pews, and the sun filtering through the clear glass window panes. On the end window, a cross, unfamiliar to the women, was etched into the glass. They found out later that it was a Celtic cross. This was a church quite different to any that they had known. There were no candles to light and no pictures or statues of Jesus or his mother Mary, which Encarnita did find strange but, in spite of that, she liked it and could imagine Conal sitting in a pew, his head bowed in prayer, even though he had told her, all those years ago, that he did not think he believed in God. No matter. He must have liked the peace to be found here.

They sat for almost an hour before returning to the shop. Then, silently, they rose and walked, hand-in-hand, back to the store. Encarnita was tiring a little.

The shopkeeper helped them to find a B&B without en-suite, which suited them, since it was cheaper than the one they'd had in Edinburgh. This B&B landlady was an elderly widow, who told them that she liked to take in boarders every now and then, for the company, mainly. She had lived for many years in the village. Over a cup of tea and short-bread biscuits, which she had offered them, Encarnita decided to confide in her, just a little.

'You know Mr MacDonald?' she asked.

'Which Mr MacDonald would that be?'

'Mr Conal Alexander Roderick.'

'Ah, Conal! Yes, I knew him well. He and his wife came to live in Kincraig when he retired. In his youth, his family had had a house up here. He was a keen hill walker, loved the mountains. A lovely man. How do you know him?'

'He come to Spain once.'

'That's interesting. I don't ever remember them going to Spain. France and Italy, yes. Must have been before their time here. Margaret, his wife, was especially fond of Tuscany. She spoke fluent Italian. Such a nice woman. He was devastated when she died.'

Without volunteering any more information Encarnita managed to find out where Conal had lived. After they had drunk their tea she took Concepción with her and sought out the house.

It was a modern bungalow with nothing very special about it, except that it had a nice garden fringed with silver birch trees. A child's swing hung there now so a family must have bought it. While they were standing at the gate a woman came out of the front door to ask if they were looking for someone.

'Mr Conal MacDonald,' said Encarnita. 'But he dead now.'

'I'm afraid so. We didn't ever know him. We lived in Inverness before we came here.'

'Who you buy the house from?'

'It belonged to his son and daughter. It was the daughter we dealt with. She showed us round.'

'Come on, Mama,' muttered Concepción, tugging at her arm.

'Do you have a special interest?'

'Conal old friend,' said Encarnita. 'His daughter? You know where she live?'

'Why, yes, I do. In Edinburgh.'

'You have address?'

'I should have it somewhere. Come in for a moment while I look.'

JOURNEY'S END

The three women walk past the house the first time without stopping. The second time, after making sure that no one is watching them at the window, they go more slowly, allowing themselves to take a lingering look at the façade and its tall, astragal windows. It's Georgian, similar to the ones in Heriot Row, Effie tells them, built around 1820. By now they are getting a grasp of what Georgian New Town means. They are slowly coming to terms with the city. Conal's city. Encarnita is conscious of that with every step she takes. Some of the buildings in this street have been divided into flats but Conal's daughter and her husband appear to occupy the whole house since there is only one bell and one name beside the front door. Their name is inscribed on a brass plate. MARJORIBANKS. Effie tells them that it is pronounced Marshbanks. Encarnita repeats the word and Concepción hushes her, worried that they might be overheard.

'Brass plate needs cleaning,' observes Encarnita. 'Bell-pull, too, and handle for door. Maybe they need cleaner.'

After the second look, they go to a café and drink insipid cups of *cappuccino* and discuss the way forward. Encarnita has turned down the idea of going up the step and ringing the bell and announcing to Celia Marjoribanks that Concepción is her sister and that, she, Encarnita, was once her father's lover.

'She probably shut door in face. Probably not believe. Think we try to get money.'

'We could write her a letter,' suggests Effie, 'and say you'd like to meet her.'

'She might not reply. Might tear up letter.'

'It's tricky,' agrees Effie.

Encarnita thinks they need to find a way to get inside the house. Once they were in, it would be more difficult for Conal's daughter to get rid of them. She would have to listen to what they had to say and, once she did, Encarnita is sure she will recognise the truth. The problem, as Effie sees it, is getting inside the house, legally. Encarnita has an idea.

'We go as cleaners.'

'But how that happen?' demands Concepción.

Effie thinks about Encarnita's proposal. She considers it to be not a bad idea for she knows that people who live in large houses have a problem finding good, reliable cleaners who don't cost the earth, especially in central Edinburgh where parking is difficult. She has a couple of patients who are constantly bemoaning the fact. Encarnita and Concepción can get the gist of most of what Effie says, without understanding every word and phrase. They are left behind when she uses phrases like 'cost the earth'. When she sees them looking blank, she says, 'Cost a fortune.'

'Ah,' says Encarnita, *'cuesta mucha pasta.'*

They return to Effie's flat, where she sets about constructing an advertisement on her computer. She reads it out as she goes along. 'Mother and Daughter Team. Two for the price of one.' You wouldn't mind doing that, would you? It would be a good come-on. And you probably won't end up doing much cleaning, anyway, once you tell her what's what. "Mother will do dusting and cleaning of silver and brasses. Daughter, all other work. Phone Connie."' Effie puts down her own telephone number. She then prints the leaflet in two colours, red and blue, putting little fancy twirls at the top and bottom, and the potential cleaners examine it approvingly. After that, all that remains is to pop it through the Marjoribanks' letter box. Effie offers to do that herself after dark.

'If the door does open and I am confronted by Celia I shall simply tell her the truth. That I am helping to distribute flyers for two friends and that I can recommend you highly.'

Effie manages to deliver the flyer without being accosted by anyone. Encarnita senses that she is a little disappointed by this.

Encarnita and Concepción settle down to wait. They are sleeping on the pull-down double settee in Effie's living room now. Their money was running out and Effie kindly offered. There is only one bedroom in her apartment since she uses the third room for her therapy sessions, but she says they are welcome to stay with her until Morna returns from Canada. A picture postcard of the Rocky Mountains has come from her, saying she saw a moose the day before and is having a wonderful time.

After three days pass without any phone call from Celia Marjoribanks, the two women begin to get restless. Concepción is spending some time in studying her English phrase book so that she is able to tell her mother that she frequently forgets to use the articles 'a' and 'the' in front of words. This annoys Encarnita.

'All these years, and you wouldn't pay any attention when I tried to teach you English! Now you think you are an expert.'

'I want to be able to talk to my relatives, don't I?'

They walk past the Marjoribanks' house again and see that the brass plate, bell pull and doorknob are still in need of cleaning.

On the fourth day, Effie admits that her plan may not be working. It's likely that a number of assorted leaflets are stuffed through the Marjoribanks' letter box daily. 'There is so much junk mail these days that people tend to put it straight into the bin. We may have to think of something else,' she concedes.

Encarnita has been thinking. 'Why not we go to door and say we are cleaners from leaflet. When she see us maybe she think we honest women and let us in.'

'You could try,' says Effie doubtfully. 'I suppose I could write you a reference.'

She types it out on her computer, saying what excellent, reliable cleaners the two women are, all of which is true, since they have been cleaning her flat relentlessly since their arrival. At times she has had to come through from her therapy room to ask them to turn off the vacuum cleaner. The noise is distracting. And in such a small apartment it is not really necessary to vacuum so many hours a day. The carpets will soon be threadbare.

Armed with the reference, and a copy of the flyer, the two women set out for the Marjoribanks' house. Encarnita goes up the steps, followed by Concepción, and pulls the bell.

The lady of the house opens the door herself. Encarnita knows straightaway that it is Celia, for the similarity between Conal MacDonald's two daughters is striking, even though there must be several years in age between them. She wonders if they will notice it themselves, but thinks possibly not. She is inclined to believe that we do not see ourselves as others see us. She has observed that in her own daughter. Sometimes Concepción, from the way she dresses, seems to think she's still thirty years old. When she has told her so Concepción has retaliated, saying that women of all ages can dress the same now. Encarnita, having watched tourists of every age and shape parade through Nerja in shorts, is inclined to believe it.

'Yes?' Celia Marjoribanks smiles politely.

'Good morning,' says Encarnita, equally polite. They have gone through a rehearsal with Effie, who is hovering a few doors along the street, waiting to see if they will be admitted. 'We are the cleaners in this leaflet. I am Encarnita, and this is my daughter Concepción. You can call her Connie.' She holds out the flyer.

Celia Marjoribanks takes it and says, 'Oh yes, I believe you put one through my door a few days ago?'

'We have very good references,' Encarnita continues, handing Effie's over. 'This is a recent one.'

Celia reads it and nods. 'It is very good.'

'You would like to have something done?'

'I daresay I could do with some help. The last woman I had vanished a few weeks ago, without a word.'

'We can start now.'

'Now?'

'Yes, we are free. We can offer you a free trial for today.'

'Oh, I wouldn't dream of letting you work for me for nothing.'

'We can start?'

Concepción moves up a step to stand level with her mother.

'Well, I suppose so.' Celia's mood appears to shift. 'Why not, for goodness sake! The place is in a bit of a mess and we're having visitors at the week-end and I don't know how I'm going to cope with cleaning it myself.'

Encarnita and Concepción are admitted, and the door closes behind them. Effie goes home to await their news on their return.

Encarnita is dusting *To the Lighthouse*. She jabs the spine of the book with a blunt forefinger and says, 'I know that woman.'

Celia Marjoribanks goes over to look. She frowns as she reads the title. '*Really*? You know her? Virginia Woolf? I mean, you *knew* her? She's dead.'

Encarnita nods. 'She must be dead. She older than me. She wear nice shoes with buttons. Nice leather shoes. Soft. I feel them.'

'Did you work for her?'

'No, not work. She come to my village.'

'In Spain?' A light is beginning to dawn behind Celia's eyes. 'In Spain. Did she by any chance come to visit Gerald Brenan?'

'Don Geraldo, we call him. He teach me English.'

Celia says her husband will be most interested, since he teaches English Literature at the university. 'So, remind me, the name of your village is —?'

'Yegen.'

'Of course! I should have remembered. In the Alpujarra. My husband and I spent a couple of weeks there a few years back.'

'You went to Alpujarra?'

'Yes, indeed. Marvellous far away from the world feeling. We went to Yegen to see the house where Gerald Brenan lived. We had read *South from Granada*.'

'I not live in Yegen now. I move to Nerja, on coast, many years ago.'

'We went to Nerja, too. We had a wonderful week staying in the *parador*.'

'You were in Nerja? And I not see you!'

'Even if you had seen me you wouldn't have known me, would you?'

'Oh, but I would! I sure I knowed you.'

'I don't see how,' says Celia gently.

There is much that Celia does not yet see, thinks Encarnita.

At that moment, the telephone rings and Celia goes to answer it in the hall, leaving the drawing room door ajar. Encarnita knows that it is so that she can still see her.

Encarnita puts *To the Lighthouse* back in the bookcase and takes out *Mrs Dalloway*. As she dusts it, she hears snatches of conversation coming from the hall.

Celia is telling her friend about them. She sounds defensive. Encarnita thinks possibly her friend disapproves of her allowing two strange foreign women to come into her house.

There is a slight disruption when Concepción yells over the bannisters from upstairs, 'No find plug for electrics in study,' and Celia cries out in alarm, 'Don't touch study! It is my husband's study. Leave, please, *leave*!' She then goes back to her telephone call, to continue reassuring her friend Lilias. 'I am sure they are absolutely fine. They will be finished, anyway, before Cuthbert gets back.'

In the warm, elegant drawing room, scented with yellow freesias, delicately arranged in a shallow orange-coloured bowl, Encarnita continues with her work. The sun streaming in through the three almost floor-length windows warms her back. She moves from the bookcase to the grand piano, on top of which stand a series of photographs in silver frames. Family photographs. Groups of various kinds on days of celebration. There is Celia on her wedding day with her husband. That must be Cuthbert. Celia is wearing a white silky-looking dress with a long train that has been arranged in a swirl around her feet like a big comma. She holds a sheath of red roses against the white dress and she is smiling. The man is wearing a kilt with knee socks and a black jacket with silver buttons. He has a straight back and a small, neat moustache. He looks proud to have such a lovely bride on his arm. It is not possible from this picture to know what kind of a man he is but Encarnita will find out when she meets him for she knows that she will. The next photograph is of three small children, a boy and two girls. None of these people are familiar to her but here is a young man whom she once knew and recognises still even though he had wild tangled hair and a beard when she knew him and in this picture he is clean-shaven. He is sitting under a silver birch tree on a summer's day, with a book on his lap. The leaves above his head are shimmering in the sunshine lighting up his golden-red hair. He is smiling directly at the camera. He is smiling directly at her. She gently slides the duster over the glass and replaces the frame on top of the shiny piano.

In the hall, Celia carries on talking to her friend in a soft, low voice, too soft and low for Encarnita to make out what she is saying. But she is content. She has made her journey and when Celia has finished talking to her friend and comes back into the room then she, Encarnita, will tell her story.

Celia listens without attempting to interrupt the flow of Encarnita's narrative. She frowns. That is the only emotion she betrays. When finally the story ends, in this very room, silence falls. Eventually, she speaks, her voice still well modulated and polite.

'I think there must be some mistake.'

Encarnita shakes her head. 'No mistake. Conal Alexander Roderick MacDonald the father of Concepción.'

'What proof do you have?'

'You look at Concepción. You look at you in mirror.'

Celia makes no move to go and examine herself in the oval gilt-edged mirror on the wall. She says in a low voice, 'That is not proof. Many people look similar. They say everyone has a double in the world.'

'That so?' Encarnita is interested. 'So somewhere another me. Maybe I find her sometime.'

'If you did it would not mean that you were necessarily related by blood.' Celia's voice is gaining strength from this diversion in the conversation. 'Doesn't Saddam Hussein have several doubles? The man in Iraq,' she adds.

'We see him on television,' says Concepción, huffed by the implication that they might not know about world affairs.

'Conal have birthmark on stomach, just above belly button,' says Encarnita, who is not to be diverted. 'Like upside down quarter-moon.' They had laughed about that.

Celia looks startled.

'That true, yes?'

'Yes, that may be, but, well, I mean to say, other people could have similar marks…' Celia's voice trails away.

'Also bad injury to right leg above ankle which I clean. Must have left long scar?'

'Possibly. Even so…'

'Not many men with same name, same colour, same marks on body.'

'I suppose not…'

'This big shock for you, I understand. Maybe need drink?'

'Yes, perhaps we could do with one.'

Celia gets up and goes to a cupboard and takes out a decanter of sherry and three fine glasses of Edinburgh crystal. The two women, seated on the settee, still wearing their overalls, watch her in silence. Encarnita feels as if she has run dry and Concepción is trying to take in the knowledge that this unknown well-mannered, well-groomed woman is related to her by blood, is, in fact, her sister.

Celia's hand shakes a little as she pours the sherry. She comes back to join them and each take a glass from the tray. They drink without a toast being proposed.

The room is warm. The gilded clock on the mantelpiece emits a quiet tick-tock and the tyres of passing cars make a soft swishing sound on the wet street. It has started to rain. Large drops slide down the window panes.

And then they hear the front door opening and are jolted out of their trance. A cheerful male voice calls out. Can this be Cuthbert, wonders Encarnita. But when the door opens and she sees the young man she thinks for a moment that it is Felipe come to fetch them home. He may be a few years younger but, apart from that, he could be his double.

'Alex,' says Celia, getting to her feet and going to embrace the newcomer. 'I didn't know you were coming.'

'Thought I'd look in.' Alex glances past her at the two women on the settee.

'This is my son Alex,' says Celia, a little flustered. 'Alex, let me introduce you to Encarnita, and her daughter Concepción. They've come from Nerja. That's in Spain, on the coast. Do you remember Dad and I went there a few years ago?' She is talking too much, and too fast. She realises this and slows down. 'Why don't you pour yourself a whisky? I have something to tell you.'

While she haltingly retells Encarnita's tale he listens attentively, his head cocked slightly to one side, the way his mother had. He smiles at the end and says, 'That's quite a story! What a shame Grandfather died before you got here.'

Encarnita nods. 'I liked to see him. But I see you. You are his image.'

'So I've always been told. We were very close. He talked a lot to me about Spain. In fact, he talked to me about you.'

'He talked about *me*?'

'He told me how he'd been wounded when he was fighting with the International Brigades during the Civil War and how a wonderful Spanish girl called Encarnita had saved his life.'

'He told you that?' Celia sounds stunned.

'He remember me?' says Encarnita, catching her breath.

'Of course he remembered you! After he came out of the army – he fought in the Second World War – he went back to Spain to look for you.'

'But not find me.'

'Mama!' cries Concepción. 'Oh, Mama! Imagine —'

For a fleeting moment Encarnita allows herself to imagine what their life might have been had Conal found them. Then she pats her daughter's hand.

'He went to the place where you'd been living,' says Alex.

'Almuñecar?'

'Yes, that was it. But he couldn't find anyone who knew where you were. That was where Laurie Lee ended up, wasn't it, in his book *I walked Out One Midsummer Morning*?'

'Laurie Lee?' says Encarnita, puzzled. 'I knew English boy Lorenzo Lee in Hotel Mediterráneo. He play violin with German boy Jacobo. '

'That's the one.'

'So Lorenzo write a book? I will read it.'

'You've had quite a life, haven't you?' Alex shakes his head in admiration.

'Most of the time I live quietly.'

'Mother, imagine, you've got a sister!' Alex turns to Celia. 'You always said you wished you'd had one.'

The sisters eye each other uncomfortably.

'You'll have to meet the rest of the family,' says Alex. 'Dad, and Lucinda and Clarissa. My sisters,' he adds.

'We would like,' says Encarnita, who is feeling tired now and is ready to leave.

They hear the outside door opening again and Celia starts up in alarm.

'That'll be Cuthbert. I think I'd better go and warn him.' She hastens out of the room, closing the door behind her, though they are able to hear the conversation that ensues between husband and wife. She breaks the news quietly but when he responds his voice is raised.

'This is ridiculous, Celia! Don't tell me you've fallen for a cock-and-bull story like that! You're far too gullible, always have been.'

'Hush, Cuthbert, they'll hear.'

'They'll have to hear. They can't come waltzing in here out of the blue claiming that this woman is your father's daughter!'

'She does look like Father. And me, I think. We could have a blood test.'

'Blood test nothing. I am going to go in now and ask them to leave.'

'Alex says —'

'I don't give a damn what Alex says!'

The door opens abruptly and Cuthbert enters the room. He stops dead.

Alex springs up. 'Dad, come and meet Encarnita and Concepción.'

'I must ask you two ladies to leave now,' says Cuthbert, ignoring him. 'I do not believe you have any claim on my wife's family.'

'But, Dad,' says Alex, 'Grandfather told me all about Encarnita.'

Cuthbert's eyes bulge behind their glasses.

'Concepción willing to have blood test,' says Encarnita and Concepción looks horrified as she hates having needles stuck into her.

'There's DNA,' says Alex. 'That would settle it. If we need to. As far as I'm concerned, Concepción looks just like Mother.'

His mother does not look greatly flattered but she says to Concepción, 'I have to admit I got a jolt when I saw you. I think we do probably look somewhat alike.'

'Have you lost your senses, Celia?' demands Cuthbert.

'We not come for money,' Encarnita says to him.

'What have you come for then?'

'To find what happen to Conal. Big shock for you all, I

know, us coming.'

'Very big shock,' he declares and leaves the room, after giving his wife a look that says he will talk to her later.

'Don't let Cuthbert upset you,' she says. 'He hates surprises.'

'Especially when he senses he's losing a battle,' his son adds with a grin.

'Time we go,' says Encarnita, making to rise.

'But you will come back, won't you?' asks Alex anxiously. He comes to help her up. 'We can't lose you now that we've just found you. We must have a family party to celebrate. Don't you agree, Mother?'

'Yes, of course.' Celia manages a smile, even if it is a little wan.

Alex takes Encarnita's arm and walks with her to the front door.

'You so like my grandson Felipe,' she tells him. 'The son of Concepción. The double. What do you do in your life?'

'I'm a lawyer,' he says.

She is not surprised.

In the evening, she phones Felipe and tells him, 'We have found your family. You must come.'

Two days later, Felipe arrives from Spain and is met at the airport by his cousin Alex. They agree that they had no problem recognising each other! 'It's uncanny,' says Alex. They hit it off together straightaway. Felipe's English is good and Alex has a smattering of Spanish from travelling in South America as a student. He says he will take Spanish lessons so that when he comes to visit them in Spain he will be able to talk to his relatives in their own tongue.

The family gathering is organised. Felipe buys new outfits for his mother and grandmother in Jenners department store. Morna would be happy to know that, thinks Encarnita, as she is borne down the escalator carrying her bags. The purchase she is best pleased with is a pair of dove-grey kid shoes that fit her feet as if made for them. They go to a hairdresser and have their hair washed and blown dry and Concepción has a manicure and a facial followed by a full make-up. Encarnita declines. She says she is long past all that.

At the elected time, they arrive at the Marjoribanks' house in a taxi with Felipe. Concepción, in royal blue silk, is fidgeting a little nervously. Encarnita, wearing burgundy velvet, is perfectly calm. Cuthbert and Celia come to the door together. He greets them civilly, extending his hand, but not offering his cheek. Encarnita suspects that he has had warnings issued to him by his wife and offspring. He is wearing a slight air of martyrdom. Celia is more welcoming and kisses them on both cheeks, Spanish-style. The two daughters, tall, attractive, well-mannered girls, like Celia herself, greet them warmly. They do not have their mother's or their brother's colouring. Their hair is mid-brown, their eyes hazel-coloured; in that, they resemble their father.

Celia has had caterers lay on a sumptuous buffet. The visitors are amazed by the amount of food for just eight people. A whole salmon with a lemon in its mouth, decorated with scales of cucumber, several kinds of meat and fowl, stuffed eggs, numerous bowls of salad, several kinds of cheese as well as deserts. The Spanish women's eyes go to the Scotch trifle and chocolate mousse and raspberry meringues. They both have a sweet tooth. Encarnita appreciates that Conal's daughter wants to make amends and do what her father would have wished her to do.

Alex and his sisters chat non-stop with Felipe. Laughter erupts from the little group at regular intervals. Encarnita is content to sit and watch and listen to the rise and fall of their conversation, making out a few phrases here and there. She is proud that Felipe can speak English so well for it was she who taught him his first words in the language, the ones taught to her by Don Geraldo. Tree. Flower. Goat. Clouds. The memory of that sunny day on the hillside comes back to her. She can smell the warmth of the earth and its scents of lavender and thyme.

'Grandmother,' says Felipe, bending down to her, startling her out of her reverie, 'Lucinda is going to study Spanish at university. Because her grandfather got her interested in Spain!'

'*Our* grandfather,' Alex corrects him.

'Yes, *our* grandfather,' agrees Felipe with a smile.

Lucinda, who is the younger of the two sisters, says she will try to do her year abroad in Granada. 'That would give me the chance to get to know my new relatives!'

'We should like that very much,' says Felipe.

Lucinda says she was thrilled when she found out that they had a Spanish connection. 'Imagine Grandpa!' she says admiringly.

'As a matter of fact, I can easily imagine Grandpa,' says Alex.

Clarissa, who has already qualified as a chartered accountant, declares that she, too, will come to Spain. She is planning a holiday in the summer with her boyfriend, who works for the same firm. 'We might come to Nerja! Perhaps you could suggest somewhere for us to stay?'

Felipe says he is sure they could do that.

Encarnita imagines entertaining Clarissa and her boyfriend, whom she imagines to be like Hubert, the Pilkingtons' son, when he was in his early twenties. They will seem very tall in her small house but she will receive them well and lay out a spread of good Spanish food and wine on her table.

Encarnita and Concepción are glad to have Felipe with them, so that he can talk for them. After telling her story, Encarnita does not want to say much more. She has a short exchange with Celia in which the latter comments that she seems very close to her daughter. Very close, agrees Encarnita. They are together always, every day of life. Celia says that is very unusual these days when children fly the nest as soon as they can get the money together for a flat. Encarnita does not ask if she is close to her daughters and is glad when Celia excuses herself to go and see to the food.

Encarnita cannot think of anything at all to say to Cuthbert, who still looks somewhat horrified at what is going on in his house. He does not ask her anything about her memories of Virginia Woolf.

The next morning, Encarnita and Concepción take affectionate leave of Effie and set off for the airport. Felipe escorts them there in a taxi but he will not travel further with them. He is to stay on for a few days. He wants to spend some time getting to know his cousins. The girls are keen to show him the sights of Edinburgh and Alex plans to take him hill walking. They will go up to the Cairngorms and visit their grandfather's grave. Encarnita is happy to think of the friendship between the two young men blossoming. She is sure that Conal, if he were to know it, would be pleased too.

As they are fastening their seat belts, Concepción says, 'I don't think I will find all that much in common with Celia even though she is my sister.'

'Maybe you won't,' agrees Encarnita. But it does not matter.

Celia has promised to come out to Nerja to see them. They suspect she will not be accompanied by Cuthbert. Effie, too, plans a visit and they have told her that she would be welcome to stay in their house though they have not extended the same invitation to their relatives. They will surely stay in the *parador*. Effie said that wild horses would not keep her away, another of her turns of phrase that has puzzled the two women.

'It was kind of Celia to give us the money, though.' In her handbag Concepción has a banker's draft for *euros* equivalent to ten thousand pounds sterling. They wonder if Celia has told her husband.

'She is a good woman and she felt you had a right to something from your father,' says Encarnita. ' I think that is fair. He would have wished it.'

Celia has also given ten thousand pounds to Encarnita, who did not want to take it. 'I not need. At my age.' Celia said she should spend a little on herself at least and perhaps give some to her other grandchildren, or their children, as she saw fit. After all, they are family, too. What a large extended family they have become! Encarnita has something in her bag that she treasures more than the money: a picture of Conal Alexander Roderick MacDonald as a young man, sitting under a silver birch tree on a summer's day, with a book on his lap. The leaves above his head are shimmering in the sunshine lighting up his golden-red hair. He is smiling directly at the camera. He is smiling directly at her.

'I'm glad Jorge is coming to meet us,' says Concepción. 'It'll save us the taxi fare.'

Jorge has forsaken his motor bike for a clapped-out car. He said he thought he was getting too old for the bike and maybe Encarnita would be more comfortable in the car than riding pillion. They might manage a little jaunt up to Toledo. She has always wanted to go there. Encarnita told him that she would like that. She will spend part of Celia's money on the trip. And then, after that, who knows where they might go? She spoke to Jorge on his mobile phone the night before. It is another thing he has acquired.

They are ready for take-off. Encarnita takes hold of her daughter's hand and braces herself for the ordeal, telling herself that in no more than three or four hours she will have her feet on the ground, and after that she will have no need to fly again.

Acknowledgements

I wish to acknowledge the following sources:

Gerald Brenan: *South from Granada*
The Face of Spain
A Life of One's Own
Personal Record
Best of Friends: The Brenan-Partridge Letters (with Ralph Partridge)
Jonathan Gathorne-Hardy: *The Interior Castle, A life of Gerald Brenan*
Antonio Ramos Espejo ed.: *Ciega en Granada*
Gamel Woolsey: *Death's Other Kingdom*
Laurie Lee: *As I walked Out One Midsummer's Morning*
Valerie Grove: *Laurie Lee, The Well-loved Stranger*
Maria Carlota Hallama Palm: *Almuñecar en la obra de Laurie Lee y en el recuerdo de sus habitantes*
Shirley Deane: *Tomorrow is Mañana*
Valerie Cunningham ed.: *Writers on the Civil War*
Nina Epton: *Andalucía*

Special thanks to Isobel Murray and Tom Adair for their advice and encouragement.